SEAN CUMMINGS

snowbooks

Proudly Published by Snowbooks in 2010

Snowbooks Ltd.
120 Pentonville Road
London
N1 9JN
Tel: 0207 837 6482
Fax: 0207 837 6348
email: info@snowbooks.com
www.snowbooks.com

British Library Cataloguing in Publication Data
A catalogue record for this book is available from the British Library.

ISBN   978-1-906727-46-8

Printed and bound in the UK by J F Print Ltd., Sparkford, Somerset

CHAPTER 1

My boyfriend drives a dump truck.

I know — it's not the most glamorous job in the world, but one does crave some measure of predictability when life spins wildly out of control — like a when a car hits a patch of black ice or worse, when everything you've ever known or loved simply vanishes.

I mean, how do you cope with that?

You wake up one morning, you kiss the man you intended to marry and discuss what to make for supper, only to find the apartment picked clean when you arrive home from work. A snapshot of him standing next to his precious BMW and a pile of ripped up wedding invitations that were supposed to go out in the mail are scattered across the living room floor. There are three stalks of celery in the fridge and a can of tomato soup in the cupboard. The only reminder of what you thought was a functional relationship is the stack of unpaid bills in both your names that he neatly piled on the toilet seat so you wouldn't miss them.

My therapist has strongly suggested that I learn how to "be alone", lest I condemn myself to continued failed relationships and a referral to a psychiatrist, because nobody, absolutely nobody, experiences breakups on the scale that I do.

Dave Webber drives a dump truck, and he's seemingly found the elusive balance we strive for in life. You know the one — it has something to do with total job satisfaction and the sense that you've carried out something meaningful when you punch the clock at the end of the day. When Dave isn't working, he's an avid reader, a home improvement enthusiast, and he's recently taken up photography, because he believes that Chapters needs a good coffee table book with glossy photographs showing the history of dump trucks over the past sixty years. Who knew?

All my girlfriends believe I'm crazy to have fallen for a dump truck driver, but after half a dozen failed relationships with well-paid professionals such as lawyers or oil industry analysts, I've learned avoid men in expensive business suits. They can't be trusted.

Before Dave, I had always looked down on blue-collar types. I assumed that tradesmen were beer chugging sexists who aspired to scratching their testicles while watching Monday Night Football with their cronies. We met after he had delivered a load of gravel for the new driveway that Dad was laying for the fifth-wheel he'd just brought home from Gerry's RV World. Mom and I were sitting on the terrace, watching what Mom refers to as "man's work" — she's a traditionalist that way. The last thing I expected was to see a truck driver with a gunslinger mustache and a white t-shirt with the words, "Get in touch with your inner Mozart" emblazoned across the front in gold letters. My ears pricked up when I heard *Die Entführung aus dem Serail* pouring from the cab of his truck, and he sang along as he measured the area of Dad's driveway with some kind of roller doo-dad.

That I love the opera is no secret, and it's the main reason I decided to strike up a conversation with this strange man as he began poking at the pile of gravel with a steel-toed boot.

"Okay, I'll bite," I shouted, as I sauntered over. "I can name three people in the entire city of Calgary who know the words to even one Mozart composition."

"Mozart is life-affirming," he shouted back, as he reached for the shovel conveniently stowed on the side of his dump truck. "Kind of surprising when you consider that he lived hard and died young."

"What do you mean?"

"The guy was a party machine," he said, as he wiped the sweat from his brow with a gloved hand. "He was the late-1700's equivalent of a rock star — you know, extreme living, debauchery, and women aplenty. He managed to pump out over six hundred compositions and still found time to get married and father six children."

My jaw dropped — perhaps the gods were playing a cruel joke on me.

Every man I'd ever been involved with had to be dragged kicking and screaming to a performance of the Calgary Opera, and the last one liked to make farting sounds to amuse himself twenty minutes into *La clemenza di Tito*. Naturally, I just had to ask the strange man now standing shirtless on a pile of topsoil for a date.

"There's a performance at the Jack Singer next week; would you like to go?" I blurted out in a voice that sounded embarrassingly close to a squeak. Dave stuck his shovel into the pile of dirt and wiped his brow with a dirty forearm.

"Hmmmm, not sure on that — you mean, like a date?" he asked.

"Yeah — sure, a date," I bleated.

"I dunno — I mean, I think that going out with a client's daughter might be bad for business."

"I'll buy you dinner!" I gushed, astonished that I was asking someone out for a date, because role-reversal had never been my strong suit. Dave leaned on his shovel while I handed him my business card. He held it up to shade his eyes from the midmorning sun and examined it for a second.

"Valerie Stevens, huh?" he said, cocking his right eyebrow. I watched the corners of his mustache curl up into an amused smile, and it was at this point that I began wondering just how desperate I looked.

"That's me," I said, trying hard not to sound like a complete imbecile.

"What's with the pentagram next to the Government of Canada logo? Don't tell me — the civil service has taken up devil worship!" he chuckled.

"Nope," I said, my normal voice returning. "It's a long story, and that's what first dates are for, right?"

He shrugged his shoulders and stuffed my business card into his back pocket, then wiped his brow again.

"Since I've never been asked out by a woman before, I suppose I should say yes — even if you do work for the Prince of Darkness," he said with a smile. "No need for you to buy me dinner, either — there's a good pizza place about a block from the Jack Singer, and they make home brew."

"Beer and pizza?"

"Beer, pizza AND opera."

"Done," I announced, turning on my heels and heading back to the terrace. "Call me, and we can make plans."

"Yep," he grunted, as he resumed shoveling the gravel.

Now, try to understand that my asking him out was the first time in my life I'd ever done something that impulsive in the romance department. If I had a sordid past, which I don't, I'd say that I've always been attracted to guys who seemed intent on generating income and acquiring the best in leather furnishings, home electronics and Lexus products. Dave, on the other hand, drives a Chevrolet Nova that he's lovingly restored, and his TV still has knobs, believe it or not. His motto is "keep it simple, stupid", and with my troublesome history of relationship angst, I'm inclined to agree with him.

The old me, the one who couldn't make love work to save her life, is a stark contrast to the new me. I've found love. Blessed, lasting love. Passionate, hopeful and spirit-enriching love. Sure, we have our occasional tiffs, but Dave is the first man I've met who is happy to sit on a park bench and watch the leaves turn in the autumn. We make grilled cheese sandwiches together, and we're content to watch British drama on PBS each night. I bake and he cooks. I complain and he listens. In fact, we both excel at finding that happy medium which guarantees domestic peace.

As an added bonus, he doesn't fear me — a refreshing change. More on that later.

Neither of us stakes his or her ground, like it's disputed territory where game-playing is the currency. Jeez, even my Dad likes Dave and isn't bothered by the fact that my suitor aspires to nothing more than a quiet life and continued employment with the Demarco Construction Company.

Of course, our careers were not the immediate topic of discussion when we started dating. In truth, Dave Webber learned about my day job quite by accident, after waking up to the whip-snapping sound of a series of bullets slamming into the wall above the headboard, narrowly missing us both. That he soiled the bed sheets was a forgivable sin, since we'd nearly become members of the dearly departed, so I was happily prepared to cut him some slack. I calmly rolled up the dirty linens and stuffed them in the washing machine, then hummed a pleasant melody while I made the bed. Dave gulped down a tumbler of scotch to calm his nerves and then asked me why my condominium was a target of a drive by shooting.

I told Dave that I collect things.

I also told him that what I collect can only be described as unconventional, and that it's a bloody miracle my employer remains discreetly hidden from taxpayers, because I'm worth every penny of the forty percent commission I receive at the time of delivery. Don't get me wrong — I pay Revenue Canada when I owe them money, and my job is legitimate — I'm a civil servant, for crying out loud! You won't find my name on the government ledger, but I will disclose that my employer is a division of *Government Services and Infrastructure Canada.*

It might be troubling to learn that your tax dollars pay for items that cause drive-by shootings in the middle of the night. Then again, the nature of what I collect justifies the creative accounting by the bigwigs that work for the Finance Minister, and the market for the items I've recovered produces roughly three percent of the revenue the government needs to balance the federal budget. When you think about it, I'm actually contributing to lower taxes, in the grand scheme of things.

Of course, these commodities exist beyond that which most people would consider reasonable. Indeed, my collection straddles the line between reality and the supernatural. When I say supernatural, I'm talking about something more substantive than strange sightings, UFO's and bleeding staircases — that's what they *want* you to believe in.

Dave takes it all in stride. God, the man is a rock. He didn't even blink when I dispatched the demon who tried to slit his throat after Dave fell asleep in the bathtub. I captured its essence in a Tupperware container and FedEx'd it to one of the two hundred or so storage facilities that most people believe are grain elevators straddling the U.S. border. Tupperware is absolutely vital in my line of work, by the way.

Did I mention that Dave has met the Prime Minister, and both are huge fans of the Toronto Maple Leafs?

The saps.

I used to think the hotline to my condo was for emergency calls from the Prime Minister's Office. Imagine my surprise to learn that Canada's national leader uses it to talk with Dave about the Leaf's playoff prospects or the score of a hockey game that went to overtime. There's an amusing photo of both of them in my living room during last year's play-offs, and from the mischievous grins on their faces, you can tell they'd just consumed a case of beer and two De Niro's pizza's between them.

I don't have the heart to tell either of them I like the Chicago Blackhawks.

Some people consider me to be a mystic, but that's far from the truth. I've been accused of witchcraft by a certain fundamentalist neighbor of mine, and while sorcery is listed on my resume, I'm not in the habit of luring young children to my condo in order to bake them in an enchanted oven. I fell into this job quite by accident when I discovered that I possessed the ability to see the preternatural world. There are a handful of people with similar abilities, and part of my job is to locate them, since Government Services and Infrastructure Canada likes to keep track of these things. Don't ask me why.

What is the preternatural world?

It's part myth and part reality, where magic and turmoil fly in the face of the laws of physics and pure science that we apply to the near world, which is where we live. The preternatural world made up in large part of beings possessing qualities that would take scholars a lifetime to wrap their collective heads around, assuming they're open to what can only be described as, well, unnatural. It exists within our world, but it's a place that is rarely seen by near world residents, because we're too busy sitting in the drive thru at Tim Horton's or grinding through gridlock on the Deerfoot Trail to notice.

Here's an example.

Have you ever read a newspaper article about a mysterious event? Something that's inexplicable? Perhaps the headline reads, "Scientists Baffled by Mass Death of Songbirds in the Cariboo". Conventional resources will try to find a scientific explanation why thousands of songbirds suddenly die for no clear reason. They'll do air quality tests in the bird's habitat to look for toxins. Hundreds of bird carcasses will be dissected to find out if they were somehow poisoned. They'll even research any unexplainable meteorological phenomenon that might have occurred at the same time the birds died. Once conventional science comes up empty-handed, that's when my phone rings. Within hours, I'm on a plane so I can discover a cause.

In the case of the dead songbirds, I wasn't in the back forty for longer than thirty minutes before I spotted what had killed them: A forest imp.

He wasn't your average, run-of-the-mill forest imp either. This particular imp was three sheets to the wind as he crouched over a bubbling stew in a cast iron pot, chanting wildly as a murky vapor collected above his head. His incantation supercharged the vapor with gray malice, a little-known dark spell designed to wipe out the source of the sorcerer's frustration. In this case, it was the songbirds.

You see, forest imps dislike songbirds for two very critical reasons: songbirds are competition for the various insects that are the primary source of the forest imp diet, and because most imps demand silence in the woodlands. If you're ever walking through a woods in a provincial park or a national forest, and you happen on a place that is eerily quiet, where you feel like you're the only person in the known universe, you're probably in the heart of a forest imp domain. Don't worry — they're not known for attacking humans, so long as they respect the silence of the woods.

Of course, the damage was done, and part of my job description is to act as a broker with the goal of negotiating the way in which this creature of the preternatural world remained unseen. Sometimes I barter information about a predator that might be a direct threat to a specific race of unnatural beings. Other times, I'm forced to resort to my own abilities, which, when applied correctly, can be convincing to a recalcitrant waif or even a river troll, for that matter.

Yes, trolls exist.

In fact, they are quite common. They don't normally hang out underneath bridges, as popular Norwegian mythology would suggest, either. Instead, they prefer to live in the many small suburban green spaces within walking distance of middle class neighborhoods, because our disposable society is addicted to fast-food and microwavable meals, and trolls are addicted to our refuse. It's their crack.

Ever wake up one morning and find your garbage cans overturned and trash strewn about your neatly manicured lawn? That's the work of a common troll and not a raccoon.

I know, these revelations are difficult to imagine — I get that. Still, someone has to do this kind of work, and before I came along, the job of policing the preternatural world and preventing large-scale calamity was left to exorcists and folk sorcerers, who often wound up on the wrong end of a poorly delivered spell. Naturally, they would only succeed in complicating the mess they'd intended to clean up, so really, it's a wonder humanity survived this long.

I'm serious.

In the past one hundred years, we've experienced five major "incidents" that had the potential to destroy life as we know it. The reason we can laugh about it nowadays is because most people won't accept that, for example, the Cuban Missile Crisis happened primarily because Nikita Khrushchev was possessed at the time, and none of Kennedy's people spoke demon.

Each morning I wake up and read the personal ads in the Calgary Meteor. I know — I agree it's a rag, but darn it, they have the best advertisements for inexplicable phenomenon, and Dave (who doesn't live with me — god, while I adore the guy, I'm just not ready to go shopping for drapes — not yet, anyway) circled a big, bold-lettered advertisement in the Lost and Found section before he went to work:

LOST - Grain Bin in Hidden Valley. It was here two nights ago. Owner baffled. Anyone with information, please contact me ASAP. E-mail responses only: wheresmystuff@accumail.net.

"You have my undivided attention, Farmer Bob," I said, as I sipped my coffee and tore out the ad. I shuffled to my office and logged into Outlook Express, then began typing:

From: Valerie@mail.org

To: wheresmystuff@accumail.net

Subject: Where's your bin?

To Whom It May Concern:

I read your advertisement in the Meteor. Are there any trees surrounding the missing item, and if so, are they devoid of foliage? Feel free to contact me at: 1-888-64-VALERIE. I might be able to help.

I clicked "send", and within thirty minutes, my cell phone was ringing.

CHAPTER 2

"Valerie Stevens," I chirped, stirring another cup of coffee.

There was dead air for about ten seconds and then a man's wheezing voice.

"How did you know about the dead trees?" He coughed and then cleared his throat with a loud hork.

I smiled into the phone. "Well… I didn't say the trees were dead in my e-mail; I asked if they were devoid of foliage."

"You mean, like leaves?"

"Yes, sir, are there any leaves on the trees surrounding your missing bin?" I asked, politely.

"Nope." he coughed.

"What did you do with all of the leaves? Did you burn them?"

"What I'm sayin' is there ain't no leaves on none of them trees — they're just *gone*. Them damned trees just died."

I reached over to my book case and pulled out a red binder I'd labeled "Missing Items" and then flipped to the divider that read "Large Items". I flipped a few more pages until

I found a snapshot I'd taken of a large hole in the ground, where a lawn shed once stood.

"When did you last see it?" I asked, noticing the hedges in the background of the snapshot were bare, and every flower in the adjacent flower bed was dead.

"Two days ago," he said. "It was there when I went to bed, and it was gone the next morning. I looked for tire tracks, because I thought it might be the work of vandals, but shit... they'd have made a helluva lot of noise, and the dogs would have been on 'em faster than you can say 'what the hell'."

"Hmmmm... is there a hole in the ground where your bin used to be?"

"Yer damned right there is!" he snapped. "Listen lady, if you're the one behind this, I won't press charges or nothing — the joke's on me. Just return the bin, alright?"

I closed the binder and took a large slug of my coffee.

"I didn't steal your bin, Mister..."

"Peter Orlowski," he said, finishing my sentence. "Who the hell are you?"

"My name is Valerie Stevens, and I think I can help you find your bin," I said.

There was another brief period of dead air, and I half thought the man would hang up on me.

"Damned bin ain't worth no more than a couple of hundred bucks, eh?" he grumbled. "Not the end of the world if I don't get it back, but it's just the principle of the whole thing."

"I understand," I said, nodding into the phone. "Mr. Orlowski, I'm wondering if you'd be agreeable to a meeting — I'd like to take a look at that hole in the ground."

"How come?"

I'd like to take some soil samples and snap a few pictures, if that's alright."

I heard a loud THUNK as he dropped the phone, and then I heard him shouting.

"Bern... okay if we have company today? I got someone on the horn who might know what happened to the bin!"

"Are they staying for dinner?" a raspy female voice rang out. "I don't feel like entertaining guests."

"Nope — they just want to look around," he shouted back.

"That's fine with me," Bern's voice answered.

There was a scuffling sound, and then I heard Mr. Orlowski's wheezing voice.

He sniffled and then blew his nose. "Yep — you can come out here and have a look. Meet me at the Tim Horton's in Okotoks, and you can follow me out to the farm. I'll wait in my truck... you can't miss it, because it'll be the only truck in the parking lot that's older than whale shit."

"Do you have a cell phone?" I asked.

He made another horking sound. "Nope. Been farming this land for the past forty-eight years. We didn't have cell phones then, and I don't need one now."

"Fair enough," I said. "Two hours is enough time?"

"Yeah, that's fine. Meet you at the Tim's at eleven-thirty."

He hung up the phone, so I wandered over to the bathroom and turned on the shower. I slung my bathrobe over the toilet and grabbed a fresh towel from inside the vanity, then placed it on top of my robe. I poked my hand inside the shower to test the water temperature and then hopped in.

The hot splashing water pulsed against my back and felt heavenly. I reached for my loofa and wondered how it would be possible to pilfer a grain bin without leaving at least some evidence that you'd been there. The darned things are made of galvanized steel, and they have to weigh at least a thousand pounds, so it's not something you can just throw on the back of a pickup truck in the middle of the night. I massaged some conditioner in my hair and chewed my lip as I thought about the trees the old farmer had told me about. While a missing bin might be of great concern to a farmer at harvest time, the fact that the trees surrounding the bin had lost their foliage was a sure sign that whoever took the bin probably wouldn't need a truck.

"Are you thinking it's space aliens, Valerie? Dear God, I hope not."

"DAMMIT, BILL!" I choked, nearly slipping on in the tub and landing flat on my ass. My heart pounded in my throat as I got back to my feet and threw my loofa through the shower curtain. "You scared the hell out of me!"

CHAPTER 3

"Fifty-Dollar Bill, get out of my bathroom!" I barked. "I mean it!"

"I'm just trying to be helpful," said Bill, trying to sound apologetic. "I'm not a dirty old man, you know."

There was a muffled hissing sound, so I poked my head around the shower curtain to make sure the coast was clear. Satisfied, I finished rinsing the conditioner out of my hair and turned off the shower.

"I'm pretty sure that little old men didn't hang out in attractive young ladies' bathrooms in your day!" I growled, still fuming. "For a dead guy, you have crummy manners."

"I have excellent manners," Bill's voice rang out from the hallway. "I'll have you know that I've dined with FDR, Churchill *and* Stalin. Mind you, Stalin was a boor. He'd be the one to hide out in the ladies' room, not me."

I dried myself off and ran a comb through my hair, then threw on my robe.

"I don't have time for a history lesson, Bill," I grumbled, as I stomped down the hall to my bedroom. "What do you know about large farm implements that disappear into thin air and trees that suddenly die?"

Bill appeared in the doorway and made a slicing motion across his neck with an index finger. He tilted his head to the left, and it promptly fell off, landing in his left hand.

"You know I hate it when young people forget their history," his head snipped. "In life, I was very important man."

"You talked to your dead mother through your dog!" I huffed, throwing on a pair of jeans and a sweatshirt. "Nobody asked you to hang around, either – you could easily cross over."

"Speak no ill of my mother, missy!" he choked. "That woman was a saint!"

I gave Bill a sour look as I pulled up my socks.

"Put your head back on; you look ridiculous," I groaned, rolling my eyes.

"Fine!"

Fifty-Dollar Bill is my name for the spirit of William Lyon Mackenzie King, Canada's tenth Prime Minister and the guy whose face is on the fifty-dollar bank note. With over twenty-one years as Canada's national leader, he holds the record as the longest serving Prime Minister in the British Commonwealth. He was also a closet occultist and liked to commune with the spirits of Leonardo da Vinci, Sir Wilfrid Laurier, his dead mother, and several of his Irish terrier dogs, all named Pat. That now, nearly sixty years after his death, the guy likes to commune with the world of the living, well... let's just say the irony isn't lost on me.

I asked him why he refuses to cross over, and he told me that dead people were boring, plus he gives political advice to a certain federal leader whose party will never form a government in a thousand years. While I can't explain why he'd back a losing party, I can say that despite his questionable manners, he's proven to be a valuable, albeit irritating, resource. During his life, he amassed a crap-pile of influential contacts among the departed. Better still, because he was a head of state and a highly educated man, his spirit contacts are far more reliable than, oh, say, the ghost of a dead chicken farmer.

"I need a favor, Bill," I said, slipping my feet into my Danner boots.

"Why should I do a favor for someone so utterly rude?" he asked, still sounding indignant.

"Look, I'm sorry for what I said about your mother — alright?"

"I didn't talk to her through any of my dogs. That is a myth made up by the Tory controlled news-media."

"I said I was sorry…"

He floated across the main hall and sat down on the antique chair next to my front door, then crossed his legs.

"Apology accepted," he said, obviously pleased with himself. "What kind of favor is it?"

"I need you to shake a few bones in the local cemeteries. See if any of your contemporaries have ever heard of large, inanimate objects that suddenly disappear and why." I said, throwing on my leather jacket.

Bill adjusted his tie and gave me a very serious look.

"This is about the dead trees, isn't it?" he asked.

I spun around and gave Bill a surprised look.

"You've seen dead trees? Where?"

He adjusted is spectral glasses and gave me a hard stare for a moment.

"Well… just a few clusters of dead tress and shrubbery on the outskirts of the city. I'm sure it's nothing to worry about."

"Nothing to worry about?" I groaned. "Bill, I just got off the horn with an old farmer in Okotoks, whose grain bin apparently vanished into thin air, and the trees in the local vicinity are either dead or devoid of foliage. What do you think would cause that?"

Bill frittered with a red scarf in his tunic and frowned.

"How many creatures are you aware of whose sheer presence causes organic matter to suddenly die?"

"Reapers," I said, in a matter of fact voice. "That's what they do, isn't it?"

"What interest might a reaper have in a farm implement, then?" he asked, sounding like an old headmaster. "Don't you agree that it would be uncharacteristic for a reaper to make its presence known to those in the living world, outside of claiming the life of its intended?"

"Yeah, I know." I said with a nod.

"It's entirely possible that we're dealing with a creature far more sinister — perhaps something from the dark place."

"It's also possible that this old farmer is full of crap, and he's begging to have his picture in the Western Producer," I added. "I'm no skeptic, Bill; you know me."

"That I do," he said. "I shall make a few inquiries and report to you before day's end. In the meantime, I recommend that you bring your satchel, because you don't have a clue what you're potentially walking into."

"Agreed," I said, as I grabbed my leather jacket. "Talk to you tonight."

CHAPTER 4

It should be noted that what I do falls somewhere in between sorcery and dumb luck.

I'm mentioning this because I've been interviewed at length by the Mounties, and they've deemed me to be a security threat, even though I'm paid my the Government of Canada.

Gotta love those guys.

It's true; I'm not a sorceress — at least not in the traditional sense. While sorcery is the practice of magic from supernatural or occult sources, the word magic is a misnomer — it's only part of what I do. Because of this, I prefer to describe myself as an *alchemist*: someone who combines their knowledge of sorcery with that of chemistry, metallurgy, medicine, astrology, and mysticism. I'm also clairvoyant, and yes, I can see dead people, as the nature of my relationship with Fifty-Dollar Bill would attest.

As mentioned, I sort of fell into this profession, and if I had to do it all over again, I'd have been happy to simply go to medical school and become a doctor, like my Dad. Unfortunately, life rarely works out the way we expect it to, and the fact that I brokered a peace treaty with a poltergeist at our summer cottage when I was fourteen suggested that perhaps the study of medicine might be wasted on me.

You see, the darned place was haunted by a collection of spirits who still claimed ownership to the land our cottage sat on. I suppose we should have been more vigilant, since my parents bought the place for eighty thousand dollars below the property value, but hey, Dad wanted out of the city in the summer. To this day, he considers the purchase to have been a bargain, despite the fact that one of the aforementioned undead occupants nearly strangled him to death while he was sitting on the toilet.

Since I could actually see the malevolent spirits who were busily chucking plates against the wall and smashing our small dinette into a thousand pieces, it seemed reasonable that I should ask them to stop, which I did. Mom wanted to know whom I was talking to, and as I recall, I might have said something smart like, "The guys who are destroying your kitchen... NO! Hush up, for crying out loud!"

It turns out the spirits hadn't received a good Christian funeral when the trio died of the Spanish Flu on the property, back in 1918. Because the area was very remote in those days, their remains weren't discovered until 1955, when the cheapskate who bought the land decided to build the existing cottage. How cheap was he?

Cheap enough to dig three large holes about four hundred yards behind the cottage near the tree line. Cheap enough to simply dump the human remains.

Well, darn, I'd be pretty steamed, too, wouldn't you?

Anyway, I led Mom and Dad to the location of the graves, and Dad found a femur sticking out of the ground, so he called the authorities. The bodies were exhumed, next of kin were contacted, and within weeks, the trio received a proper burial. Amazingly, the slamming of doors in the cottage at all hours abruptly ended.

See?

Too easy!

You just have to *want* to listen, and for culture in perpetual denial about death, that's generally considered to be difficult. But I do listen; I have to. Heck, in most cases, I have no choice!

As for the trio of spooks from the cottage, well, they had some advice for me prior to leaving this plane of existence. They informed me that if I could see them, I should keep my eyes open, because the world as I knew it was a lie.

I took their advice to heart, and in the twenty years since that day at William's Lake, I've seen everything from undead flesh to Orchard Faeries who are responsible for ensuring that "good farmers" in the Okanogan have a plentiful crop of cherries each year.

You won't find any orchards as you head out of Calgary on Highway 22X, and the rolling farmland blasts by at a hundred kilometers an hour for about ten minutes before you take the turn into Okotoks. It was a moderately pleasant late August afternoon, and I opened the sunroof on my Nissan Maxima, because the dank smell of recycled air simply can't compete with a good, old Southern Alberta breeze. The warm wind blew my baseball hat off, so I reached into the backseat and grabbed it, then closed the sunroof and opened my windows a crack. Within minutes, I spotted the Tim Horton's, and, as always, there was a huge lineup at the drive thru. I pulled into the parking lot and drove in circles until I saw an ancient Ford pickup truck with a grizzled looking man seated behind the wheel, smoking a pipe. I assumed this was Peter Orlowski, so I backed into the parking spot next to his driver-side door and rolled down the passenger window.

"Mr. Orlowski?" I asked, pushing my sunglasses against my forehead.

He took off his *Roundup Ready Herbicide* baseball hat and tapped his pipe on the side of his truck, spilling ash onto the pavement.

"That would be me," he said, sliding his pipe into the breast pocket of his plaid shirt. "You ready to come out to the farm?"

"Sure thing," I said, with an unusually chipper smile. "Lead on."

He nodded and slipped his ball cap back on his head, rolled up his window and put the old Ford in gear with a loud THUNK! I followed him back onto Highway 22X for about fifteen minutes, until he put on his right signal light and slowed down. I flicked my signal light and geared down as we both turned off the highway and onto a dirt road.

Since my car was leased, I didn't want to wind up with a boat load of paint chips or a cracked windshield, so I slowed down until I was satisfied that the cloud of dust from his old pickup no longer posed a thread to my paint job. We drove for another five or so minutes, until he turned right and crossed a Texas gate, and then parked his truck. I slowly drove over the gate, hoping against hope that the independent suspension in my Maxima was as forgiving as the pickup's, and pulled up beside Orlowski.

As soon as I got out of my car, my knees buckled.

I hate it when that happens.

CHAPTER 5

"You alright Miss, er..."

"Stevens," I exhaled heavily, as Peter Orlowski helped me to my feet. "Just call me Valerie."

"Alright, then," he said, as he took a tentative step backward, just in case my knees planned on giving way again. "I never did ask you what you do for a living... you with the Mounties?"

"No, I'm not a police officer," I muttered, brushing myself off and feeling embarrassed as hell. "I'm a consultant."

Orlowski's grey eyes narrowed, revealing a deeply chiseled set of crow's feet.

"Sheeoot... this is gonna cost me some money, is that it?"

"No... not at all," I half-groaned, as my stomach started doing back flips. "Would you reach into the back seat of my car and grab the large leather satchel? I'm going to need it."

"Sure enough," he said, exhaling in relief as he opened the back door of the Maxima and reached inside. "Money's been tight lately, with the missus needing her medication and all. Goddamned Alberta Health Care don't cover crap."

I climbed into the box of the old Ford pickup and surveyed the area.

We'd parked along the forward slope of a waist-high stand of wheat that bobbed and weaved in the warm breeze. An ancient Massey Ferguson combine sat idly along the ridge of the hillside, and I could see the glint of the sun bouncing off the cone-shaped lid top of a series of eight grain bins. There was a noticeable gap between bin number six and bin number eight.

"I take it that's the location of your missing bin," I said, flipping down my sunglasses.

"Yep," grunted Orlowski. "Just what the hell happened when you got out of your car? You're not sick are you?"

I hopped off the box of the pickup, grimacing when I landed.

"No, I'm not sick... at least, I don't think so," I said, forcing another smile. "Mr. Orlowski, how long have you lived on this farm?"

Orlowski pumped out his chest and smiled proudly.

"I've been farming here for over forty years," he said. "My father farmed this land before me, and my grandfather cleared this land after it was granted to him by the Canadian Pacific Railway... why do you ask?"

It's rare that I'm immediately affected by negative energy, or what I like to call bad joo joo. When I walk past a cemetery, I normally experience some light-headedness or slight nausea if a murder victim or a criminal is buried there, and I'll often see a procession of spirits who've chosen not to cross over holding vigil at their final resting place. In the case of Peter Orlowski's farm, I assumed that a grave or two existed somewhere on his land, but the circumstances of their deaths shouldn't have affected me at all. Since the intensity of bad joo joo has to build up considerably before I feel any ill effects, the suddenness of my bout of nausea told me this was a serious case of hard-ass menace aimed squarely at me.

"I was just wondering," I said, holding my stomach. "Why don't you lead me to where you last saw your bin?"

Orlowski nodded and motioned for me to follow, so we headed along a cut line and up the hill. As we crested the hill, I spotted a depression in the ground between the bins, and I noticed a tidy row of dead poplars surrounding the barn.

"It's the twentieth of August, and you tell me why the hell those trees are dead," Orlowski griped, pointing to the barn.

I knelt down and placed my left hand on the ground, hoping there was enough spiritual energy in the earth to catch a glimpse of who or what had stolen the grain bin.

"I'm not sure," I said, concentrating, as I picked up handfuls of soil. "Nope, I've got nothing so far. Let's take a look at that hole."

Orlowski grunted in agreement and led me to a perfectly formed circle in the ground where the bin used to be. Just as he told me on the phone, there were no tire tracks or footprints in the dirt surrounding any of the bins.

I had to admit, I was impressed.

The ridge of the hole looked like a giant cookie cutter had pushed into the ground with tremendous force and the inside surface was smooth — as if the bin itself had been pulled into the earth. I grabbed my flashlight out of my satchel and aimed it down the hole.

"Jeez, that's a deep hole," I said in astonishment. "Hand me a rock, Mr. Orlowski".

"Why?"

"Well, do you see the bottom of the hole? I sure as heck can't."

"What are you gonna do?"

"Drop the rock in the hole and time how long it takes until I hear a thud."

Orlowski handed me a rock, so I held it over the centre of the hole and let go.

"One thousand one, one thousand two, one thousand three, one thousand four…"

We heard a faint thump before I could reached five, so I assumed the rock had hit bottom, and then something unexpected happened.

The rock shot out of the hole as if it had just been launched from a catapult and flew high into the air.

"Sonofa — oh, *sheeit!*" Orlowski gulped. His face turned three shades of pale as he staggered backward and then promptly fainted. I scrambled to my feet and was about to shake him out of his stupor when the ground surrounding the hole started shaking. Dust filled my nostrils as the hole belched a huge jet of dirt high into the air, knocking me flat on my ass.

I took off my ball cap and shook off the dirt, then I noticed a bleached-white human skull, along with what appeared to be a pelvis, lying on the rim of the hole. I raced over and opened my satchel, then frantically stuffed the remains inside. Mr. Orlowski groaned weakly from about ten feet away, so I spun around to see if he needed first aid.

"Mr. Orlowski… sir, are you okay?" I squeaked, as I reached over and shook his chest. My satchel was nestled snugly beneath my left arm, and I hoped like hell he hadn't seen me stuff the skull and pelvis into my satchel.

He coughed hard as he got up and then ran about fifty feet from the hole, almost doing a face plant into one of the dead trees.

"I don't know what the hell kind of game you're playing, missy, but I'm an old man with a heart condition, and the last thing I need at my age are big ass holes in the ground that spew rocks at me!" he shouted, his voice shaking.

I motioned for him to calm down, hoping he wouldn't have a stroke.

"I had nothing to do with this, Mr. Orlowski, but if we're going to find your bin, you're going to have to trust me," I said, in the best soothing voice I could muster.

"To hell with that!" he snapped. "I'll just fill in that Goddamned hole and forget about the bin. You can get the hell off my land and forget we ever met!"

Orlowski wasn't being rational, so I decided to play the civil servant angle. I reached into my satchel and grabbed my wallet, and then I pulled out my government identification card.

"Mr. Orlowski, I work for the federal government — here's some ID," I said, handing him the card.

He held the card about three inches from his nose and frowned.

"Government Services and Infrastructure Canada, eh?" he mused. "My missing bin is now a matter for those freaking retards in Ottawa?"

"No, Mr. Orlowski." I said calmly. "The Government of Canada doesn't care what happened to your bin. They're likely more interested in why there's a geometrically perfect hole in the ground that is probably three hundred feet deep, which apparently spews out anything that you drop inside."

Orlowski handed back my card and gave me another very suspicious look.

"Where are you going with this, missy?" he asked, tapping his foot in the dirt.

I shrugged hard. "It's entirely possible there some kind of geological anomaly causing this…"

"You mean like a sink hole?" he interrupted.

"It's possible," I said, reassuringly.

Orlowski's frown rose into a full-blown grin, and he let out a boisterous laugh.

"Jesus H. Christ, you government types really believe that farmers are dumb as a post, don't you?" he chuckled. "This farm is in the Alberta foothills, honey — the soil only runs so deep. Beneath the soil is solid rock, for Christ's sake! Are you trying to tell me there's a geological explanation for this?"

"I can't rule that out," I said.

"Uh-huh… so geology is the reason that rock you dropped in the hole flew fifty feet into the air, is that it?"

"I'm not sure, Mr. Orlowski. The only way we'll know is if we get a team of people to go down that hole and have a look, and that means that a bunch of scientists from the University of Calgary will be out here with their four-wheel drives and surveying equipment."

Orlowski made a huge effort of rolling his eyes.

"Shit, I'm in the middle of a harvest here… I don't have time for that!"

"I understand, but we can't have sink holes popping up in farmer's fields, can we?" I asked, matching his frustrated tone. "There is another option, though…"

"What's that?"

"Forget about your missing bin and fill that hole in today…

do you have a front end loader on your property?"

"No," he shrugged. "But I can fill it in with my tractor — so long as you don't report this to your bosses in Ottawa. Seriously, this is my busiest time of year, and if I can avoid an invasion of taxpayer-funded Poindexters, I'd like to do it."

I looked at my watch; it was 2:30 P.M.

I decided I would leave Mr. Orlowski to fill in the hole, and when he wasn't looking, I grabbed a sprig of wretched oak from inside my satchel and dropped it down the hole. Then I reached inside the satchel again and pulled out a small Tupperware container that I promptly filled with soil.

Orlowski snorted. "Tupperware, huh? That don't look too scientific."

"You should be pleased," I joked. "Do you know how much they charge the government for petri dishes these days?"

"I can well imagine," he said, his voice laced with cynicism. "You can make it back to your car without me, right?"

"Sure can," I said. "Before I leave, though, you mentioned this property has been in your family for generations, and that your grandparents were homesteaders. Are there any graves on your land, or is there a cemetery nearby?"

"Why?"

"Just so I can make a note of it for the vital statistics people."

"Yeah, my grandparents are buried a quarter section over, as well as two uncles who died in the 1930s."

I scribbled the information on a notepad and stuffed it into my satchel, then stuck out my hand.

"I'm sorry about the bin, Mr. Orlowski... sorry about the sinkhole too. If there are any more mysterious occurrences out here, would you be kind enough to give me a call?"

"Guess so," he said, shaking my hand. "Thanks for your help, anyway."

"Not a problem," I said, as I turned around and headed down the hill toward my car.

CHAPTER 6

When I returned to my condo, there was a message from
Dave on my voicemail, saying that he'd hoped I could sleep
over at his place, as he'd been experimenting with his new set
of Greek cookbooks again. While the prospect of a gourmet
meal and a quiet evening in front of the television sounded
appealing, the fact whatever was inside that hole at Orlowski's
farm had spewed a human skull and pelvis at me suggested
that I'd have to take a rain check. I called Dave back and
broke the news to him, and being the good sport that he is, he
didn't kick up a fuss.

"Got your message," I said. "Are you on the road?"

"Naaa, just pulling into Demarco's," he said, turning down
the stereo in his dump truck. "So are you up for a fabulous
night of Greek food and possibly a DVD?"

I bit my lip; it sounded wonderful, but the nausea in the
pit of my stomach was just starting to subside and I had to
consult with Fifty-Dollar Bill.

"Something came up," I sighed. "Remember that
advertisement you circled in the Meteor?"

"Yeah…"

"Well, it's a doozy... hey I have a question about ditch digging."

"I drive a dump truck," Dave said, sourly. "It's more glamorous than driving a front end loader, you know."

"Gotcha... well, you're the closest thing I know to a heavy equipment operator, so I was just wondering, how fast can a backhoe dig a hole in the ground?"

"Hmm... assuming the ground isn't frozen, I've seen them dig a ten foot deep hole in about five minutes... why?"

"Oh, just a big hole in the ground where that farmer's grain bin used to be, that's all."

"As in how big?" Dave asked.

"Big." I said, cryptically.

Dave let out an amused chuckle, and I heard a loud hiss, so I assumed he'd just parked his truck.

"You sound like you're trying to get your head around one of those unnatural occurrences."

"You sound like you're starting to understand the woman in your life," I laughed, in a lusty voice. "If you're nice to me, I might just perform some unnatural acts on you when I'm done this case."

"Promises," Dave snickered. "So what you're saying is I'm going to be snuggling up to my body pillow until I hear from you again, is that it?"

"Yeah, sorry about that — but this is what I do for a living."

"Are you going to be a target for another one of those mysterious assassins? You know I worry about you."

"Hopefully not," I said, trying to sound confident when my gut told me that whatever was down in that hole would probably take a shot at me. "Anyway, I'll take some precautions."

"Do so," Dave said, sternly. "Hey, I lo — "

"Do *not* say that word to me for the first time over the phone, Dave," I lectured. "We need to say it to each other face to face... ideally when I'm corrupting you."

"Is that a promise?" he teased.

"Count on it... look, I have to go. Call you tonight."

Dave let out a disappointed sounding sigh. "Talk to you then," he said.

I hung up the phone and dropped my satchel on the kitchen counter. A small cloud of Orlowski's topsoil drifted into the air, filling my nostrils and causing my stomach to heave again.

"You know, that kind of language is pure filth, Valerie," Bill snipped, in a disgusted tone. "Men and women never talked dirty like that in my day..."

"Cripes, Bill... how the hell would you know? You never married, and half the scholars in the country think you died a virgin."

He rolled is near transparent eyes. "Enough with the potty talk, young lady; what's in your satchel?"

"Just the leavings from a southern Alberta farm, oh, and human remains."

Bill rubbed his hands together and grinned in anticipation. "Ooooo, this *is* a mystery — I do so love a good mystery," he said, dreamily.

"I imagine you do," I grunted, as I reached into the satchel and pulled out the bleached skull. "What have you learned about the dead trees?"

"Well, it wasn't a reaper – I was wrong on that hunch."

"Great," I huffed. "This is going to be more difficult than I expected."

"You can always make the skull talk," said Bill. "Surely you've got something in that satchel to compel the history of those old bones."

Bill was right, of course. There was always something in my satchel that could be put to good use, because my satchel is enchanted. That said, were I to pack it with what I really need when dealing with the preternatural world, I'd have a satchel the size of a Chevrolet Silverado. No, enchantment in this case means the satchel responds to the strength of my spirit and not only offers a small measure of physical protection from physical or spiritual attack, but veils whatever is inside to anyone who might acquire it. In short, the satchel works for one person and one person only. Me.

As an alchemist, I collect ingredients for spellcraft, or what I like to call, "magic on the fly". You'll note that use of two important words here, "alchemist" and "spellcraft", because they are two fundamentally different beasts. While spellcraft implies the use of magic, alchemy deals with the investigation of nature using chemistry, metallurgy, physics, medicine, astronomy, and a host of other disciplines. It's not "witchcraft", an art entirely different from what I do, and it's a far cry from wizardry, as wizards deal in the art of thaumaturgy, or, the working of magic and feats.

Yeah, that's right. I said *wizards*.

I know a wizard or two, and frankly, I would hate their job. While they interact with the preternatural world, they're also bogged down with archival practices, and there's this nasty business of wearing pointy hats, not to mention long, flowing robes. I don't do pointy hats unless I'm drunk and it's New Year's Eve, and the only long, flowing robe I own is my bathrobe, which is decidedly un-wizardly, because it's covered with pictures of friendly cows. Unlike me, wizards are cantankerous at the best of times, and because wizardry is still an all boys club, all wizards are required to grow a beard of sufficient length as a membership requisite. Personally, I think the beard thing is a rule designed to keep women out – therefore, sexism does indeed exist among those with supernatural abilities.

Call it a supernatural glass ceiling.

My satchel acts as a catalyst to somehow charge items I've placed inside with a supernatural energy that I am only now beginning to understand. What I've learned so far is that if I put an ingredient inside that is to be used for spellcraft, that ingredient is enhanced, somehow making for very strong magic. Take the sprig of wretched oak I dropped in the mouth of the hole at Orlowski's farm. My satchel enhanced the sprig, thereby allowing it to immediately take root the instant it came in contact with the soil. In the case of Orlowski, I used it to seal off whatever was in the bottom of that hole. Would I be lost without my satchel? You bet. Have I ever misplaced my satchel? Not yet, but give me time.

The smell of old leather and arctic dubbin filled my nostrils as I unbuckled the satchel.

"Are you absolutely certain you're an alchemist?" Bill whispered from the ceiling.

"Most days," I mumbled, as I reached inside and pulled out a small vial containing a clear oily liquid, and held it up to the fluorescent light over the sink.

"What's that?"

"Egyptian Hibiscus oil," I said.

"What's it do?

I glanced at Bill and decided I would use my patient voice, because I was getting tired of playing twenty questions with a dead guy.

"Bill, I know you find this entertaining, but I need you to just stand there and shut up, because the skull won't talk to you — you're already dead."

"Yes — yes… fine," Bill grunted impatiently. "Just get on with the show."

I placed the skull in the sink as a safety precaution, in case it started bleed ectoplasm all over my new granite countertop, and pulled the small cork out of the vial. I poured a tiny drop that landed on the crown, forming a perfect bead, then took a step backward in case the skull did something unexpected – you know, like explode.

Bill looked pleased as punch and rubbed his hands in anticipation, as a thin mist rose from the sink in wispy, vaporous tendrils. A dense, grey cloud comprised of static electricity took shape a foot above the skull, and the jaw started opening and closing as if attached to the hand of a puppeteer. It was time to talk.

"Who are you?" I asked the skull, politely.

The cloud came alive with tiny bursts of electrical energy as my cupboard doors started banging. I could hear a stack of plates rattling away, and then a cup flew off my coffee cup tree, straight through Bill's nearly translucent head, smashing against the dining room wall. Then the skull let out a haunting, raspy whisper that sounded like it was talking through the end of a very long and very hollow tube.

"I am who I was… this is not the hereafter."

"You've passed on," I said, calmly. "I found your skull quite by accident."

"This was no accident," it griped. *"I was perfectly happy on the other side when something pulled me through..."*

"What is your family name?" I asked.

"Sedgewick... I mean, I was William Morrow Sedgewick. I was buried on my land after the consumption got me in nineteen hundred and four. Who are you?"

"Someone who'll help you cross over to the other side, if you'll let me."

"Ask him if he voted for Laurier," Bill whispered in my ear. "He'll be very pleased when I tell him."

"Shut up, Bill," I hissed.

Suddenly a God-awful stench like rotting garbage began filling my kitchen. The cloud grew dense as the electro-static bursts grew in intensity.

"I-It said it needed my bones to bring him," the voice groaned. *"It violated the compact between the creator, the living, and the dead."*

"Who?" I asked.

"I-I don't know its name... but it knew me. It knows you, and it knows what it wants."

"What does it want?"

"Death... it wants death," the voice softened. *"It holds malice and contempt above all else; it rejoices at the suffering of all who've lived and died."*

"Heaven, help us... it sounds like the Tories," whispered Bill.

"I mean it Bill — *shut up!*" I growled, baring my teeth. I turned my attention to the skull and decided to ask one final question before I helped the spirit of William Sedgewick cross over.

"Why did it want your bones, Mr. Sedgewick?"

"To pull me back into your world," the voice sighed. *"It needs the energy of a host of spirits like me, and it will stop at nothing to find them. That which lives will die, if it falls into its shadow. It is a parasite, and it knows who you are... it knows you pose a threat. That's why the earth gave up my bones in your very presence."*

I had heard enough.

I decided to release Sedgewick's spirit, so I closed my eyes and focused my thoughts on the magical energies that trapped Sedgewick in the mortal realm. I reached out my hand, feeling through a slurry of tiny spectral particles that tingled against my skin and collected them into a small compressed ball of force.

"Cross over, William Sedgewick. Find the peace you've sought, and spirits bless us all!" I said, in a resolute voice.

The cloud began swirling into a funnel, spreading out tendrils of super-charged energy in every direction. Suddenly, there was a brilliant flash of light, and the spirit of William Sedgewick was gone.

I exhaled slowly and wiped a bead of perspiration from my forehead with my sleeve. Fifty-Dollar Bill was dabbing at his eyes with a handkerchief he'd pulled out of his tunic, and I felt a little bit lost.

"That was so touching," sniffed Bill. "It almost makes me want to cross over too."

"Wouldn't I just *love* that," I groaned. "I might get a little privacy around here."

"Yes, yes... well, of course, I'm content to stay here and perform my civic duty to the world of the living."

I nodded, half listening to Bill, as I took Sedgewick's skull out of the sink and shoved it inside my satchel. Tomorrow, I would slip it into a Fed Ex box and ship it to the usual place, but I'd leave a note asking that it be returned to the land it was buried in all those years ago. It was the least I could do.

CHAPTER 7

Bill had decided to do a little spiritual snooping, so I spent the remainder of the day analyzing the soil content from Orlowski's farm. I found a highly concentrated level of spectral discharge, which seemed to bond the clumps of soil into something that emitted a small static electric shock whenever I tried to invoke a spell to track the magical signature of whatever took the grain bin.

"Damned thing acts like a spiritual countermeasure," I grunted, snapping the Tupperware lid tightly on the container.

I stuffed the container inside my satchel and chewed my lip as I ran over the facts.

There were two missing pieces of the puzzle.

The first was the lost grain bin, and the second – and more ominous – was that I didn't have a clue as to who or what kind of entity or spirit would steal the bones of William Sedgewick in a vain attempt to live again.

I plopped myself down at my computer, scanned the bookshelf adjacent to my desk and reached for a dusty old manuscript entitled *Arcane Notes,* written by Edgar Cayce, the noted American psychic and occultist. Why it was never published remains a mystery, and though the United States government has offered to pay me a boat load of money if I sell it to them, I've always refused.

Why?

Because it is a dangerous piece of literature that foretells a series of events, leading up to what Cayce believed was the end of days. Being the practical person that I am, it stands to reason that were I to accept the offer of payment, I might very well piss off the supreme being. (There has to be one, when you consider that I've stood toe to toe with creatures from the abyss.) Naturally, I refused partly out of the aforementioned fear of divine wrath, but also because you just *know* the White House might do something stupid with it. Of course, the American intelligence community don't take kindly to a refusal of good old American greenbacks, so they tried to steal the manuscript. That didn't go over well, because it is protected by a spell and can never leave my condominium.

What kind of spell, you ask?

Well, let's just assume that Cayce's manuscript causes shrinkage when it's in the hands of someone other than me, and we'll leave it at that.

I flipped through the first ten chapters, until I came to what Cayce described as "the naming of eight", or what I like to call "Edgar Cayce's Top Eight Malevolent Entities Of Total Bad Assedness".

Surely I'd find a description that might fit who or whatever the heck sucked Peter Orlowski's grain bin into a three-hundred-foot hole.

Entity Or Spirit Characteristics

1) *GEELBRIX*   Poisoner of fresh water.
2) *SECTOFIDE*   Spirit of malice
3) *ENTOBINE*   Wind demon
4) *LEEK*   Commands the river of death
5) *NOTSTOB*   Spirit of thieves
7) *SHADE*   Spirit or imprint left on person, place or thing.
8) *RUNESPITE*   Spirit of malevolent text and dark spells

   I remembered Sedgewick's spirit telling me that whatever
had stolen his bones wanted to live again and that it saw me
as a direct threat to its plans. That likely explained why I
had doubled over the moment I set foot on Peter Orlowski's
farm — whatever or whoever it was knew I was coming. But
how? I decided to consult with the only person I knew who
commiserated regularly with Edgar Cayce: Fifty-Dollar Bill.
   Now try to understand — the nature of my relationship
with William Lyon Mackenzie King's spirit is such that I try
to avoid seeking him out unless it's absolutely necessary. The
reason is that while he has proven to be a valuable source of
information about the spirit world, I truly wish that he would
cross over, because he is a pitiable character. He was a life-
long bachelor who never married or fathered children, and
there's an air of loneliness to him that completely bums me
out.
   Yes, I feel sorry for the guy, okay?
   That being said, I don't ever wish to give him the
impression that he *shouldn't* cross over, because while he
might have been a brilliant politician, he is thick as a bag full
of hammers when it comes to what constitutes appropriate

and inappropriate conduct — like when he showed up in my bathroom while I was showering. In short, I'm always afraid that if I seek him out, he simply won't leave, and frankly, my boyfriend Dave is terrified of him.

I'm serious.

You try to get intimate with a loved one when the ghost of a chubby old man in a in a pin-striped suit is floating above your bed — it tends to spoil the mood.

I bit my lip and decided I needed Bill's insights, so I summoned him.

"William Lyon Mackenzie King, I summon you!" I grumbled, reluctantly. Within seconds, a bright red vapor shot through my office window, and Bill materialized in the leather couch beside my filing cabinet.

"Oh, this is exciting!" Bill grinned from ear to ear. "You actually said my name properly."

I made a huge effort of rolling my eyes and let out a heavy sigh. "Bill, what do you know about Edgar Cayce?"

"Everything!" he squealed. "We wrote to each other every Sunday for over twenty years, and he was a frequent guest at twenty-four Sussex Drive."

"He liked to hang out at the Prime Minister's residence, eh? So you were both very good friends, I take it."

"Absolutely — you know, of all the mediums I'd ever met, Edgar Cayce was the only one who contacted my mother. He also gave me incredible insights into the economic crisis our nation faced during the 1930's and the coming war."

"So he was accurate beyond the shadow of a doubt?" I asked.

Bill nodded as he stretched out on the couch. "Do you mind if I make myself comfortable?"

"Go nuts," I said, surprised by his enthusiasm. "So you know about the naming of eight?"

"Absolutely," he said with a nod. "As a matter of fact, I sent one of my staffers to help him research his manuscript. A dreadful shame it couldn't be published, but it was a dangerous time."

"It's still a dangerous time, Bill," I said, nodding back. "In your opinion, which of the eight would be the one William Sedgewick referred to?"

Bill scratched his chin and frowned. "Well, a Sectofide would certainly posses enough malice to smash a grain bin into a perfectly round hole about three hundred feet deep, but they have little interest in re-animation. A Leek could conceivably resurrect, but that's unlikely because it covets the fare that certain cultures pay as they cross the river of death. My hunch is that we're dealing with a Shade."

"Why's that?"

"Because they exist exclusively in the mortal plane, and they leave their imprint wherever they go… in this case, I'd think that big hole in the ground is a mighty convincing imprint, don't you agree?"

"Possibly," I said. "But aren't shades simply a presence? I didn't think they were known for carrying out acts of pure rage."

"Like when you became sick at the farm?" he asked.

"Exactly."

Bill sat up and gave me a stern look. "That feeling of menace that so sickened you might very well have been a shade leaving its imprint."

"Because it perceives me as a threat?" I asked, innocently.

"Because you *are* a threat," said Bill, dead serious.

"Considering the possibility of a resurrected life, would it be fair to argue that one's desire to live again might possibly become an obsession?"

"Of course… why do you ask?"

"I'm asking for no other reason than to warn you about the very real possibility that this particular shade might want you dead and will stop at nothing to make it happen," he said, grimly. "It can bide its time and strike when you're asleep, or when you're driving your car on the freeway. It can command the laws that govern chaos and strike you down if you don't remain vigilant."

There was silence in my office as I considered what Bill had just disclosed, and a chill went up my spine. Despite my unique gifts, it was entirely possible that Peter Orlowski's missing grain bin was a ruse to lure me to that farm. What happened next confirmed my suspicions.

I hate it when I'm right.

CHAPTER 8

Since I am the only person I know who can communicate with the dearly departed as easily as picking up a phone or waving at someone in the street, I can understand why I might be a person of interest to the shade in question. That being said, it's not as if those who've passed away are clamoring at my feet to engage in idle chit-chat — it doesn't work that way.

First off, the overwhelming majority of men, women, and children who die *choose* to cross over, but there's a large number who prefer to hang around, like Fifty-Dollar Bill. Sometimes they appear as spirits, forever holding vigil over the places that meant something to them in life, and more often than not, they pay little regard to the comings and goings of those in the mortal realm.

Secondly, the word *haunting* is a mortal word that implies some measure of mischief on the part of a spirit, and there's a distinction here: we are dealing with *spirits* and not *ghosts*. The word "ghost" implies that a spirit has nothing better to do than scare the living crap out of people, a popular misconception. Those who choose against crossing over do so for reasons known only to them. It might be that they were not ready to die; it could also be that a spirit doesn't yet know that it passed away, and it could be out of concern for loved ones. Either way, the overwhelming majority of spirits I've encountered are lonely souls who seem trapped between moving on and staying here. If it were me, I would move on, but I'm not dead. Not yet, anyway.

While I haven't a clue what's on the other side when you cross over, my suspicion is that it's either a very happy place or a place of torment and punishment: in short, heaven and hell. It stands to reason that some of us might try to avoid going to the bad place, but why wouldn't someone wish to go to the happy place, and more importantly, why would a spirit care to live again when everything they've ever known or loved has probably crossed over in its own right?

Good question — and one I suspected was central to the motivations of the entity that had stolen the bones of William Sedgewick.

Fifty-Dollar Bill left my condo, and I was nuking a frozen dinner with the CBC Calgary News playing in the background. My head was swimming with questions about how I was supposed to find the shade in question when it could be anywhere, and I was in a sour mood because I could have been munching away at *spanikopita* with a certain mustachioed dump truck driver rather than trying to solve the mystery of the missing grain bin.

That was about to change.

I'd just taken my meal out of the microwave when I heard the news anchor's voice.

"A mysterious case of grave vandalism at Kingsview Cemetery has authorities baffled..."

I raced into the living room and plopped my butt on the coffee table, then turned up the volume on my TV.

The camera flashed to a neat row of headstones connected by a long line of yellow police tape, then to a tiny crowd of grieving onlookers dabbing at their eyes with Kleenex. The lawn in the immediate vicinity of the graves was crisp and brown, contrasting the emerald green of the perpetually cared for landscape.

Crisp, brown grass.

Dead grass.

My gut told me the shade was upping the ante and was sending me another message, so I listened to the reporter covering the story.

"Grave vandalism isn't common in the Calgary area, and police are investigating. Management at Kingsview Cemetery can't explain what happened to the bodies or why these four graves in four separate areas of the cemetery were targeted."

I clicked off my TV because I just knew there were probably four geometrically perfect, rectangular holes in the ground about three hundred feet deep, and it was only a matter of time until this would happen again. I needed some help on this one.

It was time to contact Vishesh.

Who is he?

Vishesh Rajwani works for the *Canada Border Services Agency* — at least, that's what his government ID says, and that's what they want you to believe. What they don't tell you is that Vishesh is a senior civil servant who has worked in the public service for the past twenty-three years, and he's also the chief archivist for all those little trinkets I've been sending via FedEx. I've never met the man in person; we communicate exclusively via secure cell lines and web conferencing software that is entirely hacker-proof, thanks to a nifty spell I'd concocted from a recipe I'd smuggled into our realm. (When one of Vishesh's staff tried to hack it during the testing phase, her hair fell out, and her desktop burst into flames.)

I logged onto my laptop and clicked on my web cam, then paged Vishesh. In less than a minute, I saw his bespectacled face and pronounced nose looking at his web cam as if he were peeking out the peephole at the front door of his house.

"Oh my God, you've got a dilemma, yes?" he asked, in a voice with a deep East Indian accent.

"You might say that, Vishesh," I said with a nod. "Are you up on what happened today at that cemetery in Calgary?"

Vishesh smiled, revealing a set of pearl-white teeth behind a scraggly, gray goatee. "Yes, we've got some people thinking up a big story about where those bodies disappeared to."

"So, where did they really go?"

"I'm trying to work that out right now, because our story about grave robbery will be dismissed by the conspiracy theorists sooner than either of us would like — and you know what *that* means."

"Yeah, I know — another alien autopsy documentary on the Sci-Fi Channel."

Vishesh rolled back in his chair and reached for something, then produced a small Tupperware container that he held in front of his web cam. "You see this? You see this?"

I snorted. "Well, duh, Vishesh. I bought that container at a garage sale, for crying out loud."

"You need to make sure these receptacles are properly sealed," he snipped, admonishing me. "The specter you trapped in this container nearly destroyed my database and could have opened the many other receptacles you've sent me."

"Don't blame me, blame FedEx... I made sure there was a retaining band on the lid. It's not my fault the damned thing came off because the people they hire don't understand the word fragile."

Vishesh gave me a sour look and started clicking away at his keyboard.

"I'm checking my latest report from Environment Canada, and there's been an unusually large amount of magnetic activity in the Calgary area," he said, still typing. "Unfortunately, it keeps moving, so they've been unable to get a bead on it."

"What do you think it is?" I asked.

"I'm not entirely sure, but I am concerned the intensity of spectral energy on that farm you visited could have killed you... you must be more careful, Ms. Stevens; you're a valuable asset."

"Holy crap, Vishesh!" I snapped. "When I visited that farm, I assumed we were dealing with a reaper!"

"Reapers don't make large objects disappear," he shot back. "I thought I'd taught you that."

Of course, Vishesh was right. He's always right.

He's the reason I work for the government, by the way. He recruited me via one of his undead contacts, and he possesses enough knowledge of the arcane to fill an office building. He lives and works in the tiny prairie village of North Portal, because he needs to be within a short drive of those grain elevators and for security reasons: while there are unnatural beings that would love to see me dead, Vishesh is still number one on their hit list.

"You'll be more careful with this one, yes? I have a bad feeling about it."

"I'll try," I said, sounding conciliatory. "I'm just not entirely sure what we're dealing with. Fifty-Dollar Bill seems to think it's a shade."

"Oh my God, he's still here?"

"Like old luggage," I laughed.

"He might be onto something," Vishesh grunted. "I'm assuming you talked to that skull you sent to me? What did you learn?"

"That its name was William Sedgewick, and that something with the goal of resurrecting itself yanked him clear into our realm — it stands to reason those four bodies met with the same fate."

"How did you acquire the skull and pelvis?"

"Think bones flying out of a deep hole at Mach 3 — I have to assume something about me caused that to happen."

"Perhaps your above-average chakra did it," he said. "I will assume the spirit returned to the other side without putting up a fight?"

"That's right," I said. "It did give me a warning that whatever grabbed him will probably take a swipe at me."

"I have to agree — you're taking steps to protect yourself? You still have your satchel?"

I dangled the old leather bag over the webcam for Vishesh to see. "My butt is covered — see?"

"Very good, then," said Vishesh, still clicking away at his keyboard. "I'm sending you some information regarding how you might better locate this shade... assuming it's the culprit."

A window popped up on my computer to show a digitally enhanced photograph of a vaporous, black, human-like form hovering over the freshly cut trunk of a giant Sequoia that had just been felled. The background of the picture was a mural of dead trees, and there was no living vegetation on the forest floor.

I grimaced. "That is one ugly shade."

"It's unpleasant to look at because it chose to take that form," he nodded. "You know that shades can occupy everything from trees to people to toaster ovens... I suspect the one in the picture was released when they cut that tree down."

"You're probably right — I'll keep my guard up. I do have one question for you..."

"What's that?"

"Is this dark magic we're dealing with, or just plain malice?"

Vishesh scratched his beard and leaned back in his chair.

"I don't believe this is dark magic," he said, grimly. "There's no evidence yet that a human being is behind this activity."

I exhaled slowly. "That's what I was afraid of... talk to you later."

"Very good, then — do be careful."

CHAPTER 9

I decided that paying a visit to Kingsview Cemetery might not go over so well with the families of the four missing bodies if their bones flew into the air at my very presence.

I'm sensitive that way.

Obviously their remains could be anywhere between the physical realm and the spirit world, so it made sense that I should attempt to send their spirits back to the great beyond. This meant I needed a spell that would command their bones to return to their final resting place.

Well, it sounded good, anyway.

After I consulted with Vishesh, I dispatched Fifty-Dollar Bill to collect the names of the missing bodies from their headstones while I did a little research on how to conduct a powerful enough spell to draw their spirits away from whatever the shade had been using to yank them out from other side. This meant I'd be straddling the line between pure and dark magic, and it's not a happy place to be.

Ahhh… what can be said about dark magic?

Well, for starters, a spell — or even a potion, for that matter — relies on two things in order for it to function properly: the spell recipe and the ability of the person casting the spell to bend it to their will. What makes a dark spell or potion inherently evil can be summed up in one word: malice.

Let's face it, you're not going to use dark magic if, for example, you're a sprite with a penchant for filling the air with the scent of apple blossoms, and it just happens to be a snowy December morning. You'll use elemental magic because the scent of apple blossoms can't be a bad thing, right? On the flip-side, assume there is someone you want dead — *that's* the domain of dark magic. Not only because the magic requires that the spell is being cast for menacing reasons, but also because the ingredients of your spell or potion aren't exactly, well... *pleasant*. (Think blood, dead animals and possibly even brimstone.)

With this in mind, I decided my safest bet was to use a potion I'd stolen from a coven of devil worshipping anarchists in Edmonton. (They planned to summon a demon with the goal of possessing an unpopular university professor's soul and instead summoned the spirit of dead Methodist minister, who promptly chased them out of Fort Edmonton Park.)

I grabbed my satchel and headed to the roof of my building. It was just past 11:30 P.M., and there was a faint hint of autumn in the air. I reached into my satchel and pulled out a stick of white chalk, then drew four concentric summoning circles on the tar surface. I drew a fifth circle that I'd hop into just in case an angry looking shade showed up, wanting my head on a pike.

Summoning circles, incidentally, are probably the most effective protection device known to anyone who studies sorcery. Nothing can get in or get out unless the line is broken somehow, and God help you if that happens, because you will be done like dinner.

Fifty-Dollar Bill arrived with the names he'd read off the headstones shortly after midnight, so I wrote each name on a scrap of sacred parchment and stapled each name to the surface of the roof inside each of the four circles. Once I added the potion to each name, their spirits would be suspended in the summoning circles, and it would be a simple matter of releasing them to the other side. Everyone would be happy, right?

Well, not everyone.

I expected this move might possibly draw the shade out into the open, and that was fine by me. I wasn't too keen on the prospect of my chakra, or whatever the hell Vishesh had called it, being added to the shade's growing collection of souls, and since I often act as a broker, I assumed it was still possible to negotiate my way out of this.

I'm naive that way — or just plain dumb.

Bill sat on an exhaust vent and looked unimpressed.

"You think this will work, then?" he asked, sounding skeptical.

"It should," I said, shaking the potion I'd just pulled from my satchel.

Bill started pacing and gave me a worried look. "Are you quite certain that's all you intend to do, because I have to assume that fifth summoning circle is for you."

"You assume correctly," I said.

"Then you intend that your actions on the roof tonight will provoke this shade, is that right?"

"That's right."

"And what will you do when it shows up, looking for the

four spirits you've sent away?" he asked.

"I'm not entirely sure on that one, Bill… maybe I'll trap it with another spell and capture its essence in Tupperware."

Bill rubbed his chin and gave me a disapproving frown. "Suppose this shade turns its attention to me… then what?"

I pointed to the fifth summoning circle and shook my head. "If you're worried, then you should get inside that summoning circle with me," I said, sourly.

His face lit up, and he clapped his hands in apparent agreement. "Right then, in I go… are you ready for this?"

I nodded and flipped the cap off the small jar of potion and measured a drop with an eyedropper on each of the scraps of sacred parchment, then ran as fast as my legs could carry me into the summoning circle with Bill.

It should be noted that what happened next was not entirely unexpected. In fact, I planned on it happening.

Yeah, right.

The potion was having its desired effect, and I'd no sooner stepped into the summoning circle with Fifty-Dollar Bill when the spirits of the four souls appeared from within their own respective summoning circles, bobbing and weaving as their corporeal forms began to take shape.

"What are your names?" I shouted in a commanding voice.

"Where are our bones?" the four cried, in unison.

"They've been stolen from your graves," I said. "What are your names?"

The visage of a woman dressed in early twentieth century attire hissed. *"You know our names — they're not worth repeating…"*

I glanced at Bill, and then gave the four a puzzled look. "I need you to state your names so that I might send you back… why are they not worth repeating?"

"It knows we're gone," she said, this time sounding conciliatory. If we state our names, it will find us and take us."

"The one who stole your bones," I asked. "Is he a shade?"

"Yessss and noooo… It is coming… it is coming. We cannot say our names… it will find us!"

This wasn't good.

In order to send them back to the other side, the four spirits or I would have to state their names, allowing me to command their return. If I was going to do it, I would have to step out of the protection offered by the summoning circle, and that meant I'd be exposed to the shade, if it attacked. I flashed my eyes to Bill and gave him a sugary sweet smile.

"Absolutely NOT, young lady," he protested, angrily. "You're the one with supernatural powers, not me."

"Bill, if I step out of this summoning circle, you know what could happen," I pleaded.

"I also know what could happen if *I* step out of the circle too! You started this, young lady; you're going to have to finish it."

He was right — the jerk.

"Fine!" I said, icily, as I took a tentative step over the summoning circle. I glanced back at Bill, who was smiling as if he'd just won a point of order during Question Period.

"He is coming!" the spirits cried, this time there was an air of panic to their voices.

I raced past the four circles and shouted their names. *"Ronald Shaw, Elmer Holowaychuk, Delores Wilson, Charles Yeung… return to your place of rest, and may your souls find eternal peace!"*

The temperature dropped like a stone as a cold blast of icy wind appeared out of nowhere. The spirits began circling around me, and I felt a surge of energy building inside my chest. I shut my eyes tight, focused the energy to my fingertips, and made a hurling motion. A blinding blue ball of compressed spectral energy flew out of my hands and opened a rift between the mortal world and the realm of the dead.

"I command you to return!" I shouted, as the frigid breeze blew back my ponytail. "Find your peace!"

"WE'RE FREE!" they shouted, and their visages flew into the rift. The howling wind ceased, and the rift disappeared from sight as I dropped to my knees, feeling slightly dazed.

"That was beautiful," Bill sniffled from behind me. "It almost made me want to leave."

"T-Thanks, Bill," I said weakly. "Anytime you want to go, just…"

Suddenly, there was an explosion of thunder from the intersection next to my condominium. The power on my block immediately went out, and the few cars that were traveling up and down 17th Avenue screeched to a halt. There was an eerie silence for about ten seconds, and then the ground shook as a roar like a freight train going off the rails filled the air, followed by a metallic groan.

I heard voices shouting from the intersection of 17th Avenue and 8th Street. The power quickly restored, and the streetlights flickered to life, so I ran over to the edge of my roof and looked down at the street below.

"H-Holy crap!" I squeaked.

Peter Orlowski's missing grain bin had hit the intersection with enough force to leave an impact crater. Grain spilled out in every direction from the crushed steel that had burst on impact with the street, and I couldn't help thinking the bin looked like a giant, squashed coffee cup. Motorists got out of their cars and gathered around the bin; a few pointed to the sky, and a few more were taking pictures with cell phone cameras.

"Consider that grain bin lying there in the intersection to be a shot across the bow," said Bill, as he brushed up beside me and peered over the edge of the roof.

"Rats," I muttered, under my breath. "That wasn't supposed to happen."

Bill shook his head and hovered back to the exhaust vent, then sat down. "Well, you've obviously made an enemy… good thing his aim was off, otherwise you'd be flat as a pancake, and there'd be a rather large hole in the roof of this building."

"Yes, well, thank heavens for little miracles," I said, dryly.

Of course, I was unsure whether this was a shot across the bow, as Bill suggested, or the result of a poorly executed spell. I was certain that by summoning the four spirits and sending them back, I would draw out the shade. So where had I gone wrong? Within fifteen minutes, my handheld was ringing with a very irritated Vishesh Rajwani on the other end of the line.

"Oh my God, what did you do, Valerie?" Vishesh barked. It was the first time he had ever raised his voice to me.

"I did what you guys pay me to do!" I snapped, as I grabbed my satchel and headed down the stairs to my condo. "You know damned well this isn't exactly a precise science."

"Do you want to know what else isn't a precise science?" he shot back. "Explaining how a grain bin suddenly appears out of thin air and crashes into a busy intersection. Oh, and there's the issue of why a decomposed body landed in the middle of a dance floor at the Ranchman's Country Bar. Did I mention another body mysteriously appearing in the back seat of a taxi cab, or the two bodies sitting in a booth at Wendy's on Southland Drive?"

All I could manage was a curious gurgling sound.

"You know well enough that we hired you to *prevent* the knowledge of unexplainable phenomenon from ever seeing the light of day. If the truth about what we do was to be revealed, it could have devastating effects on not only the public's trust in its federal institutions, but also on the mortal and preternatural worlds."

"I know, Vishesh… look, I'm doing the best I can with what I've got," I explained, as I exited the building and headed over to the grain bin. "I'm going to see if there's anything from the other side I can scrape off that bin, and I'll use it to locate the shade."

"Make sure you do it right this time, Valerie," he snapped. "I'm going to dispatch some cleanup crews, and we're already working on the press coverage."

"Will do," I said, then stuffed my phone into my pocket.

I could hear the fire and police sirens approaching, so I pushed my way through the crowd of onlookers until I was next to the bin. There was a splattering of spectral ooze in all directions, so I knelt down and collected a large quantity in a Tupperware container, then shoved it in my satchel.

"What are you doing with that?" asked a shirtless man who was sucking on a Super Big Gulp.

"I'm going to analyze it," I said, pushing my way past him.

"Sweet!" he chirped. "I'm gonna get me some of that!"

"No you're not," I grumbled, as I reached into the pocket of my jeans and pulled out my wallet. Inside was a small envelope of a white powder I keep in case the public gets too close to something they really don't need to know about. I palmed my government ID and flashed it to the crowd.

"Everyone step back, I'm with *Health Canada* and this is a potentially infectious area. Step back!"

I shut my eyes tight, and then threw the enveloped onto the pavement in front of me. It exploded with a blinding flash as soon as it hit the asphalt, and instantly, everyone standing around the bin stood frozen in place and stared into space with a dead look in their eyes. Bill flew down from the roof of my building and hovered next to me as I crossed 17th Avenue.

"What was that?" he asked.

"Zombie bomb," I grunted. "They'll be standing there for the next three hours, and when they come to, they probably won't remember a thing."

"Well, that's convenient — I take it you've acquired some ectoplasmic discharge?"

"Yep," I said, as I headed to my car that was parked in front of my building.

"Care to enlighten me as to what you intend to do next?"

I flipped the unlock button on my key fob and the tail lights on the Maxima blinked twice. "I'm going to the pay a visit to an old friend," I said calmly, as I opened the door and hopped in the driver's seat.

"So you're not worried about dead bodies showing up in taxi cabs or fast foot restaurants?" Bill asked, poking his head through the roof.

"Nope," I said, starting the car and slipping it into gear. "That's the least of my worries right now."

I pulled out onto the street, squealing my tires and tore up 17th Avenue.

It was time to talk to Caroline.

CHAPTER 10

Caroline is a family lawyer — or she *used* to be, until she started her nasty habit of eating dead things.

Don't worry — she's far too left-leaning to actually eat people, which is something zombies are exceedingly good at. How she came to become one of the walking dead is quite a miraculous story, given that she'd actually been bitten by the rotting husk of a long-dead magistrate who was under the control of a necromancer. The only thing that kept Caroline from completing the transformation into a full-fledged zombie is that the necromancer had a weak heart and died of a coronary embolism at the precise moment the zombie magistrate took a chunk out of Caroline's left shoulder. That I'd just blasted the necromancer with a bolt of lightening probably helped speed up the massive heart attack.

I am, if anything, helpful.

Somehow the necromancer's magic infected Caroline, and as a result, she retains all her pre-zombie faculties, with one or two small exceptions. She *is* technically dead because she doesn't have a pulse, and her body temperature is lower than ten degrees Celsius. (She still breathes air, and her body isn't decomposing, though she is unnaturally thin, so I'm not exactly sure how that works.) As well, there's this nasty business of eating small mammals and assorted sundry, you know, *alive*. I asked her why she doesn't eat people; her response? Because she'd feel guilty.

Yes, Caroline is a zombie with a conscience.

She lives in a comfortable one-bedroom flat above the old Freedom Baptist Church, which, believe it or not, Caroline owns and rents out to a small fundamentalist congregation that have no idea their landlord could eat them, should they fail to pay the rent on time. I'm not saying she *would* eat them, mind you — but she could if she wanted to. She could also eat me quite handily, and it is for this reason that while she technically owes me what she calls a "life debt", because I dispatched the necromancer and saved her from becoming a mindless killing machine in Prada shoes, I don't entirely trust her. After all, she *is* a lawyer.

I pulled up the alley behind Freedom Baptist Church and dimmed my headlights. I stopped short of the fence surrounding the church courtyard and looked up at a picture window to see the flickering amber glow of one of Caroline's many candles that she makes from bees' wax. (Her hobby of candle making pre-dates her life as a zombie. She's also into scrap booking and has been trying for six months to recruit me into her online scrap booking web-ring.) For some strange reason, she's sensitive to anything above a ten-watt bulb, so not only was I about to visit the flat of a zombie, the candle light would only make the experience creepier than it already was.

I slipped my car into park, grabbed my satchel, and headed up the wrought iron staircase that led to an arched doorway. It was too dark to see what was beneath my feet, but I just knew the crunching sound beneath my Danner boots had to be the remains of a variety of small rodents. As I reached the top of the staircase, I didn't know whether to feel revolted or genuinely spooked.

"Who's there?" A sultry voice called out from behind the door.

Yes, Caroline has a sexy voice. That I am envious of the fact a zombie has a sexier voice than me is consistent with how things work out in my happy little life.

"It's Valerie," I called back. "You aren't, ugh, *eating* anything, are you?"

The door swung open, and Caroline stood before me wearing a pink bathrobe. The pale, waxy skin on her face gave way to bruise-like discoloration that spread from her lifeless eyes to the bridge of her cheekbones. A beaded necklace hung loosely from her ash-colored neck, and I could see the bony outline of her collarbone and sternum through her thin, dead skin. Her hair was a mass of giant, green curlers, and her black lips curled down into a disapproving frown.

"Your inability deal with my eating habits is *your* issue, Valerie," she snipped. "Seeing as how you're at my doorstep at ten o'clock at night, I take it you've chanced on something that tried to kill you, right?"

"Does a grain bin that fell out of a hole in reality and crash landed on 17th Avenue count as an assassination attempt?"

"That was you?" she asked. Her hollow, dead eyes opened wide, and a chill ran up my spine.

"Yep."

"Well, come on in!" Caroline said with a grin, which revealed a full set of stained, brown teeth.

"Thanks," I sniffed, stepping into her flat.

Caroline led me down a short hallway until she made a left turn into her small office and plopped herself down in a big leather chair behind an antique oak desk. Still grinning, she reached inside her desk drawer and pulled out a handful of crawling insects that she popped and into her mouth like M & M's.

"That's really gross, Caroline," I said, wincing.

"Yeah, I get that," she said, crunching away as if the bugs were popcorn. "I like how *I'm* suddenly responsible for how my eating habits make *you* feel. Cripes, Val… a girl's gotta eat, for crying out loud."

I sat down on a chair opposite the desk and placed my satchel on my lap. Caroline's eyes shifted from me, to my satchel and back.

"You have trust issues," she said, dryly. "You don't need that arsenal you call a satchel when we get together. Besides, when have I ever let you down?"

I relaxed my grip on my satchel and tried to force a smile. "Never."

She nodded slowly. "Never is right, Val… anyway, it's not like I'm going to drop a grain bin on your head."

"Thanks for pointing that out."

"No problem."

I pulled out the Tupperware container of spectral discharge and threw it to Caroline. She caught it one-handed without even blinking.

"What's this?" she asked.

"Goop from that bin," I said. "Does the color look right to you? It's supposed to be clear — not cloudy and yellow."

Caroline flipped off the lid and stuck a long bony finger inside. She scooped a gob of the slime on her fingertip, and then stuck her finger in her mouth.

"It does taste a bit off," she said, as I tried not to pitch the remnants of my last meal on the floor.

"What?" Caroline asked, innocently.

"That's just nasty," I admitted, sounding revolted.

"Oooooo — big, tough sorceress," she snickered. "Freaked out by a bit of slime and a talking dead chick."

"Undead," I corrected.

"Thanks," she said with a smile, again revealing her disgusting, brown teeth. "Yeah, this stuff has gone bad. Fresh ectoplasm tingles the palate, and this stuff, well, it just tastes… *dead*."

I tried not to laugh at the irony of a zombie telling me that something tastes dead, and instead nodded politely. If anyone knew why the spectral discharge was off, it would be Caroline. Why? Because in the seconds after she was bitten by the magistrate, her soul crossed over to the bad place we mortals call Hell with a capital H. The moment the necromancer died, Caroline's soul returned to her lifeless body, only to find that she would be spending eternity (or until someone lops her head off) sucking the innards out of live rats and eating cockroaches by the handful. On the plus side, though, her body isn't decomposing, and I suspect her eating habits must have something to do with that.

"How dead?" I asked.

"Long dead," Caroline said, sounding ominous. "More than fifty years, I'd say. What do you think you're dealing with?"

"A shade," I said. "A really freaking strong one that can drop grain bins into downtown Calgary."

Caroline got out of the chair and adjusted her robe as she walked over to me.

"Give me your hand," she said, kneeling down. She stuck out her bone white right hand and looked me square in the eye. "I need to check something."

I tentatively reached out with my left hand and immediately felt my blood run cold at the touch of her cold and waxy skin.

"Caroline, if you bite me, I swear to God you will rue the day!"

"Relax," she said, as she turned over my hand and started examining my fingertips. "I just ate, and you're too damned skinny for my tastes."

"Thanks," I said, gripping my satchel tight in my left hand. "What are you looking for?"

"To see if you got any of that gunk on you."

"Why?"

Caroline dropped my hand and it landed on my lap with a dull thump. I was numb from the elbow down and could barely move my fingers.

"Because you're not the only one with trust issues," she said, standing up and leaning against her desk. "That gunk can and will infect you with heaven-knows-what. I just want to make sure I'm talking with Valerie Stevens and not some third party who is using you to achieve some undetermined purpose."

I rolled back the chair to a more comfortable distance and cocked an eyebrow at Caroline.

"*You* don't trust *me*?" I asked, innocently. "Care to explain that one?"

Her eyes again shift to my satchel as her smile disappeared into a serious frown.

"Yeah, I don't trust you," she said, icily. "You're like a time bomb that doesn't know when to explode."

"Excuse me?" I asked, not sure whether I had just been insulted or not.

Caroline let out an impatient sigh.

"Valerie, it's me here. I've seen what you're capable of."

"So?" I said, still unsure where Caroline was going with this.

"I've seen you call up funnel clouds; you can channel the power of an electrical storm, and you can bring down a river troll from a hundred yards away just by touching the earth. I might be a member of the living dead, but, honey, at least I know my limitations — you don't."

She was right.

As mentioned, I'm learning as I go, and very often when I'm forced to rely on spellcraft, I don't consider the magnitude of what I can do. It would be easy for me to dismiss bringing down a four-story office building simply by manipulating the contour lines on a topographical map as just another technical glitch, but Caroline had a point. My lack of control often brings about significant damage to property, not to mention the injuries to a variety of unnatural creatures that choose to engage me in something resembling combat.

"I'm working on it, Caroline," I said quietly. "It's not like there's a technical manual for this stuff."

"Welcome to my world," she grunted. "Sucks to be me, sometimes — still, I'd rather have you as an ally, and I know you're only going to come after me if I suddenly develop a hankering for human flesh."

"And I would in a heartbeat," I said, dead serious. "The last thing anyone needs is an army of the hungry zombies roaming down the Stephen Avenue Mall."

"Oh please… the place is dead, anyway," Caroline joked. "It would liven everything up!"

"Ha-ha." I said, in a sarcastic tone. "Listen, I have no idea where to even begin looking for this thing. I thought you'd have a few ideas and, you know, maybe tag along."

Caroline leaned on her emaciated arms gave me a very serious frown. She knew what I was up to.

"Let me get this straight," Caroline said, sourly. "You're dealing with what you believe to be a shade, and you think that during my stay in the netherworld, I simply accumulated an encyclopedic knowledge of all things evil, is that it?"

"Something like that," I said, nodding.

"What makes you think this thing is evil? It could just be a mischievous spirit looking to stir up the shit."

I gave Caroline a sugary sweet smile and decided to try Plan B.

"I could *pay* you," I said, my voice lilting up an octave.

"Uh-huh," she grunted again, this time sounding wholly unimpressed. "You once tried to pay me for helping you by giving me a toy poodle for Thanksgiving, and then you kidnapped it while I was changing into a new outfit."

"It was a puppy, Caroline… a *puppy!*"

"And puppies taste good!" she snapped. "Just because you have a problem with what I eat doesn't give you a right to steal my food."

"I gave you a bag of live goldfish instead," I said, trying to sound conciliatory.

She rolled her eyes. "Who pays people with fish, Valerie? Honestly…"

I decided to wait a few seconds before I would dangle something she'd really want. If everything worked, Caroline would agree, and I'd have a virtually un-killable zombie backing me up, should my investigation into the shade go ugly.

"Caroline," I said, leaning into the desk. "I know what you want more than anything. I can help you get it."

She cocked what was left of an eyebrow and leaned back on her desk.

"Really — you know how to get my soul into another living body? Whose body?"

"Yours." I said. "I think I might know a way to resurrect you."

"How?"

I tapped my satchel for extra effect and really started to lay it on thick.

"A few ingredients I traded during an encounter with a former necromancer. He couldn't pay my full fee, so he is in my debt."

"Former necromancer?" she asked, her voice laced with skepticism. "I suppose he had an epiphany and mended his ways, is that it?"

"Yep," I said.

"I see — and did this guy teach you all the tricks of the trade?"

"Nope, but I'm fairly confident he can be convinced of the value associated with paying his debt on time."

Caroline stood up and began to pace around the room. I decided to keep my mouth shut and let her consider her options. After about two minutes, she sat down on the edge of her desk. The disapproving frown was gone, and in its place was a sly smile.

"You'll excuse me if I'm not hopping up and down with joy about this," she said. "You're asking me for help, and you don't even know what you're up against. From where I sit, that's a recipe for disaster."

"I know."

"Then you'll also know the few seconds I was clinically dead was the equivalent of about a jillion years while I was in the dark place."

I nodded silently.

"I have no desire to go back there, Valerie," she griped. "It's bad enough I have to walk around with saggy gray skin and that I'm losing my hair. I used to be smoking hot, you know."

I put a tentative hand on Caroline's shoulder and smiled gently.

"And you will again," I said. "I promise."

Caroline reached for my hand and swatted it from her shoulder like it was an annoying bug.

"You promise? That's what I'm afraid of," she groaned.

CHAPTER 11

The ultimate spy is not a dashing, black-haired Englishman in a white tuxedo jacket, with a penchant for martinis.

No, the best kinds of spies are the ones who nobody ever notices as they go about their business each day, and who can see or hear everything.

And I mean *everything*.

The Calgary Board of Education is located a stone's throw from the W.R. Castell Library, one of my favorite haunts in the entire city, and across the road from police headquarters. Its offices were built some time in the 1960's and offer a bit of mid-twentieth-century feel to a downtown that is bursting with shiny, glass skyscrapers and few green spaces. On the west side of the building, facing McLeod Trail, are a group of ten statues. Each stands twenty-one feet tall, and each is a nude representation of either a male or a female. (One of the statues is even clutching a baby at its side).

At first glance, their bone thin bodies and featureless faces have a haunting look, similar to that of concentration camp survivors. But looks are deceiving. Their outstretched arms and fluid movement represent community, youth and possibly even hope.

They were crafted my Mario Ammengol for the British Pavilion at Expo '67, the world fair that was held in Montreal. They were purchased shortly after the fair and donated to the Board of Education, and they've been standing in a small green space on the west side of the building for the better part of the past forty years.

First entitled "Brotherhood of Mankind" then renamed "Family of Man" prior to their official dedication by the Duke of Kent in 1968, the statues are a fixture of downtown Calgary, which thousands of people have seen, but few people have actually taken the time to learn about.

You can learn a great deal by looking at a statue.

You can learn a great deal more when you ask a statue questions, because they see and hear *everything*.

Statues are more than works of art. They carry the soul of their creator's hopes dreams and aspirations within them, and it doesn't matter if they're solid marble, like Michelangelo's David, or brushed aluminum, like the ones outside the Board of Education. There's scant information about what Mario Ammengol was trying to convey through this work, but I like to think it was a positive message, despite the loneliness of standing silent vigil over a bustling city that is too busy to notice ten of the most fascinating pieces of modern art in existence.

"Stay in the car, Caroline," I said, taking off my ball cap and handing it to her. "Cover your face with this and pretend you're sleeping."

"It's dark outside, Valerie… I can come with you," she protested.

"They don't know you, and that means they won't talk if you're there," I said, opening the driver side door. "Besides, I need you to keep anyone from breaking into the car."

"We're half a block from the cop-shop, Val!"

"Just stay here… I'll be back in a jiffy."

I shut the door and jogged across McLeod Trail. Within seconds, I was standing in the middle of the small park the statues call home, so I knelt down on the warm grass and listened closely.

If you're attuned to the things that I've seen in my thirty-two years, you'll learn very quickly that sound isn't limited to living and breathing organisms. These effigies of humanity whisper like children telling secrets, and if you listen closely enough, you'll hear them, too. I shut out the sound of the city and focused my thoughts in a kind of meditation. Immediately, I heard male and female voices whispering to each other (because statues only speak in hushed tones).

"It's the sorceress," murmured the statue to my left. "She's come for another visit!"

"We've not talked with her for a long time," said a female, in a barely audible voice.

I stood up. "Good evening, family," I said, quietly. "I've come for your help once more."

"What can we offer this night?" asked a male voice from behind me.

I stood up and started meandering through the tiny park, touching each statue on the shin or calf and weaving myself between their giant legs.

"There is a spirit that can do great harm to those in the mortal world." I said, this time a little bit louder. "I believe this spirit has the ability to become one with trees, animals, mortals and possibly even proud statues such as you."

"Impossible," a female voice protested. "For what reason would a spirit do this?"

"I'm not entirely sure," I said, standing beneath the statue of the woman with the baby. "I'm not even sure if it is evil or not. But this spirit… this shade, has the ability to pull a departed soul across the river of death and back into the mortal realm. I would be in your debt were you to offer anything that might help me locate this spirit before it does any harm to my kind."

I knelt down in obeisance and kept my mouth shut as the statues began muttering amongst themselves at a frantic pace. I shut my eyes tight and tried to concentrate, hoping to catch the gist of their deliberations, but their chattering took on a percussive tone, and as they increased their tempo, all I heard were clusters of sharp metal clangs. This continued for about two minutes, until all of a sudden, the clanging ended and one of the male statues spoke up.

"We do not know what kind of evil can bring forth the dead from their reward or punishment for their deeds in life. We agree, however, that it must be evil, because only evil can dwell in the dark places to perform feats such as this. It has come to pass that your kind is oblivious to mortal dangers that surround you, just as it has come to pass that mortals have lost much of what makes them unique among the living things."

I nodded, silently.

"Our family has not seen that which you seek; however, we know of a presence that hangs over this city like menacing fog on a winter morning. By and by, we shall aid you, good sorceress, in your search. Alas, this night, we have little to offer other than our hopes that you unravel this mystery. Go now and seek this evil. Come to us two nights hence, and we will tell you what we have learned, for it is not only you who speaks to us, but those with the gift of flight and those who dwell in the belly of the earth."

"The birds… they talk to you?" I asked in an astonished voice, and surprised as heck the statues didn't have a hate-on for them because of the whole bird poop thing.

"Little birds are our eyes," said another female voice. "They stand with us as each season passes. They nest nearby and we comfort each other on lonely cold nights. They ask nothing of us, other than our companionship."

"I didn't realize that," I said, standing up. "I'll come to visit you more often; how does that sound?" "Thank you, sorceress," they whispered in unison. "Be wary of this gathering evil — it may act to deceive or destroy you and you must be on your guard."

"I will," I said, as I started to leave. "Thank you again for your help."

CHAPTER 12

I hopped back into my car, and gave Caroline a poke.

"I'll take my hat back now," I said, holding out my hand.

She slipped it off her face and handed it to me. "Those statues gave me nightmares when I was a little girl," she said, peering out the driver side window. "I can't imagine how you're able to talk to them."

"Anyone can talk to a statue," I said, starting up the Maxima. "Your mind must be silent enough to hear what they say, that's all."

Caroline blinked a few times. "Did they tell you anything useful?"

"They sense an evil presence," I said. "They've agreed to keep eyes and ears open."

I pulled out onto McLeod Trail, and after a ten-minute drive, we were parked outside my condo, across from the intersection where the grain bin had landed. Vishesh had moved quickly to get the area cleaned up, as the bin was gone, and the crowd of curious onlookers had dispersed. Caroline poked her head through the sunroof and looked out onto the street.

"That left a nasty dent in the pavement," she chuckled. "This shade must have lousy aim, because he missed your building by more than two hundred feet."

I turned off the engine and glanced over my shoulder at the intersection. "You see anything that I might have missed?"

"You mean like a shade?" she asked.

"Yep."

Caroline dropped out of the sunroof and back onto her seat. "I don't even know what a shade looks like," she said, sounding unimpressed. "Do you?"

I let out a sigh and shook my head.

"No, never seen one up close before."

Caroline tapped a bony finger against the dashboard and said nothing for about one minute, which was surprising, given that Caroline is the most impatient creature in my circle of unnatural friends.

"So basically, what you're suggesting is we don't know what we're looking for," she huffed.

"Basically." I admitted.

"Lovely," she groaned. "And the only clue we've got is a Tupperware dish of slime."

"Yep - oh, and the grain bin, of course."

Caroline pressed the tilt button on her seat and yawned as it hummed backward into a reclining position.

"Well, *do* wake me up when you've found something worth investigating, Val."

I ignored her sarcastic comment as I examined the intersection.

"Who says I don't have something worth investigating," I grumbled, under my breath. "I've got a container of slime and a lot of contacts around town who might offer a bit of insight."

"I can hardly wait to meet them," said Caroline, still yawning. "I'm just going to assume some of these contacts dislike you a great deal and you just happened to bring me along for moral support, right?"

"Some, yes…"

Caroline interrupted me and she bolted up from her reclined position, nearly bumping her forehead on the headliner of my car.

"Great," she groaned. "So we're going to be talking to ogres, is that it? You know they creep me out, Val… I freakin' hate ogres."

I turned to Caroline and tried my best to smile politely, given there was some measure of irony in her statement. I, too, have been known to be impatient; that's part of the whole mystery-solving process. But for Caroline to be creeped out by ogres? I know they're nasty, brutish, smelly and downright mean, but Caroline *knows* that nearly every creature in the preternatural world is dead terrified of zombies, and for good reason: zombies are utterly terrifying creatures.

You can't kill them unless you take their head off or you're a crack shot and can nail them between the eyes. They are completely resistant to most spells, and even if a sorcerer calls up a spectral firestorm and then lays waste to ten city blocks that happen to be a host to a zombie infestation, the damned things *keep* coming! They consume entire settlements of everything from waifs to elves to trolls much in the same way a cloud of locusts will swoop down on a field of ripe wheat, devouring everything in their path. Yeah, zombies are bad news to the power of infinity, and the one sitting beside me was frightened of ogres.

Caroline, while retaining all of her intellectual capacity, is *still* a zombie, and as such, she is both an object of terror and scorn. She's also an extremely efficient killer and has no compunction whatsoever against ripping open the chest and pulling the heart out of anything that's trying to kill me. She is unbelievably strong, as well. I once saw her tear out the heart of a Gray Mage (the human kind) who paralyzed me with a dark spell. She ate it before death had even registered in his eyes.

"Do you have any idea how dumb that sounds?" I asked sourly. "A zombie who is creeped out by an ogre? Geez, Caroline… vampires avoid you guys, and *they're* undead too!"

"Yeah, I know," she said, with a shiver. "But it still doesn't diminish the fact that ogres are gross. We're not going to meet up with any, are we?"

"No," I said. "This is strictly a case of something from the spiritual realm."

"Good. So what's the plan?"

"I'm not sure yet — I need to talk with Fifty-Dollar Bill."

Just then, a blast of icy air hit the back seat of my car, causing the hair on the back of my neck to stand on end.

"You rang?" Bill quipped. "Oh, I see you brought *her* along."

Caroline angrily took a swipe at Bill, only to see her arm drift through the corporeal vapor that is Bill's spiritual form.

"You still a virgin?" she snapped. "Oh wait, you're *dead*."

"Piff-paff," Bill said with a shrug. "And *you're* not."

"Children!" I growled. "If you don't mind, we have work to do, and the last thing I need are you two going at it again."

Caroline's eyes narrowed as she shot a menacing glance at Bill through the rear view mirror. "He started it," she grumbled.

"I don't care who started it," I growled again, this time a bit louder. "I need everyone on the ball here, because my gut tells me we're going to be dealing with a shit storm of corpses suddenly appearing all over town, and frankly, I'd like to spare the good citizens of Calgary that kind of trauma.

Bill crossed his arms and stared at the ceiling. "Fine," he said. "Truce... for *now*."

"Thank you," I said. "Bill, what have you learned since we talked last?"

A smile formed on his nearly transparent face, and he looked genuinely excited.

"Much," he giggled. "Oh, so MUCH is about the happen."

"Care to share that information with us?" Caroline asked, barely concealing her contempt.

"Certainly - there's a spectral imbalance in the atmosphere."

"Come again?" I said.

"An imbalance that is not of your realm."

"What kind of imbalance?" I asked.

Bill stretched his ghost legs across the back seat and put his arms behind his head. "Oh... the kind of spectral imbalance that tells us your shade has access to a degree of power that might possibly be off the chart. The kind of imbalance that has the capacity to destroy all organic matter it touches."

"And you know this because of what?" Caroline sneered.

"Because you urban dwellers who rarely leave this concrete labyrinth you call downtown haven't noticed there's a small community north of the city called Airdrie, and right now you can't see the pavement because the streets are littered with hundreds of bird carcasses."

"WHAT?" I gasped. "When did this happen? And... how?"

"I'd venture to say it occurred about the same time that grain bin hit the intersection," Bill said, this time sounding ominous. "How is still a mystery, but what I can tell you is that I personally witnessed a flock of about two hundred geese fall from the sky as I was drifting north of the city. I decided to investigate, and I hit a wall of energy that was virtually impenetrable. So, being the resourceful man that I once was, I simply decided to take a subterranean route. When I poked my head out of the ground on the main street in Airdrie, I couldn't help but notice the air was filled with feathers, and the ground was littered with the corpses of every species of fowl you can possibly imagine."

"Oh, lord," Caroline gulped.

"Want to know something else?" Bill asked, leaning over my shoulder.

"What?"

"Every tree I could see was devoid of foliage. Every flower bed, every shrub and hedgerow... all *dead*. You know what *that* means, don't you?"

I shuddered at Bill's cryptic tone.

"No," I said, as panic rose in the pit of my stomach.

He leaned in closer. "That same spectral energy might very well be headed for town."

CHAPTER 13

Calgary is a city with a million inhabitants. If you drive north of town for about ten minutes, you'll see an exit leading into the bedroom community of Airdrie. It's a small city of approximately fifteen thousand people, and nearly all its inhabitants commute to Calgary for work. Airdrie is a tidy place, with a large number of young families just starting out in life and a hefty retirement contingent of farmers who cashed in during the oil boom, when their land was selling for obscene amounts of money. There is wealth in Airdrie, but the residents are reluctant to show it. Most people live in generic, four-bedroom bungalows framed by lily-white vinyl fencing. Most drive an SUV, and nearly everyone in Airdrie chooses to live there because it's *not* Calgary.

But why start with Airdrie? Why not here?

I considered what Bill had just disclosed and bit my lip as I ran over the facts in my head. A grain bin had disappeared into a three hundred foot hole in the ground. It later came crashing into a busy Calgary intersection in what may or may not have been an assassination attempt. Four bodies had appeared in four separate locations throughout the city, and their spirits had informed me that a shade was responsible. The trees at Orlowski's farm were devoid of foliage, and nearly all the vegetation that Bill surveyed in Airdrie was dead. There were possibly thousands of dead birds scattered all over the small city and a wall of spectral energy that Bill couldn't penetrate, which was growing in intensity.

Everything sounded par for the course.

I hate that.

I'm a fairly analytical person, and often I look for patterns when I'm investigating a disturbance. The laundry list of events that had transpired over the past twelve hours pointed to a shade, in theory, but a wall of spectral energy? That didn't seem consistent with what I knew about shades. Then there's the fact that Vishesh hadn't called me to let me know about the dead birds – now *that* was unsettling. As Chief Archivist, he's got access to the paranormal infrastructure his department developed to monitor all things unnatural. So why hadn't he called me? It didn't make sense.

"You guys keep the noise down for a few minutes," I said as I punched Vishesh's number in the keypad of my handheld. Caroline and Bill nodded, and I listened to the ring tone and waited for Vishesh to pick up. The line crackled loudly in my ear as I counted the number of rings. After I got to four rings, Vishesh answered.

"Hello, Valerie!" he shouted. "Can you hear me?"

"Yes, Vishesh, I can hear you," I said, raising my voice. "You sound like you're calling me from another planet."

"It might very well be another planet, Valerie. Are there any new developments?"

"Plenty — you know about the dead birds in Airdrie?"

"Yes, we've just learned of it. Are you on scene?"

"No, but I expect to be," I shouted into the phone. "Fifty Dollar Bill informs me there is a wall of spectral energy — did you know about it?"

The line crackled and popped, and I could only make out a handful of words. *"The... readings... unknown... minutes ago... investigate..."*

I shook the phone in frustration. "Hello? Vishesh... dammit!"

I glanced down at my phone's screen and saw that I'd been disconnected. "Dammit all to hell!" I snapped.

Caroline gave me a consoling smile — well, as consoling as a zombie can be.

"What did he say, Val? Did he know about the spectral energy?"

I stuffed the phone in the pocket of my jeans and let out a frustrated sigh.

"Yeah, he knew. Unfortunately, we got cut off."

"That's never happened before," said Bill from the back seat. "I thought your illustrious contact had the latest in high tech gadgets, and you'd never lose a connection."

I nodded in agreement as I turned the key and my Maxima roared to life.

"Probably lost the connection at my end," I said, again biting my lip. "If that wall of energy is as big as you've suggested, I would imagine most electronics in the city are on the fritz."

Caroline reached over to switch on the stereo, and the hissing of dead air filled the interior of my car.

"Crap," she said, as she pressed the seek button. "You're right... there's nothing on either the AM or FM band. Any suggestions?"

I gave them both a worried look as I considered what to do next. If Bill were right and the spectral energy was causing the airwaves to go dead, it was likely that television stations as well as satellite broadcasts were out too.

"I'm not entirely sure," I said, reaching for the gear shift. "I think we should probably head out toward Airdrie and see what we can learn from the… "

Just then, a crow landed smack on my windshield with a hollow thump. Its milky gray eyes stared at me, and both its legs twitched for a moment, then stopped.

"H-Holy crap!" Caroline jumped in her seat.

There was another thud, followed by another. I heard a shattering sound and I whipped my head around to see that a large Canada goose had crashed into a glass bus shelter, spraying tiny cubes of glass in every direction. Suddenly there was a series of three loud thumps on my roof, and then the sunroof shattered into a million pieces as a goose fell in through the now gaping hole and landed between the front seats.

"I am getting out of here," Bill said, tersely. "I don't care to watch the zombie eat."

I turned the key and shut off my car, then reached for the door handle and opened the driver door. "You were right about it heading for Calgary, Bill," I said trying to conceal the panic in my voice. "We should head into my condo before we get pummeled to death."

"Good plan!" Caroline said as she opened the passenger door.

We'd been out of my car for less than ten seconds when it started raining. And not a late summer evening rain, either: It started raining dead birds.

CHAPTER 14

Bill disappeared back to wherever the heck it is that he goes to, and Caroline and I tore away from the Maxima, heading for the shelter of the entrance to my building.

Birds of every size and description were falling to the ground, landing with a non-stop series of thuds that sounded like little bags of wet cement hitting the pavement. We got to the door and ran inside, stopping to brush the feathers off our clothes.

"This is insane!" Caroline screeched.

"I have a very bad feeling about this," I huffed, brushing away at my knees and looking out to the street from the doorway.

"Oh, ya think?" Caroline griped. "God, I hope I don't get the bird flu."

I gave her a sour look and then turned to watch a city transit bus slide to a grinding stop near the intersection where the grain bin had landed. Inside, passengers had their faces pressed against the windows as they looked out at 17th Avenue, which was now dotted with bird carcasses in every direction.

"This just doesn't make any sense," I said. "Why is this shade killing freakin' birds?"

"I hate to throw words back in a colleague's face, Val," Caroline said, with a hint of sarcasm in her voice. "But remember what you said about keeping the City of Calgary relatively trauma-free? I think you can shelve that notion, because this whole thing is starting to resemble a biblical plague."

I spun around and gave Caroline a surprised look.

"That's it!" I said. "Caroline, you're a genius!"

"What do you mean?" she asked, her face taking on a confused expression.

I put my hands on her bony shoulders and squeezed.

"A plague — that could be the key to all of this!"

She half-smiled and looked at me like I should be measured for a straightjacket. "Ooookay… I'm not sure where you're going with this, so I will assume you know what the heck you're doing."

Of course, I *didn't* know what I was doing, and truth be told, I rarely do.

There aren't exactly a set of handbooks sitting on the bookshelf of your local library with concise directions on how to investigate inexplicable phenomenon. You rather make it up as you go, dig your heels in, and hope against hope that a combination of your own unique abilities and good common sense will help you survive a cataclysmic event. Solving it gets you bonus points, and if you're really lucky, you get to live.

Caroline's comparing a thunderstorm of dead birds to a plague immediately got me thinking about the dead trees at Orlowski's farm and the dead vegetation in the background of the only known picture of a shade that Vishesh shared with me. People in my line of work know little about them outside of the fact that they leave a spiritual or emotional imprint on people, animals, and even vegetation. But what is an emotional imprint? Moreover, would this kind of imprint be enough to kill? The answer to that question had been staring me straight in the face, and I didn't even realize it until now.

"Why would a spectral entity like a shade start off by killing seemingly insignificant organic matter like trees and flowers, only to turn its attention to a variety of species of birds?" I asked, only half-expecting Caroline to know the answer.

"Beats me," she said with a shrug. "Maybe it started killing trees and worked its way up to birds."

I stared at her as my jaw dropped and my blood immediately ran cold. A splash of nausea twisted my stomach into a ball as I considered Caroline's hypothesis.

"Maybe this shade is working its way up to… *people*." I whispered, and panic stabbed at my heart like an ice pick.

"You know, that's frankly a terrifying thought," said Caroline. "But it kind of does make sense, when you think about it."

I nodded in agreement, as I pushed on the foyer door and headed toward my car. Caroline quickly caught up to me and grabbed my arm to slow me down.

"What's going on, Val?" she huffed, sounding confused. "You don't really believe this thing would wipe out people in the same way it just wiped out all those birds."

I stopped and knelt down and reached for a dead bird.

"Why not?" I asked, scooping up a dead sparrow with my left hand, and then holding it up for Caroline to see. "Human beings are organic matter, just like this bird. It breathes and bleeds just like we do — at least, it used to."

Caroline casually snatched the dead bird by its feet and held it up to the streetlight to examine it.

"This little bird only looks dead," she said. "But it doesn't smell like the dead."

I gave her a confused look. "Come again?" I asked.

Caroline's dead eyes squinted as she took another sniff. "It doesn't smell... *right*. Like that ectoplasmic slime in your satchel, Sonny Sparrow here is tainted somehow."

"I don't understand."

She handed me the tiny corpse, and I gently placed it inside my satchel. Caroline had a look of pure befuddlement on her face, as this was the second time tonight that her predator-like senses picked up something that I couldn't.

"Val, I eat things that you'd rather not contemplate," she said. "I know this sounds disgusting, but I'm not above picking up a dying cat and munching away at its innards for a snack."

I absolutely cringed at the thought of some poor tabby that had the misfortune of being hit by a car, only to have its body torn open by an undead creature looking for a meal. I was actually about to say something to show my disgust but decided at the last second to let Caroline continue. Who was I to know what a dead thing should or shouldn't smell like?

"Anyway," she continued, "That bird is tainted, because I can't sense the presence of decay, and the process of decomposition begins immediately at the moment of death. You know, unless you're like me and you're stuck between being dead and being alive"

I blinked a few times. "Go on," I said.

She gave me a casual shrug and then stretched a bony finger at the bird's midsection. "While the body shortly after death appears fresh from the outside, the bacteria that before death were feeding on the contents of the intestine begin to digest the intestine itself."

"And?"

"And I can smell that under normal circumstances," she said, as her black lips curled up into a self-satisfied smile. "Sonny Sparrow and the hundreds of bird corpses lying all over 17th Avenue aren't tantalizing my senses."

I pulled the drawstring on my satchel and tried to absorb what Caroline had just disclosed. The sheer scale of the carnage surrounding me suggested that if 17th Avenue were littered with dead birds, it was fair to assume that every street and cul-de-sac in the city was in the same condition.

"So what are you saying, Caroline — these birds aren't going to decompose?"

"Beats me. I mean, I'm clinically dead, and my body isn't rotting. Not yet, anyway."

"Yeah, but that's because I killed that necromancer when his minion took a chunk out of you," I said. "This is just a shade, for crying out loud! We both know that dead things can't perform magic; it's an established fact."

"I know," she said.

"What you're telling me is we've got a city full of fresh poultry that will never spoil, and there's no magic behind it."

Caroline nodded. "I can't see how, Val. All we know for certain is there won't be any vultures circling this city-sized buffet — they're probably dead too."

I clicked the unlock button on my key fob, and the tail lights on the Maxima blinked twice. I stuffed my satchel under my arm and motioned for Caroline to follow me to the car.

"I think the time has come to do a little sorcery," I said. "We've got to find out what killed these birds."

"Alright," she said, with a shrug of her bony shoulders. "Where are we headed?"

"Nose Hill Park - it's time for us to do a magical post-mortem.

CHAPTER 15

I love Nose Hill Park.

It is a natural prairie oasis that covers over ten square miles in a city that has grown too fast for its own good.

Of course, when you think of a park, your mind conjures up images of nicely manicured lawns and bright flowerbeds or picnic areas with recreational facilities.

I adore the park for reasons that have more to do with something the average person might see out of the corner of their eye late at night. The kind of something that resembles a creature you read about in a book as a child, or saw on a big screen at the drive-in while you were groping your boyfriend or girlfriend during your teen years.

First of all, it is less of a park and more of a bald-ass hill that commands a million-dollar view of Calgary's skyline. It's one of the largest municipal parks in North America, and because it's a natural environment park, everyone from mountain bike enthusiasts to young lovers regard it as a retreat from city life and a place to enjoy nature.

Nose Hill Park is, quite literally, one of the last places on the continent where people can walk on unspoiled prairie that has never been turned by till or hoe. A surprising accomplishment, given that the entire park is bordered by million-dollar homes, and land developers have for years coveted the park because of its central location and commanding view. For millennia, Nose Hill stood silent vigil as glacial Lake Calgary receded and a river surging out from the mountains carved its way through the old lake bottom. Over the centuries that followed, the hill witnessed a succession of people sculpting a unique history within and around the Bow River Valley. Of course, none of those people truly understood its significance to our world, which is just fine with those who call the park home.

You know, besides deer, coyotes, and gophers.

It is the one of the highest points in the city and is home to more than twenty species that are native to the preternatural world. Moreover, it's a place of magic and spiritual significance.

How?

Well, anthropologists believe the eight-foot diameter stone circles scattered about the park are actually teepee rings, where plains Indians once lived. Of course, the rings might resemble the stones used to secure the base of a teepee to the ground, but scientists are dead wrong. Universities don't exactly pump out students who are trained to recognize that those stone circles are in fact protective circles, which offer preternatural world residents of the park some measure of safety against netherworld predators that like to feed on everything from giant sprites to waifs. It's an honest mistake, when you think about it.

But wait… there's more.

Because Nose Hill Park's location, it is a natural conduit for magical energies. I'm not talking about some mystical swirling stew of energy that is invisible to the naked eye and just so happens to be attracted to the park because of its natural topography. No, magical energies only respond to those creatures who use magic as an everyday part of life. Just as a landfill attracts seagulls because human refuse is a large part of their diet, Nose Hill Park acts as a conduit for magic because magic is a way of life for those who dwell there.

Given that I've been known to dabble with elemental magic from time to time, I will often practice my craft late at night at the apex of a new moon. More often than not, I'm surrounded by those preternatural world residents who have grudgingly accepted my presence in their domain. I've even formed numerous acquaintanceships, including one with a dwarf troll who is over two thousand years old. His name is unpronounceable to humans, so I've named him D.T., and to date, he hasn't protested.

Who is D.T.?

First off, he resents being called a dwarf, which is entirely understandable. I'm five foot two, and I hate being called a dwarf. Heck, even little people (the human ones) are liable to punch you in the crackers if you make the mistake of calling any one of them a midget, so it makes sense that D.T. rejects the label. He's also an exceptionally gifted mage, and he has been kind enough to provide me with lessons in spellcraft, potions, and incantations. Finally, given D.T.'s age, he's a wellspring of information about the various residents of the preternatural world, their abilities, and characteristics.

Oh, and, like I said… you know, he's a troll.

It made sense that I should seek his input. If anyone could point me in the direction of why poultry was falling from the heavens, it would be him.

I parked the Maxima in the small gravel lot, overlooking 14th Street. The moon provided excellent light, so we left the parking lot and followed a worn path that meandered up the forward slope of the east hill. Caroline was cursing up a storm, because she was wearing open toed sandals, and pebbles were getting jammed between her zombie toes.

"Dammit!" she snapped, as she bent over and took off her sandals for what seemed like the hundredth time. "I wish you would give me a list of what to bring when I accompany you on these so-called 'cases' of yours."

I gave her a serious frown that told her to keep the noise down, lest she anger an ogre who would more than likely take a swipe at us with a broken tree limb.

"You should know by now to be prepared, Caroline," I whispered, as I impatiently tapped my left boot on the dirt path.

"Do you think this D.T. might have a cure for my condition?" she asked, ignoring my comment.

"I doubt it," I said, shaking my head. "He's been known to destroy flesh-eating zombies, not save them."

She pursed her black lips as she slipped her feet back in her sandals. "Great. He's gonna hate me before I've had the chance to charm him with my effervescent personality."

I rolled my eyes and turned to face a large boulder that was covered with graffiti. I shone a flashlight along its craggy surface as I searched for the summoning spell amid the spray paintings of gang tags and pornographic images.

I smiled agreeably and pointed. "There it is… you'll want to stand back about twenty feet, Caroline; I'm never sure what this boulder will do."

She gave me a confused look, shrugged her shoulders, and stepped back as I whispered the words of magic that would lead me to D.T.

Suddenly I felt the earth beneath my feet begin to vibrate as the boulder tilted to the right, revealing a three-foot diameter tunnel lit with a warm orange glow. Caroline sauntered up beside me and knelt, then poked her head inside.

"Kinda smallish, Val." She groaned. "Think we'll fit?"

"Easy-peasy" I said. "We'll have to crawl on our hands and knees, but don't worry — it's not like we'll be crawling to the center of the earth."

"Gotcha… lead on, oh wizardly one," she said, stepping back and motioning with her arms.

I slung my satchel over my shoulder and dropped onto my hands and knees, then entered the tunnel. Caroline followed closely behind, and as soon as she cleared the tunnel entrance, the earth began vibrating again as the boulder tilted back to its original position, sealing the entrance.

As we inched forward, the ambient glow became brighter, lighting the hand carved tunnel walls and revealing a series glittering scripts etched into the surface.

"What's with all the Arabic writing?" Caroline whispered. "I thought this guy was a troll?"

"They're glyphs," I whispered back. "Each one is a protective spell that is designed to keep out people like you and me."

"People like me? What's that supposed to mean?"

"It means that if you had any kind of evil intent, the magical energy that compels someone to an evil purpose would be detected by the glyphs, and your ass would be grass." I said bluntly. "I guess I should have given you a head's up on that."

Caroline gave me a hard shove from behind, and I did a face plant into the dirt.

"You should have given me a head's up?" she snapped. "You know, Val, sometimes you really piss me off."

"Hush." I snipped, as I brushed myself off. "I see the end of the tunnel ahead, so be on your best behavior."

Caroline made a grunting sound, so I assumed she heard me. We crawled another twenty or so feet, and the tunnel gave way to a tiny spiral staircase that was carved into the natural sandstone that forms the base of pretty much everything in the Calgary area. I got to my feet and hunched over as I carefully walked down the fifty or so steps that lead to a perfectly round cavern, which was decorated with tapestries and dusty, old, leather-bound books.

"What's this, his lab?" Caroline asked. "Hey… do you smell smoke?"

I felt a surge of heat headed my way, so I spun around and dove onto Caroline, knocking her flat on her back. A ball of blue flame flew over the small of my head and landed in the sandy floor of the cavern only a few feet in front of me.

"I SHALL SMITE THEE, UNCLEAN CREATURE!" a voice boomed from behind a stone cairn in the corner of the chamber.

It was D.T., and he was pissed.

CHAPTER 16

An angry, crimson glow filled up the chamber as D.T. stepped out from behind the cairn. His tiny, three-foot frame shrouded in a gray tunic that stretched from just above his four-toed feet gave the appearance of fragility, but the fierce look in his shining black eyes showed that he meant business. He stretched a gnarled hand behind his head as he prepared to throw another ball of compressed fire at Caroline, which, if I didn't act fast, would nail me square in the back.

"D.T!" I shouted. "It's me… it's Valerie."

"Stand thee aside, ally!" He snarled. "My quarrel is not with thee, but with that which follows thee into my dwelling!"

I scrambled to my feet and stomped one Danner boot onto Caroline's head, pinning her to the ground. I frantically reached into my satchel and pulled out the dead bird, then held it out for D.T. to see.

"You're the wisest mage I know, D.T," I pleaded. "The creature accompanying me is an ally. Surely, you realize that I would never align myself with forces that have a malicious purpose. I have come… we have come for your counsel. Both our realms might be at risk."

He cocked a bushy gray eyebrow that was nested in a furrow of deeply set wrinkles and grunted. His shining, black eyes shot up to my face, then shifted to Caroline, who was struggling beneath my boot, and finally to the dead bird. He pursed his lips into a disapproving frown, and then he lowered his arm as the ball of compressed fire dissolved in his hand.

"Thou art without fear, ally," he said, as he began stroking his grizzled, white beard. "The creature thou parcel into my dwelling should not have survived the sentinels surrounding this place."

I nodded in agreement, knowing that Caroline was already royally pissed with me, and nobody likes a pissed off zombie. "She is not evil, D.T.… she's a victim of dark magic, and she owes me a life debt."

"Get off me, Val!" Caroline groaned, her face squarely in the dirt.

"Don't make any sudden moves," I said, slowly taking my boot off her head. "He doesn't like zombies."

Caroline got to her knees and started brushing the sand out of her hair and off her face.

"Thanks for pointing that out."

D.T. reached for his staff, which was lying on the ground next to the cairn, still keeping his eyes on Caroline. The staff flew into his hands, and his lips curled into a satisfied smile, revealing a crooked set of yellow teeth. Then the old mage buttoned up his faded olive tunic in an effort to look dignified.

"Thou surely must know of the darkness that gathers like a thunder head on the north horizon," he said, hobbling over to a log chair covered with detailed engravings. I nodded in agreement and helped Caroline to her feet, and then I gave her a sheepish smile.

"Yes — it's why we're here."

He leaned into the chair, favoring his right side. His arthritis must have been acting up again.

"Wouldst thou pay tribute with human smoke?" he said, wincing. "'Tis a small fee for my counsel, as thou surely must know that I am the eldest of those who dwell amid your domain."

"I've brought tribute," I said, flashing him a disapproving frown. "You really shouldn't smoke, D.T."

He shifted in his seat and held out his left hand. I reached into the Mickey pocket of my leather jacket and tossed a package of Player's unfiltered cigarettes, which he snatched out of the air with ease, and then he tore off the plastic wrapping.

"Ugh, that little creep smokes?" Caroline asked, barely hiding her disgust. "Don't tell me... tobacco has some spiritual relevance to little green men who are two thousand years old."

I shook my head and let out a sigh as D.T. stuffed a cigarette into his mouth. He placed his small index finger on the tip, and with the tiniest effort of concentration, the tip glowed bright red at his touch.

"'Tis tribute, creature." he said, as he took a deep haul off the cigarette, and a look of passive satisfaction flowed across his face.

"I have a name," Caroline snapped. "My friend here does, too."

I elbowed her in the ribs so hard she exhaled a mouthful of foul-smelling breath.

"D.T. doesn't speak anyone's name." I said, giving her a frustrated glare. "He doesn't even speak *my* name."

"Because, creature, thine enemies might learn of thee and work their will against thee, should I utter thy name," he said, flicking ashes on the cavern floor. "Thou knowest thy name, but wouldst thou wish thine enemies the same? I care not for thee, creature, 'tis out of concern for my allies that I will not speak names."

Caroline grunted in acknowledgement as I carried the dead bird over to a small table he had whittled from one of the thousands of poplar trees that grow all over Nose Hill Park. D.T. rose from his seat with a loud groan and hobbled over, the cigarette drooping loosely from his lips. He picked up the dead bird and examined it like a gemologist examining a diamond. He plucked a tail feather off the carcass and pulled open a small drawer filled with glass vials of liquids and strangely colored powders. He grabbed a vial containing a cloudy fluid and placed it next to the bird carcass, and then he reached for a small clay bowl and dropped the feather inside.

"My friend here says that it doesn't smell dead… that it's tainted," I said, leaning on the table. "Something about the natural process of decomposition being halted."

"Aye," D.T. said with a nod. "The creature speaks truth. 'Tis a half dead fowl that lay before us."

"What do you think it means?"

D.T. began shaking the small vial and motioned for Caroline and me to step back from the table. He pulled off a tiny cork and held the vial over the clay bowl.

"I know not," he said, as he tapped the tiniest amount of liquid into onto the feather. "But truth can be a half-truth as surely as yon fowl is half-dead. Truth can be shaped by treachery for certain, and treachery is what killed yon fowl… behold!"

The table suddenly shook violently as a fine green mist drifted up from the bowl. D.T. rolled up his sleeves and whispered something barely audible as he thrust his hands into the mist and began making molding gestures, as if the mist were a lump of clay on a potter's wheel.

"What's he doing?" Caroline asked.

"Silence, creature!" D.T. snapped. "Thy presence is unwelcome enough… there must be silence if I am to make the dead talk."

I had a rough idea what D.T. was doing. As a mage, he possessed both the skill and knowledge to compel truth from the spirit of anything that had recently died. I'm not entirely sure as to just how he does it – after all, I'm a novice compared to D.T. – but I suspected the liquid acted as a kind of spiritual magnet that would draw out whatever residual life force remained in the dead bird. If he concentrated his focus enough, he might catch a glimpse of the moments before the bird's death, and that would give us a better idea of not only the location of the shade, but also its source of power. If we were really lucky, we might discover something resembling a motive.

The mist transformed into a floating, ectoplasmic mass and D.T. allowed himself a satisfied grin as he began to shape it into a reasonable depiction of the bird. It began to vibrate as it continued hovering above the bowl, and D.T. whispered, this time loud enough for all to hear.

"Viltus a firmus."

"Hey, that looks just like Sonny Sparrow," Caroline said.

The little troll nodded as he stepped back from the table. "Aye, creature. Stand thee aside and make way for what is yet to come,"

The small gray effigy of the bird began to flutter its spectral wings, and immediately, it took to flying around the chamber. "Behold," said D.T., his eyes fixed on his creation.

It landed on a bookcase and went through the motions of preening itself. Then it fluttered back to the small table and began hopping around and pecking at the surface, as if it were looking for the crumbs that collected between the cracks in the sidewalk on 17th Avenue. We watched closely as the bird took to the air and began circling the ceiling of the chamber.

As it flew to the highest point in the chamber, it slammed violently into what could have been a wall, had there been a wall to slam into. Then it turned upside down and fell to the floor, landing with a dull thud. We walked over to the effigy and watched as the solid object suddenly liquefied before our eyes, melting into a small pool the size of a saucer.

"Ectoplasm," I said, glancing up at the chamber ceiling. "It looks to me like the effigy hit a wall similar to the spectral wall of energy that Fifty-Dollar Bill told us about."

"The goo is bubbling, Val." said Caroline, pointing to the floor "Is that supposed to happen?"

Suddenly I felt a wave of heat as an orange plume of flame blasted through the tunnel leading out of the chamber. D.T. tumbled back and landed against my knees as the ground shook violently, knocking over the table and toppling the bookcase.

"*The sentinels!*" D.T. shouted, as he pointed to the tunnel entrance. "Evil surrounds us; be thou on thy guard!"

No sooner had the words flown out of his lips when the bubbling ectoplasm exploded into a blinding, white light. I felt a wave of nausea wash through my stomach and into my throat as I squinted to see the ectoplasm morph into something with eight legs and about the same number of eyes.

"Spirits protect us," I whispered.

And then it attacked.

CHAPTER 17

I had barely enough time to shake the cobwebs from my head as the enormous gray tarantula leaped into the air and onto Caroline. Its pedipalps pummeled her face as she balled up her left hand into a fist and drove it into one of the giant spider's eyes. The creature recoiled, then slammed her head against the cavern floor and began stabbing at her chest with its fangs.

"Get this thing off me, Val!" Caroline shrieked. "You know I'm terrified of spiders!"

I glanced over at D.T. as he staggered around like a drunk. "Where is my staff!" he shouted, clawing at the floor with his hands. "I cannot see to find my staff!"

Just then, the tarantula arched its back and shot a jet of sticky white webbing that pelted D.T in the centre of his back and sent him careening into the chamber wall. It shot another jet of webbing that immobilized the small troll and then cocked its head in my direction.

"Little help, here, Val!" Caroline shouted. "It just figured out that it can't kill me, but it can sure as hell tear my head off with its fangs!"

I tore off my leather jacket and dove behind the toppled bookshelf. "Hang on, Caroline!" I bellowed, as I fumbled at the drawstring of my satchel. I reached inside and pulled out a small water bottle filled with magnetized filings. "Can you keep it distracted for just a minute longer?"

"I don't have a minute!" Caroline screamed. I heard the sounds of her fists pounding against the spider and hoped that she'd give me enough time to work some elemental magic.

"Stay thee in thy place, ally!" D.T. shouted from across the cavern.

"Why?" I shouted back as I fumbled with the cap and poured the filings into the dirt floor.

Suddenly, a jet of blazing blue flame flew over the bookcase, missing my head by a few inches. I felt a stab of searing pain on the top of my scalp as my nostrils filled with the smell of scorched spider.

"That is why!" he bellowed, his voice shaking with fury. "I may not have my staff, but by the spirits, I shall do battle with that vile creature!"

I clued into what D.T. was doing.

Even without his staff, he possessed enough skill to call upon the power of the glyphs that protected his home and direct them onto the giant arachnid. He knew me well enough to understand that if I had enough time, I'd come up with something to kill it.

You know, in a perfect world.

"Keep it up, D.T.!" I shouted. "I just need a minute!"

"Just watch where you're aiming, troll!" Screamed Caroline, her voice filled with rage. "You nailed the spider, but it's still got me pinned to the floor, and I don't care to be incinerated!"

I poured handfuls of sand into the filings and spat onto my hands. I reached into the mixture and formed it into a slimy, brown muck with my index finger. If everything worked right, the magnetized filings would act as a conduit for the magical energies in the earth, and I'd be able to channel the energy onto the spider. I closed my eyes and focused my thoughts onto the mud, then called on the living energy with my thoughts.

"Crispus Terra!" I shrieked, as a jolt of power surged from the ground and into my body. It trembled violently as every molecule in my five-foot-two frame was vibrating. My muscles burned as my bloodstream surged with force and my body nourished itself on the living energy I had channeled from the ground. My hands became a blur as the power coursed through me, supercharging every tissue in my body. I throbbed with power as I leaped into the air as if I had been launched from a catapult, and somersaulted over the bookcase.

The tarantula hissed, and it reared up and then bolted from Caroline in a head on attack. It slammed into my body and .sent me sailing across the cavern, and I hit the cavern wall with enough force to cause dirt to fall off the ceiling.

Then it raced at me, but this time I was prepared.

I dodged to my left at the last second, and the giant spider crashed headfirst into the wall. I leaped into the air and onto its back, grasping a handful of spider hair to steady myself. I reached into my belt and pulled out my eight-inch buck knife, then drove the shining steel blade into the creature's skull.

It screamed in pain as it reared itself up again and bucked me off as easily as a Brahma bull throws a rider at the Calgary Stampede. I landed easily, rolling into a defensive position and held out my knife with both hands for protection.

"Come and get some!" I roared at the spider. Caroline scurried up beside me; she had D.T.'s staff in her hand.

"Want to trade?"

"I thought you'd never ask," I said, with some measure of relief. I handed Caroline my knife in exchange for D.T.'s staff. The enchanted branch of diamond willow surged with energy at my touch, and I readied myself for another rush at the spider.

The tarantula coiled itself back and then threw its immense body into the air, presumably intending to pounce on both of us.

"IMMOBULUS!" I cried, and a blast of force surged through the small staff and into the spider, suspending it in mid-air.

Caroline dove at the creature's abdomen, my buck knife tearing into its spectral flesh. The force of her momentum gashed a long, gaping wound into its belly, the contents of which splashed onto the floor at Caroline's feet. I spun around, and swung the staff like a baseball bat. The giant spider's body sailed into the wall hard enough to leave a large dent, and then slid onto the ground. Its legs twitched violently as it struggled to get to its feet, and then it collapsed with a hollow thud.

Caroline raced over to D.T. and cut the webbing that had pinned him to the wall. He fell to the floor, then stood up and brushed himself off as if nothing had happened.

"You're welcome, troll," said Caroline, a hint of contempt in her voice. D.T. ignored her and hobbled over to the disemboweled husk. Foul smelling smoke rose from the body as the creature's form began to melt into a large ectoplasmic puddle that gathered into a large glob, dissolving into the dirt.

"That," I said, nearly choking on another wave of nausea, "was too close for comfort."

"Aye," said D.T. "Thou art a threat to the evil that surrounds us this night. Be wary, ally; we know not the reason for this assault. Thine enemy suffered a defeat, and thou knows not what fate lies ahead."

CHAPTER 18

D.T.'s home looked like a category-five hurricane had just blasted through it. Impact craters dotted the chamber walls, and at least two bookcases lay in a smoldering ruin, victims of the inferno that had blown through the tunnel. Caroline examined the wounds on her chest courtesy of the tarantula's six-inch fangs, and I hunched myself in a corner, still shaking from the battle.

"'Tis a mighty force that can breach my dwelling," D.T. said, lighting another cigarette. His eyes surveyed the damage to his home, and he let out a weary sigh.

I nodded in silence as I slowly got to my feet. Of course, the tiny mage was right.

He had spent millennia perfecting his craft, and the protective glyphs on the tunnel walls were the result of a lifetime of practice. Obviously, the reason the glyphs didn't incinerate Caroline the moment she crawled into the tunnel was because she wasn't evil – that much I'd surmised after nearly roasting to death when the real evil decided to take a shot at us.

While it was good to know that Caroline didn't have an evil bone in her dead body, what troubled me was the sheer scale of malevolence behind the attack. Plain old menace would have triggered one or two glyphs into a defensive assault on an intruder, but a three-foot diameter jet of fire shooting through a tunnel? That kind of large-scale darkness told me that we were dealing with a spiritual energy I had never encountered before in my life; it was *that* strong.

I got up, walked over to the overturned table, and picked up the dead bird. D.T. busied himself by sorting through the smoldering pile of books and making a small stack of whatever he could salvage.

"Toss me that bird, Val," said Caroline, as she buttoned up her blouse. "I want to check something."

I nodded, and threw it to her. "You're not going to eat it, are you?" I asked, knowing that my stomach in its delicate state would not withstand the sight of a zombie having a late night snack.

"Nope," she said, catching it with one hand. "I can smell something different, that's all."

"Different in what way?"

She held the bird beneath her nose like it was a cob of Taber corn and inhaled deeply.

"It smells… *normal*," she grunted, throwing the bird back to me.

"Normal?"

"Yeah, it smells like good old fashioned death — it's not tainted like before."

"Yon fowl has reclaimed its soul," D.T. said, carrying an armful of books and placing them beside the overturned table. "The entity thou dispatched cares not for yon sparrow's soul; it has no further use for it."

"Come again?" I asked.

The little troll lifted his small worktable back onto its legs, and I dropped the tiny corpse on top. He opened the drawer and pulled out a blue crystal fastened to a hair-thin chain, and dangled it over the bird. The crystal began spinning like a top as he lowered it to within an inch of the bird's breast.

"All is as it should be," D.T. grunted. "The darkness that claimed yon bird recedes amid the power of light. Thou art free of the darkness, tiny bird, go now and be with thy creator."

As soon as the words left his lips, the crystal stopped spinning and dangled limply from the chain. D.T. slipped the crystal back in the drawer, then picked up the bird carcass and threw it into his stone fireplace.

I gave him what I hoped was a confident smile, masking a jolt of self-doubt that stabbed at my heart like a filleting knife. Ever since I had started down a supernatural path in life, I had successfully battled and destroyed everything from demons to spectral assassins bent on killing those closest to me. I had gone toe-to-toe with creatures best left for nightmares and, through it all, I'd felt some measure of confidence in my abilities — until now.

Under normal circumstances, I deal with rogue incursions into our realm by beings that often act alone. On occasion, certain creatures from the nether regions are prisoner to the will of a human conjurer to perpetrate acts, presumably, on those who the conjurer dislikes. Revenge is the primary motive for human beings to dabble with dark magic, but because revenge is a human trait, one can easily locate and subdue a predator, since they leave a trail of evidence: their victims.

A smart investigator always knows that victims have some kind of association with their killer; it's why they immediately look for a connection between a victim and a suspect. In this case, the suspect was a shade, and the only evidence before me ranged from a disappearing grain bin to thousands of dead birds. What really got under my skin was that I couldn't see a pattern or logic behind it all.

The shade, if it indeed was a shade, possessed enough power to create life from a pool of ectoplasm. It had enough malice to smash through a protective barrier that even the grim reaper tries to avoid, and the sheer scale of death surrounding its power revealed two unsettling truths: I could sense no human motive, and I was in way over my head.

"We need to talk, D.T." I said, grimly. "I'm running the numbers through my head, and something doesn't add up."

"Of course, ally," he said. "What is it that troubles thee?"

I let out a frustrated sigh and headed over to the stone staircase, then plopped myself down in near exhaustion. D.T. hobbled over, staff in hand, and Caroline leaned against a wall, a bored look on her face.

"Has anything ever gotten past your glyphs?" I asked. "We know that Caroline wasn't harmed by your protective spells because she isn't evil. What attacked us clearly was."

"'Tis not the first time evil forces have sought to destroy me," said D.T., oblivious to the shambles that he now called home.

"Look around this place!" I groaned. "It's a scene from a disaster movie! An enchanted pool of slime morphed into a big-ass spider that nearly killed us, D.T.! It subdued you, the most powerful mage I've ever known, and nearly tore Caroline apart. I need to know — has this *ever* happened before?"

He leaned heavily on his staff and stroked his beard for a moment. I searched his weathered face for a clue as he squinted his eyes and slowly shook his head.

"Nay," he said, with a look if disappointment. "Nothing has ever breached the sentinels surrounding this place. Tis a mystery yet to be solved."

"That's what I was afraid of," I huffed, kicking at the dirt floor with my boot. "I'm at a loss."

"No you're not!" chimed Caroline, from across the room. I glanced up at her and gave her a confused look.

"What are you talking about?" I asked, my voice taking on an edge of frustration.

She walked over and knelt down before me, then put a reassuring hand on my shoulder.

"Before we came to Nose Hill Park," she said. "You told me about a plague or something… do you remember?"

"Yeah, why?"

Caroline's had squeezed my shoulder hard. "Think about it, Val! There are thousands of dead birds littered on every hill and highway between here and Airdrie. You told me there was dead vegetation at that farm you visited, and creepy Bill said that all the vegetation was dead in Airdrie."

"So?"

Caroline's face lit up like a kid on Christmas morning and she gave my shoulder an optimistic shake. "There's a pattern to all this, Val… you're just not seeing it yet!"

D.T. dug his staff into the dirt and snapped the tiny green fingers of his left hand.

"Aye," he said, as he gave Caroline a cautious glance. "This creature may yet be of some use. 'Tis a pattern for certain."

120

"Really? How?" I asked.

"You were the one who told me this shade is working its way up the spiritual food chain, Valerie," Caroline continued. "It went after vegetation, birds and is probably working up to people."

"And?"

"What does missing grain bin in Okotoks that just so happens to crash land outside your condo and a full frontal assault in the home of mystical dwarf troll that you're visiting have in common?"

I slowly clued into where Caroline was leading me, and the truth hit me as hard as a locomotive slamming into a transport trailer.

"It's following… *me*." I whispered.

Holy crap.

CHAPTER 19

"Aye," D.T. said, walking into the anteroom of the main chamber. "Tis following you as certain as the moonrise on a clear winter night."

I sat there, considering the ramifications of Caroline's hypothesis. There was indeed a pattern, and if the shade was tailing me, it meant that it wouldn't be long before it decided to take another swipe. My mind raced with questions: should I warn my parents? What about Dave? His safety, anyone's safety would be in peril so long as the shade wanted me out of the picture. I got up and started pacing as a myriad of possible scenarios flooded my mind.

In the past, unseen powers had tried unsuccessfully to get to me through loved ones. From the occasional drive-by shooting to a demon suddenly materializing in my bathroom while Dave showered, those closest to me knew there was always a risk.

But what of the risk?

Everything that has tried to kill me until now possessed significantly far less power than the shade. Malevolent poltergeists liked to throw furniture around and would occasionally chuck a coffee cup at my head while I watch the evening news. A shape shifter might take the form of a mountain lion and leap out of a tree in hopes of tearing out my throat... situations like those involved a single individual or creature acting alone. In this case, the shade possessed enough power to wipe out entire species of birds in a thirty-mile radius — that kind of power represented a new threat not only to me, but also to potentially one million people.

I shuddered as I bit my lip and glanced over to see D.T. return to the main chamber, carrying a six-foot-long pole wrapped in leather.

"What's with the javelin, troll?" Caroline asked, in a sarcastic voice. "It's three feet longer than you are tall."

"Thou art to be protected by powers beyond your mortal realm, creature," he said, ignoring her. "This staff was honed by the finest craftsman among the immortals. It is of diamond willow... in the hands of a trained sorcerer, a staff is a powerful weapon."

"I *don't* want a staff, D.T.," I groaned. "I'm an alchemist, not a mage."

"Silence, ally!" he snapped, as he laid the staff at my feet. "Thou art skilled in many crafts, and through this staff, you might channel all thy power upon thine enemy."

I take alchemy seriously; it has to do with my interest in the natural elements surrounding every one of us, and my connection to living energy. Magic is one of my skills, but it's not something I'm comfortable with practicing, because it requires years of rigorous apprenticeship to master. D.T. had spent hundreds of nights like this, teaching me how to channel my thoughts and emotions into developing effective spells and convincing potions. I recognized the inherent value of a staff, but I had always considered staffs to be offensive weapons, and just like my built-in dislike for guns, the thought of carrying one went against my beliefs.

Call it a philosophical disagreement with a two thousand year old wizard.

"I *won't* use it, D.T.," I said, turning my back and crossing my arms in an attempt to look like I'd just laid down the law.

Suddenly, the amber glow of the chamber dissolved into darkness. The sound of thunder rumbled through the air as the ground shook, knocking me flat on my back.

"Take thy staff into thine hands!" D.T.'s voice boomed with an authority that absolutely demanded respect. "Thou art called upon by the spirits of the light to learn the wisdom of the ancient ones. Thou shalt not set thyself upon the gathering darkness as an innocent child was to set itself upon life without the guiding hand its mother."

"Looks like you're being drafted, Val," Caroline chuckled.

D.T. spun around, and with the wave of his tiny hand, sent a jet of invisible force into Caroline, sending her careening into the cavern wall.

"SILENCE, CREATURE!" he roared. "Lest though be consumed by my will, thou shalt silence thyself!"

Caroline motioned for D.T. to calm down, and he turned his attention to me.

"Take thy staff into thine hands, *apprentice*," he said, this time with a hint of tenderness. "Thou knowest that magic flows through thee with clarity and truth. To be a guardian of thy realm is thy true calling."

It had come to this, and somehow I always knew it would. The countless hours spent with D.T. as he'd taught me about the connection between magic, the natural elements, the creatures inhabiting the preternatural world and the nature of the soul. It had all been an indoctrination leading up to this moment.

How could I learn what had taken him more than two thousand years to learn? How could I take the few lessons he had taught me and somehow locate and destroy a force that threatened an entire city?

And what of my ability to act as a broker? I'd always considered myself to be a peacemaker of sorts, but my experience with sorcerers taught me that very often a peace cannot be made. Too often, forces beyond human understanding surround us, and in many cases, threaten our very existence.

What about my job and my responsibilities to my employer?

I had barely scratched the surface of knowing who or what acts against the mortal realm, and I'd spent more than ten years collecting material that my government kept under lock and key. Now I was supposed to just drop all that and commit myself to an apprenticeship that I didn't want and hadn't asked for?

My head was swimming with questions as I searched D.T.'s face for a something, anything that might give me a clue as to why he had chosen me. All I saw was fierce determination in his shining, black eyes and a curious, noble strength that told me I was his choice as an apprentice. That among the six billion people inhabiting our planet, I was the one he wanted.

I tentatively reached for the staff, my head swimming with emotions ranging from anger to cold terror.

"Are you certain this is the only way, D.T.?" I asked, as I wrapped my fingers around the leather bound shaft.

He nodded silently.

He nodded, and then he smiled.

CHAPTER 20

Secrets. How I hate them.

I leaned on my staff and pushed myself off the ground. My stomach was still churning, and I was both physically and emotionally exhausted.

Such is the life of an apprentice… *alchemist?*

I scratched my head as I began to pace across the dirt floor of D.T.'s cavern. It was true that while I possessed a fair degree of skill in everything from spellcraft to metallurgy, the little troll could teach me about those facets of magic I'd always wondered about. For example: what is the source of magic? I had always thought that magic flowed from perpetual slurry of energies that bound both the near and preternatural worlds. D.T. had shown me on numerous occasions that energies act much like an electrical current: they simply need something to act as a conductor, and more often than not, magic can be shaped to suit the will of a practitioner.

He'd taught me that both dark and elemental magic are essentially the same thing: it really depends on the direction those energies are projected, and too often, as we had seen with the giant tarantula, those energies are shaped by a malicious purpose.

"Thou knowest this creature shall surely strike again," said D.T., as he went back to salvaging books from his smoldering bookcase. "'Tis a mighty force gathering strength with each passing moment."

"I'm aware of that," I said with a sniff, still pacing. "I'm also aware that we don't have the time to engage in idle chit chat while this shade plans heaven-knows-what. How am I supposed to find it, kill it, or send it back to wherever the hell it came from while I'm undergoing training from you?"

D.T. gave me a pensive glance, shrugged his shoulders, and then went back to searching for salvage.

"You're not going to say anything?" I asked, my voice nearly shaking.

"'Twas planned, apprentice," he said, with a tone of hesitation "Thou art a player in a script written long ago."

I spun around and dropped my staff on the floor.

"Excuse me? What was planned?"

He carried another pile of salvaged books to his table and then pulled a scorched hardcover tablet out from the bottom of the pile.

"Secrets bind thee to a yet-to-be-determined fate, yes?" he said, flipping through the pages.

"What are you talking about D.T.? What secrets?" I asked, in frustration.

He dog-eared a page and shoved the thick volume in my chest.

"Our worlds are connected by forces thy keepers have long known about, apprentice," he sighed. "I have been bound by contracts never to reveal the truth to a peacekeeper until their will was certain."

"Peacekeeper?" Caroline groaned.

D.T. nodded silently and motioned for us to follow him up the tunnel. I grabbed my satchel and stuffed the book under my arm as Caroline handed me my staff. We crawled behind D.T., who confidently strolled up to the base of the large boulder. He slowly waved his hand, and the boulder rolled onto its side.

"Come into the shroud of darkness," he said, exiting the tunnel. "Secrets that dwell beyond the gaze of the mortal realm protect thee from forces that would destroy that which you hold dear."

Caroline nudged my shoulder as we crawled out of the tunnel and into the night.

"What's he talking about, Val?" she asked.

"I haven't a clue," I whispered, as I stood up and stepped past the boulder. D.T. turned and waved his small hand at the boulder, and it tilted back to its original position atop the tunnel.

"Time is short," he grunted, heading up the east hill of the park. "Thou shalt not harden thyself against a truth that is yet to be revealed. 'Twas a time when thy teacher was once an apprentice in search of truths. The long years I have dwelled on this good land taught me that all is not as it appears to be."

"No kidding," I huffed as I followed him up a narrow path that lead to a copse of poplars growing out at an odd angle. "It would be helpful, though, if I knew just what the hell you were talking about, D.T."

"Aye," he nodded, gesturing for me to come closer. "Behold the night."

Caroline and I caught up and knelt down so that we could see at his level. We scanned a cityscape of yellow lights in thirty-storey office towers as the droning of traffic on a thousand city streets filled the air.

"We're beholding, troll," Caroline clucked, unimpressed. "Looks like Calgary to me."

"Is it?" he asked, his voice taking on an amused tone. "Look thee closer, creature. What do thine dead eyes see?"

I squinted and tried to focus on anything that I might have missed. "I don't see anything either," I said.

He let out a tiny chuckle and grabbed my left hand. He held it out and pointed to the chain link fence that bordered the edge of Nose Hill Park and John Laurie Boulevard.

I scanned over the fence line as it stretched for more than a kilometer to the west. There were literally hundreds of vaporous faces that appeared and disappeared from sight, like a hundred ghostly lights flickering on and off.

"Spirits," I said. "Disembodied faces pressed against the fence."

"Aye, apprentice… the procession of the dead look to the great hill. Spirits of human and preternatural alike. The dead slumber not, this night."

We stopped in a small clearing surrounded by tall poplars and waist-high grass, and D.T. dug the end of his staff in the soil, digging a furrow about an inch deep, extending it into a large circle surrounding Caroline and me. Then he stepped inside and gave me his best attempt at a reassuring smile.

I stared at him hard for a long moment. Then I said, "What the hell is going on, D.T.? You've dug a summoning circle around the three of us; would you *please* explain all this?"

He let out a little coughing sound and then squatted down very quickly.

"This," he said, raising his staff into the air and slamming it into the earth like a club.

And suddenly, Nose Hill Park was gone.

CHAPTER 21

"That is the *coolest* trick I have ever seen!" Caroline cheered, clapping her hands. "Where are we?"

He stood up, his face still offering the same reassuring smile.

"Thou art between here and there, creature," he said. "'Tis a safe place for what thou must surely learn about thy fate – nay, all our fates, should we fail."

It was a shroud.

We were still inside the stand of poplars, but D.T. had used elemental magic to mask our presence from the park. The furrowed circle he'd dug into the ground was the barrier between here and there, which meant that as long as the integrity of the circle wasn't disturbed, we wouldn't be seen or heard by anything nearby. That didn't explain why he alluded to secrets, though, so I decided to press the tiny troll for information.

"Tonight I came to you for counsel," I said, abandoning my hidden suspicions and throwing my frustration out for everyone to see. "In the last hour, I've been attacked by a giant ectoplasmic spider, we've been nearly incinerated by whatever the hell got past the glyphs in your sanctuary, and there's a few hundred ghosts who are looking in on Nose Hill Park from the fence line. What the hell is going on, D.T.?"

The little troll motioned for me to settle down. He reached into his belt, pulled out what looked like a leather envelope and tossed it to me.

His face became dark. "Thou shalt bear witness of events that shape the fate of your mortal world and beings like me,"

I knelt down and picked up the envelope, staring hard at it for a moment. My instincts told me I probably wouldn't like what I was about to read, but I knew D.T. well enough to understand that if he'd been keeping secrets, it was to protect me. I exhaled hard and then broke the wax seal. My eyebrows lifted as I read over a letter dated from 1937 with the words *"The Office Of The Prime Minister of Canada"* written in faded green ink. I just about fell over when I saw the signature.

"The Right Honorable William Lyon Mackenzie King?" I gasped.

"Read..." D.T. said, passively.

I exhaled slowly and read aloud. "This office hereby appoints the bearer of this letter as guardian of the Western Provinces and the Northern Territories in the Dominion of Canada against those forces which act to disrupt the realms of common man and uncommon alike. You are hereby commanded in the name of the sovereign and his heirs to safeguard against unnatural threats by those forces whose aim is of a dark purpose."

I blinked hard a few times and gave my head a shake. "Fifty Dollar Bill wrote this?" I gasped. "Unnatural threats?"

D.T. waved his hand and cut me off.

"Aye, apprentice," he said, his voice taking on the tone of a university lecturer. "More than seventy human years pass since I became a peacekeeper, and in those years, thou surely must know that powers with an evil purpose have set upon our worlds."

"Guardian?" I gasped again, this time giving D.T. a pleading look. "Against what?"

Caroline folded her bony arms and chuckled. "I suppose the troll works for the government as well."

D.T. shook his head. "Nay, creature. I am in the employ of good versus evil. Much evil lurks amid the shadows; thy keepers rely on my use for better or for worse. Much worse has come, I fear."

"Worse than what?" I asked, still stunned at the revelation that government involvement in the arcane dated that far back. "I know of threats, D.T., but for crying out loud, you were appointed in the name of a freaking King!"

"Aye," he said, nodding. "I am marked for death by forces thy keepers know little about and know less of defending against."

I glanced at Caroline, who shrugged her shoulders and didn't appear to be surprised at all. She gave me cautious smile that revealed her stained teeth and then she shrugged again.

"Would have been nice if you told me about this… *BILL*!" I shouted in frustration.

D.T. hobbled over and reached for my hand. I offered it, reluctantly.

"It was a time of great peril," he said, giving my hand a reassuring squeeze. "Darkness set itself upon the world of man, and it was man's own doing."

"What are you talking about, D.T.?" I asked, my voice nearly shrill.

D.T. pursed his lips into a cautious frown and stroked his beard. "The first great evil," he sighed heavily. "Man set himself upon forbidden knowledge that was never intended for man's care. Mankind has a duty of care but cares not for duty, apprentice. It fell upon me to safeguard the world of men until I found a human to pass on my knowledge. Aye, my time grows short with each passing day, apprentice. It is because of this I care not to speak the darkness again, lest it consume whatever goodness remains in my soul."

I had no idea humanity was in this deep.

Most people's understanding of what governments do in the way of covert operations is limited to what they read in a book or see on the big screen. Vishesh had told me that Canada's government had been dabbling in the arcane for more than fifty years, so it would make sense they would be in contact with those who dwell in the preternatural world. But how was Fifty-Dollar Bill involved? What kinds of threats existed during the Great Depression? My mind flooded with possibilities.

Was the Canadian Security Intelligence Service involved? If so, did they know anything about why this shade had a hate on for birds? Maybe CSIS, like its American cousin, the CIA, was up to its elbows in this crap. Like most people, I'd been blissfully ignorant of the covert actions intelligence agencies undertake in the name of national security. What other secrets did our government keep? Hell, would CSIS be involved in political assassinations? Would Canada, for that matter? If so, what better assassins can you get than creatures of magic and myth, who can do everything from shape shift into a bear or morph into a shadow, only to kill you before you even know you're dead.

"This is why you want me as your apprentice, D.T.? Why the hell is it my job to suddenly become *Guardian of the Western Provinces* or whatever the hell you are?"

"Peacekeeper," he said quietly. "There is no choice to be made, apprentice. Thy keepers made it for thee."

"What do you mean by *no choice?*" Caroline growled, taking a threatening step forward. I quickly put my hand on her shoulder and squeezed.

"No, Caroline," I said in a stern voice. "My knowledge of our government's involvement in affairs relating to the near and preternatural worlds is limited. Nevertheless, they *do* employ me to collect material that is a threat to our world. It generates revenue for the government, though I haven't the foggiest idea what they are selling and to whom."

D.T. nodded slowly and appeared to shrink from his already diminutive height.

"Apprentice, I know not of the activities of thy keepers. I know well enough there are threats set forth by man and man alone. Forces work against both our worlds."

"What kind of forces?" I asked, sizing him up.

He leaned forward like a headmaster about to deliver a stern lecture. "Conspiracy surrounds those whose motivations are guided by chaos. There are those whose sole aim is the work of terror."

"Terrorists?" I gasped. "You're saying the war on terror is not limited to the human world?"

"Aye, as surely as the sun will rise. There are those who live among us whose purpose is to cast the world of man into the shadows."

Caroline chimed in. "Islamic fundamentalists?"

D.T. shook his head. "Nay, creature. The threat transcends the arguments of man about the Creator."

I stared, afraid to open my mouth.

"Know this, apprentice," said D.T. firmly. "Thy country is one that acts to serve the goodness of all whose quarrel lies with blackness and death."

"But D.T." I said, with a hint of hopelessness in my voice. "I'm just a low-end sorceress who occasionally battles undead creatures and who, as of tonight, is an apprentice mage. I have no idea how to destroy a mean-assed shade out there that just killed every bird in Calgary. Just flipping tell me… how much do you know about this shade?"

The little troll blinked a few times. "Enough to know that a human must be the source of evil this night."

"In what way?"

D.T. hunched over and drew a line in the dirt with a twig. "Thy keepers surely must know of events such as what happened to the birds tonight. If a rogue shifter kills a human, does that present a threat to a larger community?" he asked.

"Of course not."

"If a black mage sets himself upon a task such as yon fowl scattered hither, does this not become a threat to a larger community? Would it not want to use the most powerful weapons thy mind can conceive?"

"This thing has a *nuke?*" Caroline, gulped. "What the hell would a dead thing want with a nuke?"

"Nay creature," D.T shook his head again. "The scale of carnage among the fowl lying dead speaks to a sinister purpose. It speaks to a deliberate attempt to destroy as many of thy brethren as its dark will chooses."

Well, that made sense.

Perfect, logical, two-thousand-year-old dwarf troll sense.

I had been working on a hunch about the shade's next move, and now D.T. was alluding to a human motive. It was clear that I was in way over my head.

"We have few clues, D.T., and my gut tells me we're likely running out of time," I said, trying as hard as I could to sound determined. "Something tried to kill us tonight, and it will probably do it again at the earliest opportunity. I think we're going to be playing a waiting game until this shade decides to attack again. Maybe then we'll find something that leads us to a human."

D.T. nooded amiably and let out a quiet breath. "Few opportunities emerge, apprentice. Go to thy dwelling and rest while I set my will upon the darkness. Thou shalt meet me before the moon rises one night hence. Perhaps then, we will know more."

CHAPTER 22

We said our goodbyes and left Nose Hill Park.

D.T. decided it would be best to increase the power of the protective glyphs in the tunnel leading to his sanctuary, to prevent any further unwelcome guests, and it was agreed that we'd meet at the boulder at dusk to compare our findings, *assuming* we had time.

But time from what?

We had agreed it was possible that the shade was working its way up to humans, but what escaped me was a motive. As I pulled out onto 14th Street, I considered the possible reasons.

"It obviously knows about me," I said, swerving the Maxima around a pile of dead birds that the city maintenance workers had bulldozed into the middle of the southbound lane. "That implies it sees me as a threat, somehow."

Caroline nodded. "You're right... but what makes little sense is how an obscure spirit has knowledge about you. Even less sense when you think about the possibility of a human behind it. Still, I mean, the spirit world is a pretty damned big place, and you're a small fish when there are far more powerful beings like D.T. out there."

"I know. That's why I'm thinking there's some serious truth to the whole terrorism angle."

"What makes you say that?"

I turned onto John Laurie Boulevard and headed west to Bowness, and Caroline's church.

"Because if CSIS is involved, then we're talking about spying and general cloak and dagger stuff," I said.

"Yeah, but you're small potatoes," Caroline said. "Have you considered who has knowledge of what you do for a living?"

"Nobody, really," I sighed. "I mean there's you and Dave. My parents know I work for the government, but they think I'm a logistician."

"Occam's razor, then," Caroline said. "All other things being equal, the simplest solution is the best."

"Go on…"

"Well, I don't know much about the spy biz, but the simplest solution I can think of is that our shade is under the control of someone working for the federal government who knows you."

I swerved my car to the curb and jammed on the brakes.

"Son of a bitch!" I gasped. "Vishesh?"

Caroline gave me a startled look.

"What about him?"

"He's the only contact I've got in the government," I said, reaching for my cell phone.

"Surely you're not suggesting it's him?"

"No, but given that I've never even met the guy or seen where he works, it's possible that someone on his staff knows about me."

I punched the speed dial to Vishesh and waited for him to pick up. After three rings, he answered.

"Hello, Valerie," he yawned. "You have an update for me?"

"A little bit more than that," I said into the phone. "I'm working on a couple of hunches, and I have some questions to ask you about your co-workers."

"My co-workers? What on earth are you talking about?"

"I'm talking about anyone who knows about me in your office, because when a missing grain bin lands on the street outside my condo and a giant spider tries to kill me, my instincts generally lean toward the notion that something wants me out of the picture."

"Giant spider?" he gasped. "Did you capture its essence?"

"I didn't have time, Vishesh," I said. "And then there's the this whole peacekeeping thing. Why didn't you at least give me a head's up?"

There was a noticeable pause, and then Vishesh let out an audible sigh.

"Because that's how things happen when all hell is breaking loose, Valerie. We don't have time right now to get into what your role as a peacekeeper might be other than to say that what we conceal from both our enemies and our allies, we do in the name of peace."

Why should I have been surprised at the lack of information regarding the civil service and the arcane? That's government for you.

"How nice to be kept abreast of things," I snipped, my voice dripping with sarcasm.

"It's not a perfect situation, but there you have it," he said, in a bossy voice. "You'll continue to investigate the potential threat against the human world."

"Anything else?"

"Yes — get some rest, because you're going to need it."

There was a loud click and then dead air. I stared at my cell phone for a long moment.

"I think I've just been summed up by my boss," I said, unsure whether to be offended or laugh maniacally. "He basically told me to suck it up!"

Caroline let out a cool chuckle, as she stared out on the street. "That sounds about right. What's the next move?"

I shrugged. "Beats the hell out of me. It's 4:15 in the morning, and the sun will be up soon. One thing we do know is that everything from pilfering the grain bin to the mass killing of birds has happened at night. I think it's safe to assume the shade will make another move after the next sunset."

"Well, I don't sleep," Caroline said. "But you're still human, the last time I looked. Maybe you should get some rest for a couple of hours, while I hide out in my flat. The locals get a bit antsy when they see zombies walking around in broad daylight, and God knows we don't need any more panic on our hands."

"Good plan," I said, putting the Maxima in gear and heading out onto John Laurie Boulevard. "It seems like I'm in a holding pattern for now."

CHAPTER 23

Dave is my knight in shining armor.

I know, it sounds strange for me to look at him that way when you consider that I've saved his life on three occasions during our short relationship. Still, the guy has a sixth sense when it comes to anticipating my needs, and besides being great in bed, he instinctively knows what I'm thinking when I'm flustered.

My condo isn't terribly elaborate. I've never considered myself to be a girly-girl, and more often than not, the place is a pack rat's paradise, because I basically suck at housework. It was 5:00 A.M. by the time I got back after dropping Caroline off, and I was dead dog tired. My stomach growled loudly as I unlocked my door. Imagine my surprise when the smell of sizzling bacon and fresh coffee filled my nostrils as I walked in the door and hung up my leather jacket in the closet.

I beamed at him. "You are a miracle worker… *my God*… I can *see* my living room carpet! How did you know I'd be home?"

Dave was wearing his pajamas, and his hair stood out in about eight different directions. His gunslinger mustache lifted into a warm smile, as he scraped scrambled eggs onto two plates.

"Oh, this?" he said with a grin. "It's for the other woman in my life."

"Your mother's here?" I asked, sounding like a smart ass.

"Ha ha… I actually have to get going, as the City has called in civilian contractors to handle the *fabulous* task of hauling dump trucks full of dead birds to the city landfill. I'm going to assume you have an idea why God hates little birds, right?"

I gave him a serious smooch, and then plopped down at the kitchen table and started wolfing down breakfast.

"God loves birds," I said, munching away. "Shades, not so much."

Dave walked behind my chair and dug his warm hands into the back of my neck. The massage was sublime.

"Anything else going to fall from the skies?" he chuckled. "My dump truck is only so big."

"Oh, your dump truck is *more* than big enough for both of us," I purred, reaching up at his shirt and pulling his head down for a deep kiss. "You know, I have to wonder what I ever did to deserve you."

"It's your latent sexuality, sweetie. That, and short chicks are wicked hot."

I took a swig of my coffee and nibbled on a slice of whole grain toast.

"And how was your night?"

He slid into the chair next to me and sipped his coffee.

"Not bad. I came over around 10:00 P.M. and tidied up. Then I fell asleep in front of the widescreen. A good thing too, seeing as how I missed a thunderstorm of dead birds. The TV stations would be losing their minds over this, you know, assuming they were actually on the air."

"I had nothing to do with it," I said. "Though I have a hunch this shade has its eye on a bigger prize than local television"

"Like what?"

"Well, it wouldn't be a mystery if I knew the answer to that, would it?"

"Again… ha ha. You look like crap and should hit the hay. I'm gonna assume that because you look like crap, there's no num-num's tonight… err, this morning."

I spun around in my chair and draped my arms around his neck. "You," I said, lustily. "Are the greatest, most virile lover in the history of bedroom antics… but I'm afraid I'd fall asleep on you before you get my bra off."

"No problem," he snickered. "A rain check until the big mystery is solved or I run out of bird carcasses in my dump truck."

"Deal," I said, with a wink.

Dave finished his coffee and went to the bathroom as I padded down the narrow hall to my bedroom. My bed, which was normally a twisted mass of duvet, sheets, and two pillows, was made up with clean linen and my pillows were fluffed. The man is a treasure.

I slipped out of my dirty clothes and stuffed them in the hamper, then threw on a t-shirt and crawled under the sheets. I heard the shower go on, and Dave started singing something from Mozart's *Idomeneo,* and I simply let myself drift off into sleep.

A funny thing, sleep.

When you're physically and mentally exhausted, you'd think your brain is resting too, but it isn't. At least in my case, it doesn't. As I snored away, I felt my body floating above the treetops of Nose Hill Park, landing in a clearing facing west. In Calgary, you always know where west is, because that's where you'll see the mountains. In my dream, my instincts told me I was facing west, but instead of seeing the majestic snow-covered peaks of the Rockies, I saw an enormous wall of fog that stretched from the horizon line and towered into the sky.

It swirled and billowed forward, like a lumbering giant, consuming everything in its path. A dark, gray mist reached out from the forward edges of the fog bank, steadily creeping, inch by inch, touching trees and fields of emerald green grass. Then, as if the mist were a toxic stew, those trees lost their foliage, and the grass turned black. Animals of every shape and description raced ahead of the fog bank. The old, the young and those too slow to keep up were caught in the inky-white fingers of fog and instantly died. Their bodies withered and dried up, turning to dust, and then blew away as an icy wind swept in from the north.

I climbed atop a boulder and held out my staff. I focused my thoughts on an east wind and called out to the sky in a commanding voice.

"You'll go no further!" I bellowed, my voice booming over the hills and shaking the ground. A surge of crimson force swept down from the sky and combined with a blast of kinetic energy I'd drawn from the ground surrounding me,

twisting itself into a steady stream of scarlet rage that coursed through my body and into my staff.

"YOU WILL GO NO FURTHER!" I screamed, this time my voice shrill. A wall of power lashed out from the head of my staff, and my body shook violently as funnel clouds descended from the sky and waited for my will to direct them forward. Sheets of rain poured down on me like frozen daggers, drenching my body and refreshing my senses. The funnel clouds, dozens of them now, twisted and swirled as they moved forward, out of the foothills and into the path of the mist. I sent a hurricane of deafening wind forward, pushing against the fog bank, my will determined to destroy it before it killed everything it its path.

Then, a voice unlike anything I'd heard before split the air like a million artillery shells.

"For I will pass through the land of Egypt this night and will smite all the firstborn in the land of Egypt, both man and beast; and against all the gods of Egypt I will execute judgment: I am the LORD."

I felt an invisible force draw against my body, lifting me off the ground and pulling me at blinding speed over house and hilltop, faster and faster, toward the swirling fog bank. I landed with a thud on a cold, dead stretch of land and watched as the mist crept forward, inches now away from my feet.

I felt the air sucked out of my lungs as my blood boiled, my body fed the giant wave of death before me.

"No... NO!" I screamed.

Then... darkness.

"Good God, Valerie... are you alright?" Dave held me in his arms as my body trembled. I was drenched in sweat, and the sheets were soaked through to the mattress.

I blinked slowly as the room came into focus, and I looked into Dave's bright green eyes. I reached out and touched his mustache, just to make sure he was real.

"A dream," I whispered, my voice hoarse. "One very bad, very horrifying dream."

He leaned in and gently kissed my forehead. His lips were cool against my burning skin.

"Want to talk about it before I go to work?" he whispered.

"N-No, it's alright. At least I think so."

I threw my arms around him and buried my head in his chest. The smell of Irish Spring filled my nostrils, and I kissed his chest softly.

"Okay," he whispered. "I hate to be the bearer of bad news after you've had a nightmare."

"It's alright… couldn't be any worse than the dream I just had."

He nodded and gave me a bear hug.

"Okay, well… it's just that all your houseplants are dead, and the fish in the fish tank are all floating."

An icy stab of panic shot through the pit of my stomach and straight into my heart, as I bit my lip… hard. So hard, in fact, that I could taste blood in my mouth.

It was all I could do to keep from screaming.

CHAPTER 24

I flew off the bed and raced to the front closet to grab my staff.

"What the hell is going on, Val?" Dave choked, sounding half-panicked.

"Get into the center of the living room, Dave… *now*" I ordered.

I scrambled into the kitchen and started rifling through my junk drawer until I found a stick of chalk, then I ran into the living room and drew a circle around Dave.

"*Do not move*," I whispered, stepping into the circle and kneeling down beside him. "Don't even breathe."

I stretched out my right hand and gathered the magical energies surrounding me into my staff, then, I gently tapped the circle with the tip. Instantly I felt a barrier of invisible force shoot up from the chalk circle and I let out a tiny breath of relief.

"Uh… I gotta get to work, Val." Dave said, standing up. "I totally would love to hang out and play magic circle with you all day, babe, but duty calls."

I grabbed his belt with both hands and hauled him to the floor.

"Dave Webber, if you set one foot outside that ring, you'll *immediately* drop dead."

"W-What the hell are you talking about, Val?"

"Shhh…" I said, reaching out and touching the wall of force to see if anything was trying to disturb it.

Because magic is a form of energy, a spell molds that energy into whatever the conjurer desires and it generates its own magical signature that is distinct to the spell at hand. The presence of dark magic offers a magical signature that is textured by the malice associated with the person channeling it, and as such, you can literally feel when someone's magic is working against your own.

In this case, I was trying to detect the magical signature of whatever the hell had killed my fish and destroyed my house plants, since it would act against the magical energy of the summoning circle. If the foreign signature were strong enough, I might be able to send my own counter spell back through the same magical path that sent the presence in my condo.

I felt a slight ripple in the wall of invisible energy, and that told me we weren't alone.

"This is seriously freaking me out, Val," Dave whispered, nervously.

I wrapped my arm around Dave and pulled him close. "I know," I said. "But as long as the integrity of the chalk circle remains intact, we're safe."

He gave me a startled look. "Yeah, but for how long?"

I didn't have an immediate answer to that.

The longest I'd ever spent in a summoning circle was thirty

hours, and I'd had to be rescued by D.T. when he destroyed a black sprite that wanted me dead.

Wanted me dead.

I chewed by lip for half a second and wondered why we weren't dead already. I'd been asleep and in the throes of a nightmare while Dave was in the shower... why were we still alive? If whatever had killed my fish wanted us dead, it could have easily done so. How come we were both still breathing?

What if the nightmare *was* the spell?

I'd been dreaming about the massive wall of fog killing everything in its path when Dave woke me up and told me about the dead fish. It was likely the fish were still alive when I went to bed. I would have noticed a bunch of dead fishies floating at the top of my aquarium, wouldn't I?

"Were the fish still alive before I came home?" I blurted out.

"Um... yeah," Dave said, scratching his head. "I mean, I think so."

"*Think harder!*" I snapped.

"Jeez, Val, chill out," Dave growled back. "I fed them when I woke up an hour and a half ago."

"What about the plants?"

"Beats me... guys never notice plants until they're dead, I guess," he laughed, nervously. "You mind telling me what's going on?"

I kept my hand out against the barrier, closed my eyes, and concentrated. The slight rippling had disappeared, and the barrier hummed with static electricity against my fingertips.

I slowly exhaled in relief and lowered my hand. "You probably saved our lives, Dave."

He gave me an uncertain look. "H-How?"

"My nightmare," I said. "It wasn't a nightmare at all; it was a dark spell that was supposed to invade my dreams and kill me in my sleep. If you hadn't woken me up, we'd be as dead as the fishies."

Dave let out a loud gulp and huddled himself into a ball for fear of disturbing the chalk circle. "Someone can do *that?*"

"That and a helluva lot more, Dave." I whispered. "I've been chasing this shade thing around for the past twenty-four hours, thinking it was just a rogue spirit. What invaded my dream told me there absolutely *must* be a human hand behind it, and the shade might well be under the control of a someone... possibly a dark mage."

"Well, what else could it be?" Dave blinked. "That's what you magic types do, right? I mean you have to be a sorcerer to make magic work, don't you?"

I stood up and tested the barrier one last time. "Not necessarily. This could be some gifted teenager with time to kill, for all I know."

"Really?"

"I said it *could* be... though my sense is that whoever has the ability to infect someone's mind probably has attained a measure of discipline you can only get with years of study."

Dave rubbed his mustache and stood up beside me. "Well, how the hell does this guy know about you?"

"That's a good question. There are only two people outside of the government who know what I do, and one of them is a zombie. A zombie can't practice any form of magic, because it's dead."

"A zombie!" he gasped.

"Long story, sweetie, and not enough time to fill you in on the details," I said, kissing his nose. "I know you aren't behind this, because people who try to kill you generally don't clean your apartment and make you scrambled eggs and bacon."

"So… any ideas?" he asked.

"Yep," I grunted. "But I have to step out of the circle to find out."

Dave grabbed my arm and swung me against his chest. "Are you sure it's safe to step outside the circle?" he asked, his voice nearly shaking.

I flashed him my best confident smile and hoped he'd buy it. "Absolutely," I said. "I was checking for the magical signature of the spell that tried to kill us, and I'm fairly certain it's safe now."

I felt him slowly release his grip on my arm and I stood up on my toes, and then kissed him on the nose.

"If I don't drop dead when I leave the circle, it'll be safe enough for you to come out," I chuckled, grimly. "See you on the other side."

Dave gave me a helpless look as I held my foot near the edge of the circle and took a deep breath. I clutched my staff closely and leaned forward until my foot cleared the circle and touched the floor on the other side. I took a deep breath and waited a few seconds.

"Good news!" I said, grinning. "I'm not dead, and that means we can both open the circle."

Dave let out a huge sigh of relief and stepped over the ring and onto the carpet. I broke the chalk circle with the heel of my slipper while Dave slumped on the sofa, still shaking.

"I'd call in sick for work," he said. "But after this, I'd feel safer in my truck."

I sat down beside him and put a reassuring hand on his knee.

"I know," I said, softly. "And I'll be honest with you, Dave… I have a feeling that whatever killed those birds has a hate on for people. Think you can do me a favor?"

"What's that?" he asked.

"If you haven't heard from me by 10:00 P.M. tonight, I want you to get in your truck and drive east. Call my parents and tell them to get out of town… tell them I said it was a matter of life and death. Tell them to keep driving until they're as far away from town as they can get. They will understand what I mean."

"How come?"

I offered the best reassuring smile I could muster, but I could tell from the look on Dave's face that he wasn't buying it.

"Because whatever killed the birds just tried to kill us, and I'm absolutely certain that Calgary is next on its hit list."

CHAPTER 25

"We've been dating for nearly a year now, Valerie," said Dave. "During that time, I've kept a pretty open mind regarding whatever the heck it is that you do for a living."

I nodded silently, certain that I was about to get a lecture from a dump truck driver about career options. I opened my mouth to say something, but Dave held up his hand to stop me.

"I've seen a big, red guy with horns in your bathroom…"

"Class four demon, sweetie," I interrupted.

"Whatever." Dave rolled his eyes. "I've seen the ghost of a dead Prime Minister, and I've even seen some little dude with blue wings named 'Scotty' raid your refrigerator. You'll forgive me if I'm just a wee bit worried about your safety."

"And?"

"And you could get out of this line of work, Val. You could get into something with less risk."

I stared at him hard for a moment and then tried my reassuring smile bit again. "I'm well protected, Dave. Moreover, the threat to innocent people is very real, and it's for that reason that I have to do what I do… you know this."

He gave me a skeptical glance. "I don't have to like it," he grunted.

"Nobody is asking you too, honey. I love that you worry about me, but I'd ask if you would just try to see the world through my eyes, because if you did, you'd realize that sometimes people like me are the only thing standing in the way of wholesale chaos."

"I know."

"Let me ask you something: if I were a cop, would you worry about me?"

He blinked a few times. "Yeah, so?"

"If I were a firefighter, would you worry?"

"Yeah."

"Well, just try to think of me as a cop for spiritual bad guys and black magic," I said. "It might make you feel better."

He got off the couch and shuffled over to the front closet. I followed close behind and said nothing.

"I gotta get to work," he said, tying up his steel-toed boots. "We can continue this discussion when all this blows over, okay?"

"Deal," I said. "In the meantime, if you haven't heard from me by 10:00 P.M. tonight, get out of town. The same goes for my folks."

He nodded reluctantly as he took me in his arms and gave me another bear hug. Then he kissed me. Softly at first, then long and hard and purposeful.

"I just want you to know, Val, that I lo — "

"I know you do," I said, putting two fingers over his lips. "I feel the same way… I'm still not ready to say those words yet, okay?"

He kissed my fingers and nodded. "Alright… please tell me that you'll have this… *whatever* the hell this is, resolved."

"I'll try," I whispered.

He gave me a tight, worried smile and walked out the door. I watched him head up the hall and considered for a short second if maybe life in the real world might be more interesting than the life I was currently leading.

Nahhhh…

I closed the door and flipped the lock. Then I grabbed a china marker from the junk drawer and started drawing glyphs, similar to those in D.T.'s cave on the doorframe.

I didn't hear an unexpected visitor come in.

"What are you doing?"

"Jeezis God, Bill… would you *stop* scaring the crap out of me!" I shouted, angrily.

"Oh, yes… sorry. I forgot how high strung you are, Valerie," he said, his head poking through the ceiling. "Why are you drawing gang tags on your door?"

"I'm setting up some protective sentinels," I grunted. "Our shade paid me a visit while I was sleeping."

"And it didn't kill you?" asked Bill, in a voice laced with what I could have easily mistaken for disappointment.

"Nope. These sentinels will make sure it can't get back in… well, at least they *should,* if my magic is all it's cracked up to be."

I continued drawing the glyphs on my doorframe, tapping each one with my fingertip, charging it with a dose of spectral energy. After about ten minutes, I tossed the china marker onto the counter and walked over to my storeroom. Bill hovered close behind me, floating in the doorway as I rifled through my twenty or so shelves of spell ingredients.

"Chemistry assignment?" he asked.

"Supplies I'm going to need if I plan on living for the next twenty-four hours," I said.

He hovered through the doorway and floated to my grandfather's steam trunk, then sat down as if it were teatime at the Governor General's.

"The spirit world is abuzz over the dead birds," he said, grimly. "It's all the talk."

I nodded silently as I grabbed a handful of empty vials and stuffed them in my satchel.

"Anyone talking about who might be the controlling the shade?" I asked.

Bill frowned. "You're confident it's a mage of some kind?"

"Invading someone's mind isn't something listed on the resume of even the most malevolent spirits," I grunted.

Bill let out a worried little laugh. "A mage who is practiced in the dark arts might be a handful for you, young lady. Not that I don't believe you have some measure of skill, mind you. But when you're dealing with a mage, it really becomes a question of whose will is stronger… and of course, there's malice, which naturally gives him an edge."

"If it is a him," I said. "It might be a woman… hell, it might be some gifted kid with a penchant for emo music, for all I know. And by the way, Bill, thanks for the head's up about D.T. It would have been nice if you'd told me he was a freaking political appointment."

Bill looked unimpressed and folded his vaporous arms across his chest.

"I'd assumed you already knew, young lady," he said.

I stomped out of the storeroom and went into the kitchen, tossing my satchel on the counter top. Bill materialized, seated comfortably at the dinette, and for what seemed like the first time in our tenuous relationship, said nothing. I poured the remaining coffee Dave had made into a mug and gulped it down.

"You know," I said, savoring the kick of caffeine. "You were in government."

Bill gave me a sour look. "Oh my dear... I *was* the government."

"I stand corrected," I exhaled. "Bill, I don't know anything about government or how ministerial agencies function, but it's pretty clear the attacks on me point to someone who knows me... someone who knows my abilities."

"They point to a higher purpose," he said. "You yourself have suggested the attacks on the birds contain biblical connotations. That implies intelligent design, I believe, because you pose a threat to a yet-to-be-revealed plan."

I nodded and took another slug of coffee.

"I'm mindful of your concern that the attacks suggest someone is double-dealing those contacts of yours in the various ministries you associate with. It would be remiss of me to not instruct you on the way government works, though."

I gave him an impatient look and shook my head. I didn't have time for a lecture on civics from a dead guy, even if he were once the Prime Minister of Canada.

"Bill, this might not be the time or place..."

He held up his hand and gave me a stern frown. "It doesn't need to be someone who knows you, young lady... had you contemplated that?"

"What do you mean?"

Bill closed his near-transparent eyelids and looked disappointed in me. "What *are* they teaching young people these days?" he asked, his voice oozing of paternal disapproval. "My dear young lady, a government ministry is a complex beehive of departments, sub departments, civil servants, briefings, and shuffled documents. You're looking for a smoking gun, when, in fact, this person could be anyone from an assistant deputy minister right down to a mail room lackey who accidentally saw your picture on the outside of a file and decided you were pretty enough to read about. In short, government tries to incorporate appropriate security measures, but leaks happen all the time. Moreover, they're impossible to prevent."

Bill was right.

Darn it, I *hate* it when he's right.

"So you're saying that I'm looking for someone with direct knowledge of me, when it could be just a low-paid government peon?"

"In a more illuminated way, yes… that is what I'm suggesting."

"Well, how the heck do you find a peon when the civil service in Canada employs more people than the Detroit Three?"

He studied me for a minute and then his translucent lips curled up into a satisfied smile.

"You call in a political favor, my dear," he said. "You also don't go looking for him… you make him come looking for you."

CHAPTER 26

"In case you hadn't noticed, Bill, I think whoever is behind all this has no problem finding me," I said, sourly.

Bill nodded amiably. "That's true, but everything has been according to someone else's design, hasn't it? The attacks have occurred according to his plan, not yours. You simply need to arrange for another assault on *your* terms. When that inevitably happens, surely you or your little troll friend could make a counter spell that would locate the person in question or, better yet, destroy him before he destroys you."

I chewed my lip and fiddled with the handle of my coffee mug. I hadn't considered a counter spell, because I'd been too busy trying to discover the whereabouts of the shade.

Too busy trying to find the shade…

What if the shade was just a ruse?

I spun the idea through my mind for a moment and realized there was a slight chance the shade was a diversion. What better way to get my attention than to have a grain bin disappear into a three-hundred-foot-deep hole that spews human bones into the air? Whoever was behind it must have known I would investigate; it made perfect sense.

"I have a theory, Bill," I said, putting my coffee mug in the dishwasher. "But first I need some of your spiritual insights."

"Go on…" said Bill, looking very sure of himself.

"We know a shade can kill organic matter; we've already seen proof of that. In your vast, encyclopedic knowledge of the arcane, is it possible for a human to tap into a shade's power, or better yet, could a person enchant a shade to achieve their own objectives?

Bill hesitated for a second or two, and then his self-satisfied smile returned.

"A necromancer is a kind of mage, am I correct?" he asked.

I nodded silently.

"A necromancer uses dark magic to animate a corpse and bend it to his will, but a corpse is a rotting husk, isn't it?"

I blinked a few times. "What do you mean?"

"Well, it's the shell of what *used* to be a person," he continued. "It is without thought, and it is without soul. A spirit, on the other hand, is the life energy of a person who once lived. It carries the imprint of that person's thoughts, emotions and experiences, whether it chooses to cross over or not. Take me for example: I could cross over, but I choose not to, because it is a choice of my free will. A shade is a spirit by definition, and therefore, it's reasonable to assume it too possesses the life energy of what it once was. For this reason alone, it would be difficult to see how a spell could force any spirit to abandon the one thing that makes it unique: its former humanity."

I gave Bill a surprised look. The creepy old SOB *was* good.

"A spell can be shaped by a number of factors," I said. "Its effectiveness depends on the will of the spell caster, and even in cases where a dark spell infects a person's mind, it never captures that person's free will. The best it can do is to try to play on the person's emotions as a means of manipulating free will. If I hear you correctly, Bill, what you're suggesting is that spirits are resistant to this kind of manipulation."

"That's correct," he nodded.

"Then would it be fair to say the shade might be in league with a mage?"

"Occam's razor, my dear."

I threw my arms in the air, frustrated. "That's the second time in twelve hours someone has told me that. What the heck motivates a spirit to work with a dark mage, Bill? Do you have any inkling?"

Bill shrugged. "Perhaps the mage has something the shade wants. Perhaps he's manipulating the human imprint left in the shade."

"What do you mean?"

"Well, look at me… I *choose* to stay among the mortal realm for reasons that are my own. Perhaps the mage has learned how to motivate the shade to his plan and purpose by knowing something the shade values. It's entirely possible the shade is reluctantly working with this mage, young lady. You can't rule that out. Maybe the missing grain bin wasn't a ruse at all — maybe it was a plea for help."

I poured some Cascade in the dishwasher and closed the door. I was back to the question of motive, and I didn't like it one bit. The disappearing grain bin was definitely something a shade could do. Having it crash land on the street outside my home seemed improbable, but what if it *wasn't* an attempt to kill me? It could have easily dropped the bin on my building, but it didn't because…

Because innocent people could have been injured or killed.

"Son of beehive, Bill, you're a genius!"

"Why, yes," he said, pumping out his vaporous chest. "I've been called Canada's greatest Prime Minister. Perhaps there's some truth to it, after all. Why am I a genius, again?"

I raced to the bedroom and threw on a clean pair of jeans and a new sweatshirt. I stuffed my ponytail through my baseball cap and then put on my leather jacket.

"Because I think the shade might just be a good guy in a bad situation," I said, grabbing my satchel and my staff. "Meet me at my car, and I'll explain everything."

"As you wish," said Bill, disappearing through the ceiling.

CHAPTER 27

I pulled the Maxima out of the underground parking lot and turned onto 17th Avenue. The sun was just coming up, bathing the empty street with a warm, orange glow that did nothing to liven up the macabre scene of small front-end loaders lifting piles of dead birds and dumping them into the backs of dump trucks. I flipped on the radio to see if there were any reception and was pleasantly surprised to hear that life on the airwaves had apparently returned to normal.

Well, as normal as morning radio shows can be after it rained dead birds all over the city. I switched off just in time to see Fifty-Dollar Bill materialize in the back seat.

"Alright," he said. "I'm here. Where are we going?"

"Okotoks," I said, glimpsing in the rearview mirror. "To Peter Orlowski's farm."

"Any particular reason you need me to accompany you?"

"Kind of… I want to pick your brain some more, if that's alright."

Bill nodded and grinned. He liked being needed. "Pick away, young lady. What can I help you with?"

I pulled onto McLeod Trail and headed south, swerving occasionally to avoid small convoys of dump trucks that were filled with dead birds.

"Bill," I said, in a somber voice. "I'm going to guess that our government's interest in the arcane probably doesn't predate the years you were in office… fair assumption?"

"That is correct," he said with a nod. "We established a cabinet level committee of ministers who shared my interest in the occult in 1936, after I defeated that nasty Richard Bedford Bennett. I was returned to office with a majority of seats in the House of Commons, you know."

"Care to elaborate as to why, at the height of the Great Depression, you decided to do this?"

Bill made an effort of rolling his eyes, and I braced myself for yet another recrimination about my failure to have committed the entire history of Canada to memory.

"My dear," he huffed. "It is *because* of the depression that I formed the committee."

I gave him a confused look.

"Understand that at that time, more than a quarter of Canadians were out of work and on relief of some form. There was a drought on the prairie, and there were soup kitchens right across the country… people were literally starving to death. Our economic policies and, indeed, the economic policies of our trading partners simply couldn't penetrate the stifling unemployment and general sense of desperation."

I grunted. "Okay, let me get this straight. You were looking for answers to high unemployment through the occult? I don't get it."

Bill materialized in the passenger's seat and frittered with his necktie.

"We were looking for clues about the future," he whispered. "We had no idea when or where the other shoe would drop, and it was one of various methods we used to respond to the crisis."

"What were the other methods?" I asked, my voice laced with suspicion.

Bill gave me an uncomfortable glance through the corner of his eye and shifted in the seat.

"Well, we *did* try to make it rain on the prairie," he muttered.

"*Hydromancy*... you guys were dabbling in *that* kind of stuff?" I gasped. "Do you realize that if you made one small error in a spell, you might have caused a flood that not even Noah could have built an ark for?"

"Yes," Bill sighed. "We rather opened Pandora's Box, I think."

I groaned through my teeth as I turned onto Highway 22X and headed west. "Why do I get the feeling, Bill, that there's more to our government's involvement than you're telling me?"

He got his back up and gave me an icy glare. "Everyone, including a *certain bohemian corporal in a toothbrush mustache,* was involved in this."

"Hitler?" I choked, nearly driving my car off the road.

"Oh tut-tut, now," said Bill, in a dismissive tone. "It is common knowledge the Nazi's were very much working with the spirit world. Hitler had a keen interest in Teutonic mythology and Heinrich Himmler himself was a known mystic... some even think he was a satanic lord, working in concert with hellions. You must look at your history through the context of the times, Valerie."

I gripped he steering wheel hard, barely noticing a small cluster of dead cattle in a farmer's field. "Alright," I said, exhaling. "So all this stuff begins with the Nazis, is that it?" I asked.

Bill shook his head. "No, it began with a human race that was desperate. Hitler was bent on dominating Europe, indeed, the world. He devoted massive amounts of capital and infrastructure on finding anything that would help him achieve his aims. Why, the Second World War could have started two years earlier if the Americans hadn't obtained the Spear of Destiny before German Intelligence got to it."

I chewed on Bill's comments for a moment as the car bumped over a level rail crossing. I'd always wondered just how Canada became involved in the unnatural world. When Vishesh hired me, I was given a classified briefing that painted a picture of a recently discovered preternatural world and a government that was beside itself trying to keep it that way. For nearly ten years, I'd diligently faced everything from shape-shifting faeries to a rampaging, twelve-foot-tall demon, and I'd either brokered a settlement to a dispute or I settled it myself, all in the name of keeping wholesale chaos at bay. Now Fifty-Dollar Bill was telling me the utter devastation caused by The Great Depression and Adolf Hitler's megalomaniacal interest in the occult had forced our government into action.

Then there was the issue of my being a peacekeeper, whatever the hell that meant, and I chuckled at the irony of a dead guy telling me more about the government's involvement than the government itself. At least now I had an idea why taxpayers bankrolled activities involving creatures more commonly reserved for nightmares, but my instincts told me there were forces at work that went far beyond the occasional Bigfoot sighting (yes, he's real, and he's a jerk) or disappearing aircraft.

"Bill," I sighed. "This may sound rather naïve of me, but do you know which specific countries are actively involved with the arcane?"

He shifted in his seat again and gave me a hesitant glance. "Are you certain you're ready for this, young lady?" he asked.

"Lay it on me."

"If you insist, but you might want to pull over, because what I'm about to reveal may cause you to drive into the ditch," he huffed.

"It's that bad?" I asked, sounding nervous, and certain he was going to drop a bombshell.

"That depends if you believe geopolitical intrigue is no longer the exclusive domain of the mortal realm."

I pulled the Maxima onto the shoulder of the highway and gave Bill a pensive smile. "Go ahead," I whispered.

Bill turned toward me, and for the first time in our bizarre relationship, his face took on a decisive look. He pushed a pair of spectral glasses onto the bridge of his nose and straightened his tunic like he was about to give a speech. Son of a gun, *he actually looked Prime Ministerial*. I didn't think he had it in him.

"The world as you know it," he began, "is at a crossroads."

"Alright," I said, nodding slowly.

"I cannot speak for the actions of our current government, but what I can say is that all Canadian governments, be they Liberal or Conservative, inherited a series of policies that began under my tenure as Prime Minister. There are, at present, more than a dozen nations with knowledge of the preternatural world. These nations range from our closest ally, the United States, to our NATO partners and finally, to middle eastern countries like Israel and Saudi Arabia.

"To my knowledge, fundamentalist middle-eastern states such as Iran and Pakistan are uninvolved in direct negotiations with parties, for example, representing various vampire clans — thank heaven for that. The reasons for this have a great deal to do with the fact that fundamentalist Islamic countries do not benefit from the separation of church and state, and as a result, religious dogma forbids their acknowledgement of preternatural world entities, even if those entities were to make themselves known."

I blinked at Bill and said nothing.

"There is a common market within the wealthiest countries for preternatural-world-related goods and services that, in theory at least, would be of benefit to all mankind: A cure for cancer. Fantastic discoveries that might double, even *triple* life expectancy. Methods of ending global hunger and disease. Many of these discoveries contain magical or alchemical components and still others require active involvement of participants from the preternatural world. Much of what you've discovered in your brief tenure as a civil servant has been put to good use, but there is also a market for goods that serve a sinister purpose."

"Like what?" I asked, stunned at the revelation.

"Like how to assassinate a political enemy without being detected, for starters," he said, grimly. "There's also a national defense component, wherein nations actively seek to obtain weapons of destruction that cannot be explained by conventional means."

"Such as?" I asked.

Bill took on a paternal look and frowned.

"Perhaps a famine begins in a nation that is surrounded by other nations where agriculture is at an all-time high and standards of living are increasing. Perhaps crops and livestock are destroyed to the extent they cripple the economy of a political enemy, so that a corporate interest working in partnership with a government can go in there and create an economy of convenience — one that benefits the political enemy while keeping the victims of famine in the back pocket of corporations.

"You'd have to deploy biological and chemical weapons to do this using conventional means, and of course, that would be seen as a deliberate attack that would require a military response. However, were a nation to use dark magic to create the famine, there would be no act of war; you'd achieve your aims, and nobody would be the wiser."

"Anything else?" I asked, half expecting to learn that the U.S. Army has division of airborne zombies for special operations.

"Canada's role has long been that of a peacekeeper," he continued. "Under Lester Bowles Pearson, who won the Nobel Peace Prize in 1957 for preventing the Suez Crisis from escalating into World War Three, his Liberal government defined Canada's role in this new and very dangerous world. Just as Pearson advocated for United Nations Peacekeepers to oversee a peaceful resolution to the Suez Crisis, so too did he develop a formal policy of peacekeeping and peacemaking mortal involvement in the spiritual realms.

"You must realize, young lady, the cold war might be over, but an arms race, wherein magic is the weapon of choice threatens mankind's very existence. Our nation is often the only thing that stands between the continuance of humanity and the abyss."

I stared at Bill and gulped. I was speechless.

I had no idea the mortal realm had turned the discovery of the preternatural world into opportunities for power, wealth and political intrigue. It shouldn't have surprised me, mind you, yet there it was, laid out by the ghost of a former Prime Minister in surprisingly plain English: *a new arms race, where the weapon of choice is magic.*

Now I understood why I'd been identified and recruited by Vishesh. Now it made perfect sense how three percent of annual revenue came from the brokering of goods and services from the preternatural world.

But who would we sell to, what were we selling, and why?

My head filled with dozens of questions I didn't have time to ask, and my gut told me a catastrophe was about to happen if I didn't get myself to Peter Orlowski's farm. I'd ask my questions in due course, assuming I survived whatever the shade and the mage had in store for me... for everyone.

CHAPTER 28

Fifty-Dollar Bill excused himself just as I turned off the highway and headed up the dirt road leading to Peter Orlowski's farm. The last time I had visited, my stomach twisted itself in knots and I doubled over from a serious wave of nausea courtesy of what I had believed was a case of serious, hard-ass menace aimed squarely at me. Now I wasn't entirely sure if it was menace or an attempt to get my attention.

I crossed a Texas gate that led around the bottom of a hill and slowed down to where the grain bin used to be. Orlowski had filled in the hole, and the sprig of wretched oak I'd dropped at the bottom of the hole had grown into a small shrub, already two feet high. I spotted Orlowski standing on his front porch and gave him a polite wave. He took off his hat and waved back, so I assumed it was okay for me to drive up to the old two-story farmhouse. He headed over to my car as I grabbed my staff and satchel and stepped out.

"What brings you back?" Orlowski asked, with a hork. "Nothing else has gone missing, and I filled in that hole."

"I wanted to ask a few more questions, if that's alright," I said, adjusting the shoulder strap of my satchel.

Orlowski took off his baseball cap and wiped his brow with a plaid-sleeved arm. "I don't know what the hell else I can tell you, but I sure as shit have a few questions for you, lady," he grunted.

I dug the heel of my staff in the ground and nodded politely. Orlowski pulled a pouch of Borkum Riff tobacco out of his breast pocket and stuffed a large pinch into the bowl of his pipe.

"I have some questions too," I said. "Mind if we go for a walk?"

"Alright," he grunted again, lighting his pipe with a wooden match.

We headed past my car and back to where the grain bin went missing two days ago. It was shortly past sunrise, and the air was filled with the moist smell of flax, mixed with wild roses. I noticed Orlowski had a slight limp and was favoring his right leg.

"Is your back sore from when you took a tumble the last time I was out?" I asked, innocently.

"This old body ain't what it used to be," he griped. "I love this farm, but I'm ten years past too old to be working it. My goddamned kids ain't got no interest in running it, neither."

"I'm sorry to hear that — you could always sell, I suppose."

"Maybe... you still didn't tell me why you're back out here. It's just after six in the morning, for shit sake — I thought you civil service types only worked banker's hours."

"Can I level with you?" I asked, kneeling down and grabbing a handful of earth from where Orlowski had filled in the hole.

"Go on," he said.

"Well, to be honest… we don't have a clue how your grain bin went missing."

Orlowski clenched his jaw and tightened his lips. "Shit lady, your people found it sure enough, since the TV said it fell off a truck in downtown Calgary. I'm gonna assume that was my bin… it sure as shit looked like my bin on the news."

"You saw that, did you?" I asked, pleased that Vishesh had come up with a story that was more palatable than a bin falling through a fissure separating the spiritual and mortal realms.

Orlowski kicked at the small shrub of wretched oak and took a deep puff on his pipe. He leaned over and pulled off a leaf, then spun around and stuck it in front of my face.

"You want to tell me how a two foot tall shrub suddenly appears in the place where my bin vanished into a three-hundred-foot hole in the ground?" he snapped. "I've seen plenty of weird shit happen on this farm, but between this and my bin, I'm thinking there's a whole helluva lot else going on that you ain't tellin' me about."

I glanced at the leaf and chewed my lip. "What kind of weird shit?" I asked.

Orlowski tapped the bowl of his pipe against the heel of a rubber boot, and a small ball of burning tobacco fell into the dirt. He squashed it with his other boot until he was satisfied it was out.

"Just lots of shit, I suppose," he said, sounding a little defensive. "Nothing I talk to people about, since I don't like anyone whispering behind my back."

I stood up and brushed the dirt of my knees. "Oh… I don't know, Mr. Orlowski," I said, sounding very diplomatic. "I've seen a lot of strange things too. Heck, I've done plenty of investigations on crop circles… have you ever seen any of those out here?"

He took a couple of steps back and blew a hork of snot out of his left nostril. "I'm not talkin' about crop circles, little lady. I'm sayin' I seen stuff *happen* out here, that's all."

It was pretty clear that Orlowski wasn't about to voluntarily disclose what specific 'weird shit' he was talking about. He was a stereotypical southern Alberta farmer: very conservative, deeply religious, and extremely proud. He wasn't going to tell me a darned thing unless it was on his terms and until he was certain I wouldn't laugh in his face.

His reluctance made sense, really. Everyone who has ever lived can tell you at least one story about an encounter with something inexplicable, but our brains are conditioned to dismiss that which doesn't fall within our narrow view of the world around us.

For example: you can actually *see* spirits anytime you want. The trick is, you have to *want* to see them, and more importantly, your mind has to accept that a disembodied voice you hear whispering in your basement late at night is what it is. Moreover, in most cases, our minds are filled to capacity with the stresses of day-to-day life, and as such, our level of distraction is off the charts. Even if the spirit of your dead aunt were to materialize on the dining room table at Thanksgiving and start tap dancing to an Al Jolson tune, your mind has to be free enough of clutter for it to register. I sensed that Orlowski wanted to tell me some truths about his farm; I'd just have to give him a clear indication that it was safe to do so.

"Has your wife seen anything inexplicable, Mr. Orlowski… or just you?" I asked, in a passive voice.

He blinked at me a couple of times, and I could have sworn I saw his cheeks flush with embarrassment at the question.

"Bern? Hell... she sees shit all the time," he chuckled, nervously.

"Would you say that whatever it is you see tends to happen more frequently either very late at night or during certain times of the year?"

He nodded silently. I was getting through to him.

"Say... like just before Halloween?"

"Yeah — Halloween and two other times of the year."

"Just around the summer and winter solstice?" I asked, innocently.

Orlowski's red face instantly flashed from embarrassment to anger, and he kicked at the shrub of wretched oak in frustration.

"Goddammit, lady," he snapped. "How the hell are you able to know when the shit starts flying out here? I never told you squat about summer and winter solstice!"

I'd struck a raw nerve, and it was pretty obvious that Orlowski wanted to spill the beans. I decided to up the ante.

"Mr. Orlowski, I want you to know that you're not the first person to see things out of the corner of their eye." I said. "A lot of people aren't comfortable with talking about it, but I'll share something with you: there are people in the world who will believe you, and I'm one of them."

He stared at me in silence for a minute as the redness dissipated from his complexion. He let out a huge sigh and shrugged, then chuckled in embarrassment at his little outburst.

"I'm sorry about gettin' steamed, eh?" he muttered. "It's just that talkin' about spooks and wee little beasties that come outta nowhere is a free ticket to the funny farm in Ponoka."

"It's alright, Mr. Orlowski," I said, putting a reassuring hand on his shoulder. Wee little beasties, eh?"

He nodded again. "Yep… I first thought they were some kinda wild animals or something, but one time I was combining three sections over, and this little furry thing came out from behind a stump, and it was carryin' what I thought was a burlap-lookin' bag. I stopped the combine, because, you know, maybe I thought I might be havin' a stroke or something, but the Goddamned thing stopped no further away from me than you are right now, and it bloody well smiled… it *smiled* at me!"

"Did it have thin and lanky arms, a big head and no nose?" I asked, bracing myself for another possible outburst.

Orlowski's face got a little pale. "How the hell did you know that?" he gasped.

I smiled warmly and gave his shoulder a little squeeze. "Why, Mr. Orlowski, you are one of the very few people alive who've been lucky enough to see a s*kookum*!"

"A w-what?"

"A skookum," I said, still smiling. "It's a race of primitive but friendly meadow creatures in Sarcee folklore. They're kind of like a miniature Sasquatch, and they're known for being industrious and helpful to what the species believes to be honorable people. I bet you've always had good crops, right?"

He nodded. "Yeah… so what?"

"Well, the Sarcee believe that skookums are a "good luck" creature, and seeing one is considered to be a great honor, according to their tradition… it might be why your farm yields well at harvest."

Orlowski pursed his lips and fiddled with his silver wedding band. "Skookum, eh? Well, I saw it about thirty years ago, and I planned to tell my wife, Bernadette, but I was afraid she'd run from the house in her curlers. Then she told me about the little people who bring baskets of wild berries in late summer."

"Sprites?" I asked.

"Yeah, that's what Bern calls 'em. Whenever she does any baking, if she leaves out a tin of biscuits or something, well, the next morning the biscuits are gone and replaced with a hand-woven basket of wild berries. Lady, you have no idea how relieved I am to tell someone besides Bern about all this crazy stuff."

I leaned in on my staff and exhaled in relief. Orlowski was, surprisingly, one of those rare people who either accepted – or, at the very least, acknowledged – the existence of the inexplicable. Now that he'd informed me that his farm was a hotbed of preternatural phenomenon, it made sense that his grain bin would disappear like that. I decided to press for more information.

"Mr. Orlowski…"

"Call me Peter… everyone else does," he interrupted.

"Okay…" I continued. "Peter… has anything else sort of, well… you know… *disappeared* into thin air around here?"

"You mean other than my grain bin?"

I rubbed the back of my neck and nodded.

"Well, yeah," he said. "Shit goes missing here all the time… but I usually find it, eh?"

"But nothing has ever disappeared into a three hundred foot hole, right?"

"Nope… and nothin' that big, neither."

I saw a flash of movement from behind Orlowski's shoulder, and I tightened my grip on my staff.

"Ever been attacked by anything that isn't of our world?" I asked, rolling onto my toes and, this time, peering over his shoulder toward a Quonset barn about a hundred feet away.

"Nope, nothing… what are you looking at, lady?"

Suddenly the air filled with the sound of smashing glass, and I instinctively dove onto Orlowski, knocking him flat on his back. The sliding door of the Quonset flew off its hinges, and my nostrils filled with something that smelled like human sweat mixed with raw sewage.

"Jeezis H. Christ, lady… what the hell is that God-awful stench?"

I raised my head and looked at the twelve-foot-high opening to the Quonset where the door used to be and gulped.

"Rats…" I said through my teeth. I exhaled slowly and reached over my shoulder to loosen the strap to my satchel. "There's only one thing that smells like a raw sewage and can knock twelve foot tall metal door down," I groaned.

"W-What is it?" he gasped.

I clasped my hand on Orlowski's shoulder and pushed him down to the ground.

"A really, *really* pissed-off looking ogre." I whispered.

CHAPTER 29

Ogres.

You can't reason with them, they're immensely powerful, and they wield a club like an entire baseball team of Babe Ruths.

They're also the preternatural world's equivalent of a mercenary, and for that reason alone, I knew it had come for me. This was a good thing, of course, because it confirmed my hypothesis that someone with a measure of intelligence was behind the mass killing of birds in both Calgary and Airdrie.

The bad thing?

Well, I'd have to survive a duel with an ogre, and jeez, who wants that?

I leaned into Orlowski's ear and whispered. "Mr. Orlowski, would you happen to have a shotgun in the house somewhere?"

"Yep," he whispered back. "I got three of 'em."

I glanced over to the house and guessed it to be about two hundred yards from our position. If I ran, I'd easily make it there in about twenty-five seconds, but that would leave Orlowski unprotected. It would take him a lot longer because of his age, but at least it would get him out of the battle zone long enough to empty two barrels into the ten-foot tall creature.

"When I get off you... run like hell into your house and get a shotgun," I said. "Load it up and bring the entire box of shells with you. If the ogre is still standing by the time you get back, it means that I am dead, and your house is the Alamo... got it?"

He nodded and dug his hands into the dirt. I clenched my teeth and reached my own hand into the freshly dug earth, hoping to channel some energy into my staff, because ogres are remarkably adept at withstanding electrical bolts and sudden blasts of wind. If I were going to take it out, I'd have to either torch it, bleed it or bludgeon it to death. I didn't have a sword handy, and it would be impossible for me and my tiny, one-hundred-and-twenty-pound frame to club it to death, so that meant fire.

Lots and lots of fire.

I pushed my hand deeper into the earth, hoping I'd find a pocket of some kind of geothermal energy, but there was none. That meant I'd have to keep it busy and hope Orlowski got back with his shotgun in time.

"You ready?" I whispered.

"Y-Yeah... ready," he stammered.

"GO!" I shouted, leaping into the air and somersaulting into a defensive stance about fifty feet from the ogre. Orlowski scrambled to his feet and run-hobbled as fast as his nearly seventy-year-old legs could carry him.

"*Ogre*! What brings you to this peaceful farm?" I shouted. "Who is paying you?"

It took a giant step forward and slammed a hair-covered foot into the ground. Then it leaned an enormous, armor-plated shoulder forward and opened its thick lips to reveal a hideous, toothless grin.

It was about to charge.

Oh, crap.

Its muscular legs tore into the dirt floor of the Quonset as it took off. A thickly veined arm the circumference of a tree trunk reached back over its armor plated shoulder and pulled out the biggest spiked club I'd ever seen.

"*You die now!*" it bellowed with rage, as the creature threw its entire weight about ten feet in the air and swung the club down at me.

I held out my staff and drove all my focus skyward. "*Desumo!*" I cried, and the air crackled with thunder as a bolt of electrical force flew out of my staff, hitting the ogre squarely in its massive chest. It let out a surprised roar as the blast sent it jettisoning through the air. It crashed into the side of the Quonset, stumbled forward a few steps, and then shook its head.

I'd dazed the creature long enough for me to scramble behind one of the grain bins. Its yellow eyes saw me as I fumbled with my satchel and searched inside for something I could use to buy enough time for Orlowski to come out of his house and shoot the damned thing. "Come on, Orlowski," I grimaced, as I pulled out a small poke containing a teaspoon of white phosphorus. The ogre lumbered forward, club in hand and took a huge swing at the side of the bin. An earsplitting clang filled the air as the bin lilted heavily to the right and started toppling over. I dove behind a rusted-out hulk of an old station wagon at the last second as the bin crashed into the ground, spilling ripe grain in every direction.

I coughed heavily as a huge plume of grain dust billowed into the air, obscuring my vision. The ogre, who was obviously blinded by the sudden cloud of dust, swung his club furiously and screamed in frustration.

"You die now, wizard woman!" it screeched in a voice that shot through my ears and into the pit of my stomach. I tore out from behind the rusted station wagon and headed into a small dugout that was only a quarter full of water.

I needed fire to kill it, and the only thing I had was a small poke of white phosphorus, not enough to take down an enraged ogre standing in a cloud of grain dust.

Grain dust.

White phosphorus: a chemical that burns when exposed to oxygen.

I had him — that ogre's ass was about to become grass.

I stood up on the edge of the dugout and shouted, "Ogre, this is your last warning… who paid you to kill me?"

It stumbled inside the cloud, hacking at the dust with its club. *"You come out, I kill you fast!"*

"Wrong answer!" I snarled as I opened the tiny drawstring of the poke and hurtled it at the ogre.

There was a blinding flash of light, and then a deafening WHOOMP, as the white phosphorus ignited the grain dust. I dove headfirst into the mucky base of the dugout and covered my ears. It was a high-order detonation.

Crap.

A tidal wave of thermal energy and explosive force blasted out from the area surrounding the ogre. It blew through the grain bins and over top of me, as I felt a rush of intense heat pass over my back. The ground shook violently as a pressure wave sent me tumbling to the other side of the dugout, landing flat on my back. The smell of burned grain filled my nostrils, followed by a sickly sweet smell of scorched hair. I sat up, then leaned on my staff and slowly got back to my feet.

"Crap, crap, crap!" I growled, as I carefully walked up to the edge of the dugout to survey the damage. "Oh shit… Orlowski is going to be a thousand kinds of pissed."

A giant club with three six-inch-long steel spikes lay in a pile of gore that I assumed was the remains of the ogre. Bloody pulp mixed with smoldering grain stretched out in every direction, as well as dozens of sheets of bent and twisted corrugated steel. The blast had taken out all but one of Orlowski's grain bins, it bore a hole the size of a Volkswagen Beetle in the side of the Quonset hut, and every window on the west side of Orlowski's house had been shattered.

I trudged through the acrid blue smoke until I came to the bloody pile of bones and charred flesh that used to be the ogre, and spotted something shiny underneath what might have been a femur. I poked at it with the tip of my staff until it was free then knelt down to pick it up.

It was a gold bar.

I cleaned the blood off on my jeans then examined it to see if was stamped, and I spotted four distinct markings that looked like Asian script.

"Chinese?" I gasped.

CHAPTER 30

Orlowski came tearing out the front door of his house, shotgun in hand. Behind him was a portly looking woman in a fluffy pink housecoat wearing a hair net.

"Jeezis H. Christ, lady… what the hell happened?" he shrieked.

I stepped out of the blast zone and headed up the dirt road leading to the old farmhouse. "I don't think we'll be needing the shotgun, Mr. Orlowski!" I shouted. "There was a bit of an explosion… the good news is that our ogre friend has gone bye-bye."

"A bit of an explosion?" he gasped. "Shit, lady, aside from blowing out nearly every window in my house, you just destroyed half of this year's take!"

I blinked a couple of times, as Mr. and Mrs. Orlowski surveyed the damage to what used to be their grain bins. "Well," I winced. "Technically, it was the ogre that did this… I just sort of helped a little bit."

"Peter… who is this woman, and why are the bins destroyed?" bleated Orlowski's wife, her face purple with anger.

"Hush now, Bern... you saw that goddamned whatever-the-hell-it-was through our bedroom window."

"Ogre," I said, still half-expecting Orlowski to shoot me. "It *was* an Ogre. Probably about eight hundred pounds, I would imagine. Good morning, Mrs. Orlowski — I'm deeply sorry about all of this. "

She gave me an icy glare and whacked Orlowski in the arm. "Peter, who is this woman?" she demanded, her voice shrill.

"She's from the government," he said. "Came here to find out about the missing bin, and now I'm missing all of 'em for shit sake."

"Well, we're going to be talking to a lawyer," she hissed. "Missy, you're going to be paying us back for years over what you caused."

There was an instant of anger in the pit of my stomach, and I nearly lashed out at her, deciding at the last second to remember that she too could see the preternatural world.

"It's alright, ma'am," I said. "We have a government branch that will clean all this up, and you'll be reimbursed for any damage... if you'll give me a couple of minutes, I'll make some arrangements."

I reached into my Mickey pocket and pulled out my cell phone. I punched in the number for Vishesh Rajwani, and within seconds, he answered.

"Vishesh, it's Valerie," I said. "There's been an explosion at Peter Orlowski's farm. There are no casualties, but we'll need a cleanup crew at my location. There's a good deal of damage, and you'll want to send out an adjuster."

"I'm fixed on your handheld's location via satellite," he said. "Very good, then."

There was a click, and he hung up.

I breathed a little easier, secure in the knowledge that Vishesh was probably contacting local authorities to tell them to stand down. His people would be out in a matter of hours, and that would give me enough time to calm the Orlowski's, as well as do a bit of sleuthing on the farm.

"You got a dent on the roof of your car, lady," said Mr. Orlowski, his voice flat. "Looks like we can share the pain of property damage."

"Nobody was killed or injured, sir," I said, turning to Bernadette Orlowski. "Ma'am, you know what just happened out here, right?"

"Yes,' she huffed. "You killed something that wasn't quite human."

"Before it was going to kill me, and then probably both of you," I interrupted. "My name is Valerie Stevens, and I work for the federal government."

She gave me a suspicious glare. "What interest does the government have in a haunted farm?" she asked.

"It's a long story that's classified," I grunted. "It's going to stay that way, do you both understand?"

Orlowski and his wife nodded.

"Good... now if you're both agreeable, could we go inside? I have a lot of questions, and I'm pretty sure you have some too. I can't promise to answer everything, but I'll be frank about what I believe could be a serious threat to all of us if we don't stop it in time."

"That's fine," said Mr. Orlowski. "We'll go inside, and you can ask us what you need over some coffee... okay with you, Bern?"

Mrs. Orlowski's icy glare dissolved into a small frown as she scrutinized me. "I suppose that's fine," she said, grudgingly.

We headed inside, and within minutes I was seated at an antique kitchen table covered by an intricate lace tablecloth and laminated place mats decorated with pictures of combines. Peter Orlowski sat opposite me as his wife poured a decanter of water into a coffee maker.

"Coffee will be on in a minute," she said, reaching for a broom inside a small broom closet. "Go ahead and ask your questions; I'm just going to sweep up the glass that's all over the place."

I felt bad about the damage, but there wasn't much I could do to console the old couple.

"It could have been much worse," I said quietly, leaning my staff against the wall beside me.

Orlowski made a horking sound and pulled a red handkerchief out of his breast pocket. "It ain't the first time there's been damage around here," he said, blowing his nose. "It's just the first time something ten feet tall was responsible. I don't think I never seen anything that big before… you know, besides a moose in the back forty."

"It just isn't right, Peter," said Mrs. Orlowski, as she swept a pile of glass into a large dustpan. "There have always been problems out here, ever since your grandpa Bogdan got the land ceded to him from the railway."

I arched my eyebrows. "How long ago was that, Mr. Orlowski?" I asked.

He stuffed the handkerchief back into his breast pocket and picked at his nose with this thumb. "My grandfather started clearing this land around 1905," he said. "The Canadian Pacific Railway gave free land to anyone who was prepared to make the trip from Europe to what at the time was literally the end of the earth. It's why most people around these parts have Ukrainian, Polish, and Russian surnames."

"You're Ukrainian, is that right?" I asked, as I scanned my brain to draw up what little I knew about eastern European folklore.

His voice became firm. "That's right. My grandfather Bogdan and my grandmother Elena, well, they were gypsies back in the old country. They used to tell me stories about all kinds of strange sightings of bizarre lookin' creatures, and my grandmother, well, she was sort of what the Sarcee would call a medicine woman. She used to protect her family's caravan from shit like vampires and lyca... lycan..."

"Lycanthropes," I interrupted.

Orlowski nodded and smiled. "Yeah, you know... shape shifty things and such. Why, my grandfather said she knew magic and that she put a spell on him to make him fall in love with her."

Mrs. Orlowski shuffled over to an old bureau adjacent to the antique oak hutch displaying her good china, which had miraculously survived the blast. She pulled open a drawer and took out what looked like an old photo album.

"She didn't need a spell to enchant your grandpa Bogdan, Peter," she said, carrying the photo album to the table, and then taking a seat beside her husband. "He loved her with all his heart, and she loved him."

Mr. Orlowski flipped through about a dozen faded pages until he found what he was looking for, and then he spun the photo album toward me. "Here are my grandparents on their wedding day," he said with agreeable nod.

It was a picture of a thin man in a mutton chop with broad shoulders and penetrating dark eyes. His face was smooth and tight, and he had the same strong jaw as Peter Orlowski. Seated behind him to the left was a woman with a high forehead, a thin nose and dark hair pulled back into what was probably a bun. She wore a simple, white dress with tiny buttons and a collar that stretched up to the bottom of her ears, and she had a small bouquet of wild flowers in her hands.

"What a lovely couple," I said, quietly. "They had their whole lives in front of them."

"They sure as shit did," said Mr. Orlowski. "But son of a beehive, if Baba Elena wasn't the most superstitious woman I ever met in my life."

"In what way?" I asked, closing the photo album.

Orlowski scratched his neck as his wife went to the kitchen and came back with three coffee mugs and a decanter of steaming coffee.

"Shit, all kinds of stuff, I suppose. I remember my grandfather telling me a story of how she made him put large rocks every hundred feet or so around the perimeter of the entire homestead, and that was before he got working on the sod house. He told me the stones were supposed to keep to good things in and the bad things out. They're still out there, hundreds of rocks... course, they didn't work too good today, did they?"

"No they didn't," I said, quietly.

I sat in silence for a moment as I chewed things over in my mind. Elena Orlowski was clearly a superstitious woman, but maybe she was that and something more. Folk sorcery had been commonplace all over Europe for the past eight hundred years, and everyone has heard of the stereotypical gypsy fortuneteller. Among those with knowledge of the arcane, the

Roma are prized for their remarkable psychic abilities and the gift to attract good fortune or upset a life with a curse. All are born with similar gifts, but what makes their powers so innate is their relationship with nature. Their bond with the spirits of the land and sky allowed their gifts to evolve naturally.

I knew Roma believed that within their own, there are some who possess great power through the ability to perform magic with their special range of knowledge. We would call these people witches, warlocks or wizards, but within the Roma society, they are known as *chovihanis*.

"Mr. Orlowski, does the world '*chovihanis*' mean anything to you?"

He blinked for a moment and glanced at the ceiling. "Well, yeah," he said. "My grandpa used to call her his little *chovihanis* all the time. I figured it was just a term of endearment or something. You know, like how I always call Bern here, 'the best thing that ever happened to me.'"

She beamed for a second and then smacked him in the arm good and hard. "Hush up, Peter," she snipped. "You're embarrassing me."

"It's not a term of endearment," I said, admiring how cute the old couple looked. "It basically means sorceress or wizard."

"Well, that makes sense," he said. "There's a whole root cellar full of spooky old books and jars of God-knows-what about a quarter section from here."

"Really," my ears pricked up. "Did you say there were books?"

"Yep, dozens of 'em," he nodded. "That's the site of the original sod house. They built their first wood frame house beside it in 1912, and it's still there after all these years, saggy roof and all. Pretty sure they got it from the Eaton's catalogue."

I didn't see a connection between a Roma *chovihanis*, an attack by an ogre, a small gold bar with the Asian writing stamped on the back, and a shade. I knew there had to be one, mind you; there's always a connection when magic is involved.

My instincts told me there was something important about this farm. Something that would cause the shade to get me involved somehow; I just couldn't put my finger on it.

Since Elena Orlowski was a sorcerer in her own right, I decided to pay a visit to her old root cellar. Maybe the answer could be found in one of the books she'd collected.

"Mr. Orlowski," I said. "Do you think you could take me to that root cellar?"

"Sure thing, little lady," he said, standing up. "Truck's up front."

"Great," I nodded, reaching for my staff. "Just in case, though, you might want to bring that shotgun."

He nodded amiably and grabbed the shotgun and a box of shells. "Good plan," he said.

CHAPTER 31

I hopped in the driver's seat of the old Ford pickup and gave the passenger door a hard pull. Orlowski put it in gear with a loud THUNK, and soon we were headed up yet another dirt road, this time to Bogdan Orlowski's old, wood-frame farmhouse and, hopefully, some answers.

We sat in silence as the truck bounced over a series of ruts, one of which we hit so hard that it lifted me off the seat, and I bumped my head on the ceiling. "Sorry about that, Miss Stevens," he said, sheepishly. "I been meaning to get the grader out and flatten some of those ruts."

"No problem," I grunted as I clutched my satchel between my legs and tightened my grip on my staff. "How far from that old house are we?"

"Five minutes or so... listen," he said, sounding embarrassed. "My wife is all bark and no bite when it comes to things. She didn't mean we were gonna sue you for the damage to the farm."

"Don't sweat it, Mr. Orlowski," I said. "A woman's anger is one of the great mysteries of life that you men have yet to solve. I've been mad like that on more occasions than I care to remember."

"Good then... oh, and I guess I should apologize for not telling you about the strange happenings at our farm. It's just that I don't want people thinking we're crazy and all. I sure would like to know what the government's interest in spirits and wee beasties is, though. You want to let me in on that?"

I turned to Orlowski and clenched my jaw. "I'm still trying to figure that out myself," I said.

Orlowski geared down for another bump just ahead, and the truck's engine roared in protest. "You sure ain't no regular government type... the way you wielded that big ol' stick of yours, I'd be thinking you were some kinda wizard or something. My grandma Elena had one that looked kinda like yours, 'cept it was all carved up with intricate symbols and stuff."

I immediately thought about how much easier my investigation into the shade would have been had I known that Elena Orlowski was a Roma sorceress, and that Peter Orlowski and his wife were no stranger to bizarre sightings of preternatural creatures. I wasn't disappointed, mind you. I couldn't blame Orlowski for being guarded about his family history either. One thing I've learned from growing up in Southern Alberta is that, aside from being stubborn as hell, industrious and politically conservative, farmers are fiercely private and humble people who shun the limelight.

I decided that when all this was over, I'd bring Dave out to meet the Orlowski's, and I'd get him to make a casserole. They were good people, and God knows I can't cook to save my life.

We turned off the dirt road and drove for another few minutes across an open field filled with waist-high wheat, bobbing and weaving in the morning breeze. "There it is," said Orlowski, as he thrust his arm in front of my face and pointed out the passenger window. "I should have bulldozed that eyesore years ago; I just couldn't bring myself to do it, eh?"

We drove in a circle around the old homestead and parked in front of a junk pile that contained two rusted refrigerators and scrap metal. Orlowski switched off the old pickup and the engine knocked a few times, then quit.

The old farmhouse, if you could call it a farmhouse, was no more than twenty feet long. There were two windows, only one of which that still contained glass, on either side of the front door, which hung loosely from its rusted hinges and knocked against the doorframe in the morning breeze.

It was like the thousands of similar farmhouses that still dot the Canadian prairie. The paint had weathered away over the decades, thanks to the constant prairie wind that brought extreme heat from the western foothills in the summer, and frigid jets of arctic north wind in wintertime. The exterior walls, smooth now from nearly a hundred years of exposure to the elements, were bone dry to the touch and were the color of ash. Any shingles that once existed on the roof had long ago disappeared, and it sagged in the middle, dropping down a good five feet at its lowest point.

I poked my head inside to see a series of splintered floorboards stretching from the front door, past a narrow wall that had strips of ancient wallpaper hanging in loose ribbons, which fluttered in the breeze. A field mouse scurried across the middle of what once might have been a dining area and escaped into a crack between the floorboards.

"The old soddy is over this way," said Orlowski, as he motioned for me to follow him around to the back of the old house. "Watch your step – there's about a thousand years' worth of rusted junk out here, and I'd hate for you to trip up."

I nodded and followed Orlowski through a gap in an old chain-link fence that lead between the house and an eight-foot-high wall of rotting bales of hay. The rough smell of natural decomposition filled my nostrils, and I poked at the knee-high grass in front of me to make sure it was free of obstacles.

When we got around to the back of the house, I saw an old wooden door lying on what looked like a pile of uneven grass. "That's how we get in," he grunted as he unlocked an antique railway switch lock with a giant skeleton key and flipped the latch that secured the door to the doorframe. "You got a flashlight in that big ol' tote bag of yours?"

"Sure do," I said, reaching into my satchel and pulling out my mag light. "Ready to go inside?"

"Yep," he said with a nod as he pulled open the door with a loud squeak.

It landed in a small cloud of dust as Orlowski took a cautious step through the doorway and bent down low. I handed him my flashlight, and he twisted the head until the bulb came on; then he aimed it down a set of five old wooden steps that looked like they'd crumble under the weight of a toddler.

"I ain't been down in here since, God… has to be just after Grandpa Bogdan died in 1948," he said. "Only time I was ever allowed in Grandma Elena's 'stores' was whenever there was a twister bearing down on us."

"Mind if I go in first?" I asked, from outside the doorway.

Orlowski gave me a relieved look and emerged from the doorway, then handed me the flashlight. "Sure thing," he said.

I tapped the sod brick walls of the entrance with my staff to make sure it wouldn't collapse when I got inside, and took a tentative step inside. No sooner had I come through the entrance than a strange red glow lit up the walls leading down the steps, revealing a series of ornate glyphs that were carved into the surface of the cement hard bricks of Alberta soil.

"W-What the hell are those?" Orlowski gasped, pointing to the glyphs.

My lips curled up into an amused smile as a vestige of Elena Orlowski's magic tantalized my senses. I felt awash with a sense of her love for her family and concern, mixed with a pinch of good old-fashioned suspicion.

"They're her sentinels," I grinned, taking another step down. "Protective spells that act to, as you said, 'keep good things in and bad things out'. Your grandmother was *definitely* a sorceress."

Orlowski stepped into the entrance as I continued down the remaining three steps. The old cellar had an earthy, dry aroma with a faint hint of spices mixed with old newsprint. I ducked down as my flashlight revealed a twenty-foot chamber with walls shored up with burlap sandbags, and my mind immediately flashed to those old pictures of First World War soldiers in their dugouts. The ceiling slanted at a strange angle, supported by a series of four varnished poplar beams, about six inches in diameter. Between the beams was a series of planks that acted as a liner for the sod bricks that had once formed the roof.

I shone the light back to the walls to see a lengthy row of hand-made shelves of neatly stacked mason jars, old casserole dishes, and tin cans sealed with wax paper. A home made picnic table sat in the middle of the room, covered with about an inch of dust, and behind it was a five-shelf book case, again, probably hand made from local trees, stuffed with dusty, hardcover albums, thick scrapbooks and notepads.

"I never bothered to ask Baba what she kept down here," said, Orlowski, as he scratched his head. "We were always told it was a root cellar for winter storage of vegetables and cured wild game."

I leaned on the picnic table to make sure it was secure, and then sat down on the bench facing the bookcase. "It's a sanctuary," I said, quietly. "It's a private place for a sorcerer to hone their craft."

Orlowski exhaled slowly and wiped his brow with his forearm. "That's what you are," he said. "A wizard or something?"

"Alchemist," I said, correcting him. "Not quite a wizard, and not quite a science geek. I have some knowledge of spellcraft, and I can pretty much hold my own with some of the minor characters in the preternatural world, but I'm far from being a wizard."

He sat down opposite me and grabbed a jar off the shelf. He blew the dust off the lid and rubbed decades of grime off the label with his thumb.

"Blessed Thistle," he read aloud, and then shoved the jar toward me. "Never heard of it."

I took the jar and flashed my light through the brown glass. It was half-full. "It's a spell ingredient," I said. "A very common one, actually."

He pointed to the bookshelf. "A lot of them books are in Ukrainian; I could spend the next ten years translating 'em into English and still not have a clue about all this mumbo-jumbo about magic and strange creatures."

I spotted a candle inside a tin can on the bookshelf and grabbed it. I slid it to the middle of the picnic table and whispered as I touched the wick with the tip of my index finger.

"Incendia," I whispered. The wick burst into a tiny flame at the touch of my finger, and within seconds, a haunting orange glow filled the old root cellar with light.

"Magic is real, Mr. Orlowski. It surrounds our world and binds the natural and spiritual elements that govern life or death."

"Neat trick, lady," he whispered, nervously. "You sound just like my grandmother… she used to talk in parables all the time."

"Because she knew the truth," I told him quietly. "One that our modern culture, with its focus on generating wealth or increasing our standard of living, either can't conceive of, or won't."

He blinked at me a few times and let out a labored sigh. "Maybe you're right," he said. "I still don't know why the hell the government is involved, though. That's a pretty big mystery in itself."

"To maintain order," I said. "Somebody has to do it, because the average citizen isn't psychologically prepared to accept the things that you and I have seen over the last day and a half. Mr. Orlowski, your grain bin's disappearance wasn't a theft; it was an act of magic… there's no other possible explanation."

"What about the ogre that attacked you... was that thing magic?"

"Nope," I said, shaking my head. "Ogres are soldiers of fortune in the preternatural world. They'll work for pretty much anyone... even you. That is, of course, assuming you can pay them. The one that attacked us this morning was hired by someone who paid it with a small gold bar with Asian writing on the back. My hunch is it's probably a sorcerer who somehow learned that something of great value exists on this farm. That I destroyed the ogre involved a small measure of magic and a healthy dose of dumb luck."

"You sure sound like a wizard."

"I dabble in magic, among other things. I believe the creature that made your grain bin disappear is a shade."

"What's that?" he asked.

"It's a powerful spirit that has the ability to kill organic matter by its sheer presence, and apparently, it can make grain bins disappear into three hundred foot holes in the ground. I believe the shade is under the control of whoever sent the ogre to kill us, and I'm now more certain than ever the disappearance of your grain bin was intended to get my attention."

Orlowski's eyebrows arched. "How come?"

"Because I'm a known quantity among those who don't have a postal code in the mortal realm. I believe the shade wants me to free it from a kind of spiritual bondage. The good news is that I have a hunch as to who the shade might be."

Orlowski leaned forward, his face a mask of fear mixed with concern. "Who is it?" he asked.

I put my hand on his hands and gave him a reassuring squeeze.

"I think the shade is your grandmother, Mr. Orlowski."

CHAPTER 32

I found another candle and lit it with the first one, then flicked off my flashlight.

"What year did your grandmother die?" I asked.

"She passed on in 1950… she was never the same after grandpa Bogdan died," said Orlowski.

"Did she leave a will?"

Orlowski scratched his chin and then shook his head. "Nope, not that I'm aware of… but I was a young man in those days – hell, she might have left one for all I know. I was too busy chasin' skirts at the Okotoks Hotel and rough-necking for the oil companies to pay much notice."

I nodded once. "So the land went to your father, I take it?"

"Yep, and he worked it until 1960, when Mom and Dad died in a car crash outside Blackie, God rest their souls," he said, crossing himself. "That's when the farm went to me and my two brothers. They were both married off and had families and shit, so it was left to me to work the land and keep the farm in the family."

I tapped my staff on the old wood floor and ran things over in my mind.

To my knowledge, farmers are very pragmatic people who leave nothing to chance. It seemed strange that Orlowski's grandparents went to their graves without detailing who should inherit their worldly possessions, and in this case, it meant the farm. Then again, maybe it was simply an accepted fact within the Roma culture that siblings inherit everything. Still, there was a heck of a lot of knowledge about the arcane in Elena Orlowski's sod cellar. She had to know about what could happen if it fell into the wrong hands; that's why sentinels were carved into the walls of the entrance — she needed to protect her lifetime of work from someone... but whom?

"If my grandmother is this shade you're talkin' about, then where's my grandfather in all this?" asked Orlowski.

"Presumably, he's crossed over," I said, scanning the bookshelf and half-hoping for the answer to jump out at me.

Orlowski reached into his breast pocket and pulled out his trusty pipe, and his pouch of Borkum Riff tobacco. "I can't imagine her being parted from my grandfather," he said, stuffing the bowl of his pipe and then lighting it. "They were inseparable in life."

"Spirits hang around the mortal realm for deeply personal reasons," I said as I pulled a thick black book off the shelf and flipped open the cover.

"Like what?"

I shrugged. "That's the mystery — though my instincts tell me that if she's the shade, she's got some unfinished business... do you know what this writing is on the title page?"

Orlowski leaned forward and blew the dust off. I coughed and waved my hand in front of my face.

He pulled the candle closer to the book and squinted his eyes as he examined the title page. "It's backward English," he grunted.

I glanced at the title. "*Seton No Noitatrapmi — Notes on Impartation*," I read aloud. "Clever."

I flipped through the hand-written pages and noticed the page numbers weren't in order. Page one said it was page fifty, and page two said it was page eighty-three. "Very clever," I said, smiling. "Not only did she write her book back-asswards, it's missing a table of contents, and the page numbers aren't in order."

"What's impartation?" Orlowski asked.

"It deals with bending inanimate objects to your will and making them appear to come to life."

"Inanimate objects?" asked Orlwoski. "You mean that my grandmother could make dead things live again?"

"Nope, that's necromancy," I said, studying a hand-drawn diagram showing a series of formulae. "Impartation literally means to impart the basic functions of life in an inanimate object. For example, life often implies sentience or self-awareness, and I'm pretty sure that's not what she was aiming at. It's not as if she would use this book to design a spell that might bring a tree to life, because it's already alive. What she could do, though, is use a spell to give that tree a pair of arms and legs."

Orlowski gasped. "What the hell would she do *that* for?"

"Protection," I said, sternly. "Gauging from the number of books and the sheer volume of spell ingredients your grandmother collected in her lifetime, she was probably a sorceress who could pack a punch."

"And?"

"And if you're a powerful sorceress, there are those who would benefit from obtaining everything in the sanctuary. It would add to their knowledge and increase their power to boot."

"Well, who'd want to do that?" he asked, sounding a bit flustered.

"Those who value power over everything else, Mr. Orlowski", I said. "In all likelihood, a dark mage who has been trained in black magic."

He grunted as he studied the book, while I made a mental inventory of the various concoctions Elena Orlowski had stored on her hand made shelves. There had to be enough material to complete thousands of spells, and what impressed me most was that everything was still intact after all these years. Naturally, I'd have to hand everything over to Vishesh, but not until I'd had a chance to study her books and glean as much as I could, and that would have to wait until another day. My immediate priority was to discover who was controlling the shade, and most importantly, why.

"You remember when I said that my grandmother had a big ol' stick like yours?" Orlowski asked.

"Yes… her staff," I said.

"Right… Well, if memory serves me correctly, it's attached to the bottom of the table. At least, that's where I remember seeing it when I was a boy."

I grabbed my flashlight and shone it between the bench seat and the bottom of the table and then poked my head underneath. I spotted a leather tube with a large knob of twisted wood sticking out from one end. It was the Elena Orlowski's staff.

"There it is," I squealed, barely concealing the excitement in my voice. "I'll just slide it out."

I reached under the table and grabbed the knob of wood, then carefully pulled it out of the leather tube. I felt a tingling sensation run from my hands and straight up my arms, as Elena Orlowski's magic teased my senses. Once it was free of the tube, I pulled it out from between the bench and the bottom of the picnic table and laid it in front of the black book.

"H-Holy crap," said Orlowski. "Them engravings are glowing!"

They sure as hell were.

The entire top half of the shiny, wooden staff was covered with detailed engravings that contained a dozens of words and numbers, all intermingled. The word *Noitatrapmi* followed by the word *Ecaferp* and the number twenty-two emitted a bright red glow, and I instinctively looked at the page number on the bottom of the book.

"Your grandmother," I said, grinning from ear to ear, "Was one smart sorceress."

"How come?" Orlowski asked.

I pointed to the glowing words on the staff and then pointed to the title of the page the book was opened to and then to the page number.

"Her staff is the key to all these books," I said. "She crafted her staff to act as a table of contents that responds to a protective spell, which she put on the books to render them difficult — if not impossible — to read without the staff."

"I never knew that," Orlowski chuckled. "I never knew a helluva lot about my grandmother until you showed up."

"Is it alright if I take this book and her staff with me, Mr. Orlowski?" I'd like to study your grandmother's magic and see there are any other hidden messages we might have missed."

Orlowski took a deep puff on his pipe. "Be my guest," he said. "You're welcome to come back anytime you like… lord knows I won't be using any of this stuff, so you'd probably put it to better use than me."

I grabbed Elena Orlowski's staff along with mine, and stuffed the book into my satchel, then took a last look around. It seemed like it would be a shame to hand everything over to the government, just so it could be catalogued and stored in a subterranean chamber beneath a grain elevator. If Vishesh were right about how Government Services and Infrastructure Canada worked, they'd sell off anything that might bring in a few bucks for the government ledgers, but to whom? It rubbed me the wrong way that I was deliberately kept in the dark, particularly when I'd put my ass on the line more times than I'd like to admit — and to what end? Fifty-Dollar Bill had hired D.T. back in 1937, and for all I knew, Revenue Canada Taxation probably employed the ghosts of former accountants and the RCMP police dogs were shape shifters!

I made a decision to hold off on letting Vishesh know about Elena Orlowski's sanctuary for now. It would be my little secret, and since the Government of Canada had been keeping secrets from me, it seemed fair to keep a few secrets of my own — just in case.

CHAPTER 33

I left Orlowski's farm at mid-morning, and in less than an hour, I was back at my condo. I was dead tired; my head was swimming with unanswered questions, and I had a bad feeling about what might transpire when the sun went down. The only lead I had as to who might be controlling the shade, if indeed that was the case, was a small gold bar emblazoned with Asian markings, so I decided to contact Vishesh Rajwani and see what he had to say.

I plopped myself at my computer and clicked the secure link that connected me with to Visheh's office. My monitor flickered for a second, and then a window popped up with a very tired-looking Vishesh staring into a camera.

"Good morning, Vishesh," I said. "I'm back from Orlowski's farm, and the gist of what happened is that Orlowski's late grandmother was a *chovihanis*... a Roma sorceress. I have a feeling there's a dark mage behind everything that's transpired in the last two days, because after I blew up a pissed-off Ogre with grain dust and white phosphorus, I decided that malevolent spirits aren't in the habit of hiring mercenaries."

Vishesh's face took on a surprised look. "Ogres? Dear God, are you alright?" he asked.

"Yes," I said, holding up the small gold bar to my web camera. "The Ogre was paid in gold, and there are Asian markings on the back of this ingot. Any idea which country?"

Vishesh squinted as he tried to read the small stamped symbols and said nothing for a few seconds.

"I believe the script says Central Bank of the Democratic People's Republic of Korea, which is, as you know, the central bank for North Korea."

I clenched my jaw. "Okay, I'm not sure what makes you'd think I keep track of who stamps the back of little gold bars… that's why I contacted you. So… do you have any idea why North Korea has a hate-on for birds in the City of Calgary — or me, for that matter?"

Vishesh hesitated for a moment, and then stroked his beard. He exhaled slowly, and his face took on a look of extreme reluctance.

"You don't have the proper security clearance, Valerie," he said, his voice muted. "There are procedures I must follow…"

Great.

He was still in "by the book mode", and it was pissing me off.

"To hell with procedures!" I snapped. "My gut tells me there's a shit pile of bad joo-joo that's going down tonight, Vishesh. People are going to die if whoever the hell this North Korean mage might be decides to make the entire population of Calgary his next target."

He stared blankly at the screen, and gauging from his reaction, I just knew he probably had an idea who the mage was, but he was struggling with the decision as to whether he should tell me. I said nothing for a moment, letting Vishesh churn over the ramifications of breaking security protocols versus being responsible for what was starting to look like an attack on innocent people.

"You aren't ready yet, Valerie," he said, quietly. "You don't yet possess enough power to defeat him."

"So you *do* know who the mage is," I snarled. "How long have you known?"

"We've seen North Korean gold in similar cases with the mage in question... however, he's been off the grid for about two years. We knew he would eventually resurface; we just didn't know where or when. When the mass killing of birds happened, it followed his pattern of magic. Your finding the gold ingot confirms this. Try to remember that until last night, like you, we thought we were dealing with a rogue shade."

I tapped my fingers against my desk in frustration and decided to up the ante.

"Vishesh, I have it under good authority there's a lot more to Canada's involvement in the arcane than what you've led me to believe," I said, angrily.

"Yes, but..."

"Don't flipping interrupt me, Vishesh!" I growled. "I've been drafted by D.T. and you guys to be some kind of a peacekeeper, whatever the hell that entails, and I've risked my neck on more than one occasion to collect goods that my government sells to God knows whom. I want some freaking answers, and I want them now!"

"You don't have clearance," he protested.

"Screw the clearance, Vishesh!" I started shouting. "Stop thinking like a civil service drone, and start thinking like a human being for once! There isn't time to have a mindless argument about government protocols, particularly when *you guys* haven't exactly been forthcoming with me about *your* activities. I find it goddamned ironic that the spirit of a dead Prime Minister has provided more information about our involvement in affairs of the non-mortal world than living and breathing people, for shit sake! Stop being an ass and start being a goddamned realist, Vishesh — we have to move quickly if we're going to stop this thing!"

I fell silent and waited for Vishesh to provide me with something — anything that might offer a clue as to who was controlling the shade. Vishesh stared blankly into his webcam, then squared his shoulders and straightened himself.

"His name is Mago," he exhaled slowly. "I doubt very much that even your two-thousand-year-old friend has heard of him, because Mago's activities had initially been limited to acting as a broker for states that actively support international terrorism. He is a demonomancer whose sole purpose in life is to master the art of necyomancy."

I blinked at the screen. "I know that demonomancers can summon demons, what's a *necyomancer*?"

"It's one who possesses the ability to summon none other than Satan himself," he said.

"S-Satan?" I gasped, nearly choking on the word. "Oh, you've *got* to be shitting me… that's hard-ass black magic, Vishesh!"

He nodded into the screen, and the look on his face told me to brace myself for what he had to say next.

"We believe he intends to kill everyone in the city, Valerie."

I sometimes hate it when I'm right, and this was one of those times.

I sat there with what I'm sure was a stunned look on my face and leaned into my web camera. This was about as dark as dark magic could get. I'd had my suspicions that if someone were intent on wiping out every bird in Calgary, it would only be a matter of time until he or she went after people, and now it had been confirmed. I struggled to find words to respond to this unthinkable scenario, and all I could muster was a panicked-sounding gulp.

Was this intended to be an untraceable act of war on behalf of another nation, as Bill suggested? Why Calgary? Why not a far more important city with a population ten or twenty times larger than Calgary?

I swallowed hard, and I could feel my heart beating in my temples.

Why *not* Calgary?

If you wanted to strike a terrifying blow against the western world, why *wouldn't* you attack Canada? We're well regarded wherever we go. We're considered to be a quiet and peace-loving nation around the globe, and we don't involve ourselves in offensive foreign policy like our neighbor to the south. Hell, even Americans have been known to sew little Canadian flags to their bags when they go overseas because, let's face it: when you're at the top of the heap, a lot of people want to take a shot at you.

Nobody wants to take a shot at Canada, because, well, it's freaking *Canada* for crying out loud! In the community of nations, Canada is like a friendly neighbor from whom you can borrow a lawnmower, no questions asked. We're just that nice. However, wiping out the inhabitants of one of Canada's largest cities would terrify our allies to such an extent that they'd realize if ever-lovin' peaceful Canada ain't safe, nobody is.

I tapped my fingers on the desk as I remembered the voice from my nightmare of a few hours earlier:

"For I will pass through the land of Egypt this night, and will smite all the firstborn in the land of Egypt, both man and beast; and against all the gods of Egypt I will execute judgment: I am the LORD."

The voice spoke of the Angel of Death, not the Prince of Darkness. If this Mago was a demonomancer, I'm pretty sure he'd be persona-non-grata with the big guy upstairs, so why invoke the Angel of Death?

I gave Vishesh a helpless look and shook my head.

"Vishesh, I have a theory about this guy," I said, quietly.

He nodded silently.

"A few hours ago, I believe this Mago attacked me in my sleep while I was dreaming. Hell, he killed my tropical fish, my houseplants, and he nearly killed my boyfriend as well. But there was one telling facet of my dream that might be a clue as to what's going to happen to Calgary."

"What's that?" asked Vishesh.

"I heard a voice in my dream that quoted biblical scripture." I said. "He spoke as if he were the Angel of Death and were executing judgment on behalf of God."

"Except in this case, the shade is acting as the Angel of Death, and Satan must be Mago's representation of God!" Vishesh gasped. "How can a shade acquire enough power to wipe out an entire city?"

I chewed on a thumbnail and remembered that both Caroline and D.T. suggested the dead birds were tainted somehow — that their souls were missing. After we destroyed the spider that had attacked us in D.T.'s sanctuary, Caroline said the dead bird didn't smell tainted any longer and D.T. suggested that it had reclaimed its soul.

"Everything has a life-force, Vishesh," I said. "From the smallest blade of grass to the largest mammals on earth, everything generates its own living energy. The only way to gather enough power to wipe out over a million people would be to capture something's essence and channel it into a dark spell. I think this Mago needed the shade to slowly begin the process of siphoning off the living energy of plants and trees, and then as it gathered more power, it siphoned off the living energy of all those dead birds."

"So life force is like a supernatural battery for black magic?" asked Vishesh.

I grunted and clenched my jaw. "You bet — this is all part of a big ass dark spell. From the first time I talked to Orlowski and he told me about the dead trees at his farm, to the dead birds in Airdrie and Calgary, Mago has been collecting this energy in hopes of channeling it into the wholesale murder of over one million people. We've got a name, we have an idea of what his plan might be, — there are just two final pieces of the puzzle."

"And they are?"

I folded my arms and leaned back in my office chair. "Where is he storing the living energy, and why does he want to kill a million people?"

CHAPTER 34

I signed off from Vishesh and glanced at my watch. It was shortly before noon, and the midday sun beamed in through my skylight, bleaching my entire condo with its brilliant white light. My stomach growled angrily, so I shuffled to the kitchen and threw a bagel in the toaster. As I reached into the fridge to grab some cream cheese, it occurred to me that I had no idea where to find Mago or even what he looked like. The only piece of physical evidence that provided a link to the mage was the small gold ingot with the Asian markings on the back. I could start making inquiries among those less-than-savory elements of the preternatural world — it was possible someone might know something, but word travels fast among those who dwell in the shadows; the last thing I needed was to tip off the mage that I was onto him.

So how was I supposed to find him?

It was possible that a spell might locate the dark mage — but what kind of spell? Moreover, Mago was obviously a very powerful mage, and there was a strong likelihood that he'd detect my spell and corrupt it, similar to the way a virus corrupts a computer program. If that happened, he could send any number of spectral assassins to take me out.

I wasn't sure if it was his plot, the fact that Mago was dabbling in summoning Satan himself, or that his attack earlier in the morning literally hit close to home. I was dealing with a mage who possessed a set of advanced skills. I was outclassed; he was adept at keeping his plans secret until the last minute, and he'd been two steps ahead of me all along. It made me want to crawl out of my skin, to run, to get the hell out of Calgary with Dave and my parents and never look back.

But I couldn't.

Innocent people were going to die, and I was the only person who could stop it. It was at this point that cold hard reality set in, and I shuddered as an icy finger ran up my spine and my stomach twisted itself in knots: there was a good chance I wouldn't survive this.

My bagel popped out of the toaster, so I slathered on a pile of cream cheese and took a bite. I stared out my balcony window and onto 17th Avenue. The city was alive with people going about their daily business, all blissfully unaware that if I couldn't stop this guy, they'd probably be dead by morning. I thought about the spirit of Elena Orlowski as I took another bite. How could Mago force a shade into doing his bidding? What did he have on the spirit of a protective and loving woman whose life had been devoted to keeping her family and her secrets safe; what could transform her into a veritable Angel of Death?

There had to be something at Orlowski's farm that I'd missed, so I grabbed my phone and punched in Orlowski's number. Within seconds, he answered.

"Mr. Orlowski, it's Valerie Stevens," I said.

"Hello again," he said, sniffing into the phone. "You must really like me or something, lady, them government fellas have already cleaned up your little battle zone around my bins and they just cut me a cheque to cover the damages."

I glanced at Elena Orlowski's staff. "We aim to please… listen, I'm wondering if there is anything else on your farm that we might have missed. Anything that might have had some meaning to your late grandmother."

He coughed with a loud hork, and I could hear Bernadette Orlowski in the background chattering with someone about the cost of new windows. "Well, only thing we got left out here are the graves of both my grandparents… we never checked them out."

Crap.

I'd been so transfixed by the wealth of arcane material in Elena Orlowski's sanctuary that I'd completely forgotten both she and her husband were buried on the property. I kicked the cupboard door with my heel in anger at my utter stupidity.

"Damn it," growled. "I can't believe I forgot about the graves."

Orlowski was silent for a second, and I heard him strike a match and light his pipe. "About that," he said. "I remember when we first met, you'd asked me if there was anyone buried on the property. Well, after you'd left, I decided to take a drive out to my grandparent's graves, just for the hell of it. Anyway, when I got there I saw that my grandfather's plot, well, it's gone… it's just gone. I was gonna call you, but with all these government people running around here, and Bern having had such a stressful morning, I decided to wait until later this afternoon to give you a shout."

My mind flashed back to the newscast I'd heard two days ago. Four separate graves at the Kingsview Cemetery had been vandalized, and the same thing must have happened to Bogdan Orlowski's grave. The four spirits whose bones were stolen said they'd been dragged out of the other side and back into the mortal realm. When I sent them back, their bones suddenly appeared in four different locations throughout the city.

"Mr. Orlowski, when you say gone... are you suggesting there's another three hundred foot hole in the ground?" I asked.

He snorted. "It's not the same kinda hole like the one that disappeared my grain bin. Someone exhumed my Grandfather. The coffin is still there, but his body is gone."

"And your grandmother's grave is still intact?"

"Yep – not even a blade of grass has been disturbed. I'm gonna assume this is an important development."

I nodded into the phone. "You bet it is... listen, don't fill it in like you did with the hole from the grain bin. I think you've just discovered why your grandmother's spirit is under the control of a dark mage."

He coughed twice and grunted. "You might be right, little lady. Only thing that's different about this is the trees and shrubs surrounding both plots ain't dead."

"Fair enough... would you do me a favor?" I asked.

"Name it."

"If everything plays out like I hope, your grandfather's remains will be returned to your land. I'd like you to keep clear of the burial site until you've heard from me again."

"Not a problem... I'll let you go now. Bern is yelling at one of your government people, and I'd better go calm her down."

I hung up the phone and shuffled over to the front closet. I reached for my satchel and grabbed Elena Orlowski's staff, then went to the kitchen table and pulled out the old book I'd found in her sanctuary. I had the final piece of the puzzle: somehow, Mago had obtained the bones of Bogdan Orlowski, and the mage must have pulled the old farmer into the mortal realm. That meant that Mago must be holding Orlowski's soul hostage – or worse, threatening to destroy it all together – and Elena Orlowski was being forced to work for the dark mage against her will. But how do you get past a shade with the ability to destroy organic matter if you want to stop a dark mage? I chewed my lip as I glanced at the front cover of Elena Orlowski's book on impartation.

Were I to recruit an army of spirits, they wouldn't be impacted by the shade's ability to destroy organic matter — they were already dead. The problem, though, was there would be a protective barrier of spectral energy that would be impenetrable to spiritual forces; Fifty-Dollar Bill had proved that when he couldn't penetrate the barrier in Airdrie. Spirits could take a subterranean route as Bill did, but I wouldn't be able to confront the mage, since I was made of organic matter. I needed something that was invulnerable to the power of the shade, but for the life of me, I couldn't think of anything, so I grabbed her staff and held it over the book. It started glowing bright red as a series of numbers and words appeared along its polished wood surface. I examined the staff and spotted the word "noitacove" followed by the Roman numeral "XXIII".

"Evocation," I whispered. "The actual spell that will impart life on an inanimate object."

No sooner had I flipped to page twenty-three when I heard a rustling sound from my storeroom. I closed the book and grabbed the staff, then spun around and prepared to lash out, expecting another attack.

"It's just me," Fifty-Dollar Bill shouted from behind the closed door. "I remembered that you dislike being snuck up on, so I thought I'd use a little tact."

I exhaled slowly and called out to Bill. "I'm in here... thanks for that, I guess."

Bill's corporeal visage rose from the center of the table, and he had a big grin on his pudgy translucent face.

"What are you reading?" he asked. "And where *did* you find that lovely walking stick?"

"It's a sorcerer's staff, Bill," I said sourly. "The shade is a gypsy spirit who is working against her will for a dark mage named Mago."

He floated up to the ceiling, and then flew into the chair next to me. "And this would be one of her spell books?" he asked, his voice laced with curiosity.

"That's right," I said, nodding. "It's a book on how to impart life into inanimate objects."

"It sounds frightfully boring — though I could have used it on a few of my lazy caucus members. I take it you've determined the reasons the shade is working in partnership with this Mago?"

I pursed my lips as I glanced at Bill. "More like working against her will," I said. "Mago has the bones of her late husband, and that means he's pulled his spirit into our realm. I think it's being held hostage, and the shade is being forced to work for the mage."

Bill leaned back in his chair and folded his arms. His face took on a look of smug self-satisfaction, and I just knew he was waiting for me to ask what he'd discovered.

"Alright, Bill… *what*?" I asked.

"You've discovered the name of the mage," he said, in a matter of fact voice. "And *I've* discovered that by midnight tonight, every spirit in the city will have chosen to cross over — I might even choose to do so myself."

I blinked at Bill twice and gave him a startled look. "You're kidding," I asked. "Why on earth would every spirit want to cross over — hell, why would *you* want to cross over?"

Bill frittered with his vaporous, red tie and sat up straight in the chair. "Because the word among the spirit world is that the other side is a safer bet than around here," he said, in an ominous voice. "Though I quite like the pleasure of your company, I doubt very much even you will be around by the time the sun rises tomorrow, and let's face it: I've grown accustomed to helping you solve these little mysteries; it's why I haven't crossed over. Alas, with you gone, there will be nothing left for me to do, so I will cross over, and perhaps if you've led a good life, perhaps we will meet again."

My jaw dropped, and I stared at Bill.

He was scared, despite the fact that he presented a very logical-sounding reason to cross over. Under normal circumstances, I'd be flattered that the only reason he hangs around is because he likes to assist me, but this was not a normal situation. Whatever the hell was going down tonight would be big enough to scare every spirit into getting out of Dodge and cross over to the relative safety of the other side.

I clenched my jaw. *Whatever the hell was going down tonight.*

Oh… *hell*.

CHAPTER 35

I stuffed the book on impartation into my satchel and grabbed Elena Orlowski's staff. I hustled over to the front closet and slipped my feet in my Danner boots, then slipped on my ball cap.

"Meet me at my car, Bill," I said, flipping open the dead bolt on my door. "We have to move quickly."

"As you wish," he yawned and then disappeared.

I raced down the hallway, nearly clotheslining my fundamentalist neighbor who thinks I'm a witch, and then flew down the stairwell to the underground parking lot. I flicked the unlock button on my key fob and saw the Maxima's tail lights blink twice. Within minutes, I was in gear and pulling out of the lot and onto 17th Avenue.

"You know, this is twice in one day you've told me to meet you at your car," said Bill, from the back seat. "Are we going to that farm again?"

"Nope," I said, slipping on my Oakley's and pulling down the sun visor. "We're heading over to Caroline's."

"So… you've determined the best way to defeat a dark

mage is with the assistance of a zombie?" he asked, his voice oozing sarcasm. "Perhaps I should just cross over right now, because if that's your plan, I expect the city is doomed."

I glanced into the rearview mirror and gave Bill a dirty look. "No, that's not my plan," I snipped. "I'm going to pick her brain, and then we're going to be meeting with D.T."

"Ah," Bill exhaled. "Well, the more the merrier, I suppose. In the meantime, I take it you've come to a conclusion about what is supposed to happen tonight at midnight?"

"Yes," I said. "Mago is a demonomancer who I think ready to make the jump to necyomancy."

"And what exactly is necyomancy?"

"I think he's going to summon none other than Satan himself... why, I have no idea."

Bill stretched out on the back seat, the bottoms of his legs disappearing through the passenger door. "Well, that would explain why all the spirits in our area are going to cross over. I will assume, then, that this Mago's aim is to bring about the end of the world, is that it?"

I shrugged. "Beats me — I was under the assumption theologians had already determined the end of the world was governed by biblical prophesy. You went to church during your life, right?"

He nodded and smiled. "Of course. I was a devout Anglican."

"What do you know about the end of days?"

He pulled himself into a seated position and gave me a sly smile. "Why do you ask, young lady? Are you planning an eleventh-hour conversion?"

I flashed him another dirty look. "No... but it might give us a few clues as to what's going to happen tonight."

"Alright, then," Bill said. "The word of God doesn't tell us a specific date for the end of our world, but scripture proclaims that the present age — the civilization and societies we know today — will terminate in a cascade of unimaginable destruction and violence that will climax at the return of Christ. In the New Testament alone, more than three hundred verses refer to these events."

"What kind of events?"

"When Jesus' disciples asked about the end of the age, he responded by listing several warning signs. The first would be massive religious deception, including religious teachers who, while claiming to represent him, would not follow his teachings but would deceive many through a false Christianity. He also said there would be many wars and other conflicts between nations and ethnic groups, not to mention famines, massive disease epidemics, and earthquakes."

"When haven't there been wars and famines?" I huffed. "That's being going on since Christ's time."

"Exactly," he said. "Just because scripture says the end is near, it doesn't mention when or where. Moreover, the bible also doesn't talk about the existence of trolls, ogres or zombies, but you already knew that. Here's what you must remember, Valerie… *He* works in mysterious ways, as they say. Who are we to question whether the creator has a plan for all things, even little two-thousand year old trolls."

Bill had a point.

It's not that I don't believe in a supreme being, because I do. I simply don't recognize the presence of God via the traditional religious interpretation. That's not God's fault, of course — humanity has defined God for us by means of religious symbols, dogma and tradition. Too often, humanity distorts any message of love and hope to maintain control and order over the great unwashed. Given that I'm naturally inquisitive, I've long questioned the relevance of a purely human interpretation of spirituality, especially when one considers that nearly every preternatural creature I've met refers to God as *the creator*. It makes sense that if all things believe in a single intelligent being that is responsible for the combined existence of both the mortal and preternatural worlds, then logic dictates that God must exist.

Of course, there's also the issue of demons.

If you really want to find your religion damned quickly, have an encounter with a demon. You'll learn that hell is a very real place, and it's filled with countless creatures that are more than happy to do any manner of evil to either corrupt or possess your soul. They can appear in human, animal, or even corporeal form. They will tempt you, tantalize you, or subdue your will through sheer connivance, if necessary. The only thing that can stop them is faith. (That or two barrels of a shotgun, powerful supernatural energy and a Tupperware container to capture their vile essence which, by the way, smells a lot like rotting garbage.)

As I pulled up the lane behind Caroline's church, I decided the reasons for Mago's interest in Satan were less important than simply stopping him. Bill rendered himself invisible and followed me up the steps leading to Caroline's flat, and I knocked on the door. The small curtain on the window fluttered, and within seconds, I heard the deadbolt click, and the door swung open to reveal a very unimpressed looking zombie dressed in a fluffy pink housecoat. I gave her a pensive glance and poked my head in the door. The last thing I wanted to see was a gory mess of God knows what.

"I see you're back," said Caroline, flatly. "Don't worry, I ate hours ago."

"Thanks," I said, stepping inside. She closed the door behind me, and Fifty-Dollar Bill's head materialized through the ceiling.

"This is a rather tidy little flat," he said. "I have to admit, I'm surprised by that."

Caroline grabbed a broom and swung it at Bill's head. It drifted through the corporeal mass, and Bill re-materialized at the end of the hall.

"I didn't invite *him*," said Caroline, icily. "It's been ten hours since we last spoke. What's going on?"

"Plenty," I said, as I followed her into the living room and plopped myself down on a big leather chair. "The shade is under the control of a dark mage, and this guy plans on summoning the Prince of Darkness tonight. I think that whatever summoning spell he intends to use, he needs everyone in Calgary dead in order for it to work."

Caroline gushed out a shocked-sounding breath as she sat on a coffee table. "Well, that does confirm our hypothesis, but still... holy crap!"

I nodded and showed her Elena Orlowski's staff. "The shade is the grandmother of the farmer whose bin disappeared," I said, plaintively. "Turns out, she was a Roma sorceress during her life, and this is her staff."

"Gotcha... anything else?"

I nodded. "Yeah, I need to pick your brain about hell."

A look of dread washed over Caroline's ashen skin, and she pursed her black lips. "S-Sure, Val... what do you need?"

"When you crossed over to the bad place..."

"Hell," she interrupted. "It's alright to say it."

"Hell, then," I continued. "When you crossed over, did you actually… you know, meet… *him*?"

She gripped the edges of the coffee table tightly, and I could have sworn her already pale skin turned whiter.

"Uh… I really don't want to talk about this," she whispered.

I drove the Elena Orlowski's staff into the green shag carpet and snapped at Caroline. "I don't give a crap whether you want to talk about it or not! If the Prince of Darkness materializes in downtown Calgary tonight, I want to have an idea of what the heck I'm up against!"

Caroline gave me a surprised look and then started to giggle. Her giggle turned into a fit of maniacal laughter, and I glanced over at Bill.

"Oh, she's gone off the deep end," he said, whirling his finger around his right temple.

She held up her hand and motioned for us to stop talking. "No," she said, as her giggling subsided. "That's just the *dumbest* question I think I've ever heard, Val."

"Why?"

"Um… because he's *Satan*. What part of 'you don't have a chance in hell' aren't you getting?"

"She's right, you know," said Bill. "I'm no strategist, but it would seem far more prudent to eliminate the mage."

I gave them both a serious scowl. "I wasn't suggesting that I go toe-to-toe with Mephistopheles," I snapped. "I just wanted some insight into what happens should the mage be successful."

"What do you care?" asked Caroline. "You'll already be dead."

Good point.

I glanced at my watch and saw that it was just past 6:00 P.M. – sunset was in a little over three hours, and we were due to meet D.T. at the boulder in Nose Hill Park. That left us with little time to formulate a plan to prevent everyone in Calgary from being killed. I tapped the staff against the carpet as I wrung my brain, trying to think of something, anything that would work.

"Valerie," said Caroline. "When is the best time to cast a big-ass spell?"

I shrugged my shoulders and gripped the staff tight in my right hand. "Midnight is when spiritual energies are at their apex, why?"

"Okay… and do you need, like, oh, I don't know… something like an altar?"

"Not really," I said. "An altar is just a religious structure for sacrifices or offerings."

She relaxed her grip on the coffee table and half-smiled. "Well, if this guy is summoning Satan, we know that one million dead people makes for a pretty impressive offering. Wouldn't he still need an altar, and wouldn't it have to be something of spiritual significance?"

Bill made a snapping motion with his fingers. "By George, the zombie is right!" he said, enthusiastically. "The mage wouldn't be using a simple wooden altar when he can use the nerve center of all things magical in the Calgary area."

I gasped.

"Nose Hill Park!" I shouted. "That's where he'll do it."

Caroline looked at Bill and they both nodded in agreement.

"Okay," she said. "We know he's going to cast his spell at midnight in Nose Hill Park… if he's surrounded by whatever the hell he used to kill those birds, you won't get within a hundred yards of the guy, because you'll be dead too."

"That's right," said Bill. "Spirits can't penetrate that wall of spectral energy. What you need is a giant robot... has anybody invented one yet?"

"Not yet," I said as I yanked the drawstring on my satchel. "But I know something that might.'

I pulled out Elena Orlowski's book on impartation and slid it on the coffee table. I opened it to page twenty-three and placed my index finger next to the first sentence.

"What's that?" asked Caroline.

"It's a book on impartation — a guide to imparting life on inanimate objects."

She leaned over and glanced at my index finger. "You mean that if you use a spell from this book on my coffee table, it will come to life?"

I shook my head, as I reconfigured the words into plain English and scribbled down a list of spell ingredients on a scrap of paper. "I'm thinking of a group of inanimate objects about twenty-one feet tall, which have two arms and two legs each."

Caroline took a deep breath. "You're not thinking about..."

"You bet I am," I said. "The statues at the Calgary Board of Education."

CHAPTER 36

"Let me get this straight," Caroline protested. "You're going to use an impartation spell to make those ugly freaking statues come to life?"

I continued to scribble the spell ingredients and nodded. "You know it," I said. "They're not organic, so the mage can't kill them."

"So what's going to happen here... are the statues just going to march up 14th Street, climb the hill, and attack this mage?"

"Not exactly," I said, as I reached for my hand held and speed-dialed Dave's number. "We're going to smuggle them into the park."

There were two rings, and Dave answered on the third one.

"Hey there... what's up? Solve the mystery yet?" Dave asked, sounding surprisingly upbeat.

"Not yet," I said, trying to hide the nervousness in my voice. "Did you call my parents like I asked?"

"Yep," he said. "I called them first thing this morning, and they told me to tell you they've gone to the cottage."

"Good... listen, I need a favor, and before you say yes, I want you to know it's very dangerous, and you might get killed."

There was a slight pause, and then Dave said, "Well, now that you put it that way, where do I sign up?"

"I'm serious, Dave... something terrible is going to happen tonight, and I need your help. I won't lie to you, we might all die, but if I can't do what I'm planning, we're already dead."

I heard the hissing of his airbrakes, and I assumed he was pulling over his dump truck.

"Ooookay," he said, in his best 'don't piss off Valerie voice'. "What do you need?"

I folded the spell ingredients and placed the scrap paper inside Elena Orlowski's book. "Does your company have any big trucks with a tarpaulin?"

"Nope... closet thing we have are two eighteen-wheelers and a silverside trailer... why?"

"How hard would it latch onto a trailer and meet me at the Calgary Board of Education at around 10:30 P.M. tonight?" I asked.

"Well, I'd get fired for stealing a company truck, and they might press charges," he said. "Are you going to tell me what this is about?"

"Nope," I said, in a stern voice. "If I told you, your head would explode. Just do as I ask and meet me at the Calgary Board of Education at ten-thirty. Once you arrive, back the truck up to those statues facing McLeod Trail."

He let out an impatient sigh. "Alright... but if I get canned, I'll be crashing at your place, because I won't be able to pay my mortgage. I like breakfast in bed."

"If we survive tonight, I'll be your breakfast in bed, okay?"

"Sounds flavorful," he snickered.

There was a loud click and then dead air on my cell phone. I stuffed it into my Mickey pocket and flashed an optimistic smile to Bill and Caroline.

"So what's up with Dave?" asked Caroline.

"He's going to borrow a semi-trailer from work and back it onto the green space at the Board of Education. I'll use this spell from Elena Orlowski's book and animate the statues. The statues will climb into the back of Dave's trailer, and then we'll hightail it to Nose Hill Park," I said, trying to sound decisive.

Caroline gave Fifty-Dollar Bill a confused look. "Gotcha," she said, with a note of skepticism in her voice. "Assuming the spell actually works, what makes you think these statues will want to rumble with a mage?"

It was a good question.

I'd formed a solid relationship with the statues, and they'd always been more than willing to provide me with information about strange happenings in Calgary. Still, it was one thing to foster a relationship in the interest of gaining intelligence on bad joo-joo, it was another thing entirely to assume the statues would actually be willing to involve themselves in a battle.

"If I have to go on bended knee and beg them to help us, then that's what I'll do," I said, quietly.

Bill politely raised his hand like an elementary school student. "Doesn't that spell book offer a way to control the statues? To bend them to your will?"

I shook my head. "No, and frankly I wouldn't wish to control them — were I to do that, I'd be just as bad as the mage."

Caroline stood up and stomped to her hallway closet. When she came back, she was carrying a sickle in one hand and a rifle with a scope in the other. She leaned the rifle on the coffee table and handed me the sickle.

"That," she said, pointing at the rifle, "is a Mosin-Nagant sniper rifle. It can fire a 7.62 millimeter round in a one-inch grouping from more than a kilometer away."

"A-Alright," I said, staring at the long barrel "Are you planning on shooting Mago?"

She patted the rifle on the butt, and her thin black lips curled into a sly smile. "I was president of the Bow Valley Sharpshooter Association for three years. If I can get into a good position, with a clear field of vision, I can end this thing without the need for enchanted statues running amok all over Nose Hill Park."

"What's the sickle for?"

"Close quarter fighting — in case this Mago has some muscle working with him, I can plow through them like a hot knife through butter."

I smiled long and hard at Caroline.

It was heartening to know that she was ready to go to war if necessary. We'd been through enough scrapes together, and she provided valuable muscle in a tight situation.

"We don't know where Mago's precise location will be in the park, and it's a heck of a lot of area to cover," I said, turning my eyes to Bill. "There's only one person in this room who can cover that much park in a short span of time. Bill, I need your help on this."

He waved his hands to protest, and for a second, I thought I could see a splash of fear in his transparent face. "I'm a politician," he said. "I was only good at fighting during Question Period."

"Nobody's asking you to fight, Bill," I said, calmly. "All I need is for you to conduct some reconnaissance in the park from overhead... when you see Mago, scoot the heck out of there and tell me where we can find him."

Bill gave a reluctant nod. "Alright, but I'm not guaranteeing that I'll find him."

"You'll find him," I said. "If he's as smart a mage as we think he is, he'll know the best place to cast his spell will be at the highest point of the park. Besides, it's a giant, bald-ass hill; there aren't exactly tons of hiding places."

"And if he's using a shroud? Then what?"

I shrugged and shook my head. It would be difficult but not impossible to find Mago if he'd cloaked his position by using a shrouding spell. Then again, he might have grown tired of hiding in the shadows; God knows I would. Either way, if Mago were invisible to the naked eye, his shrouding spell would emit some kind of magical signature, and D.T. would most certainly notice it and find him.

"What about the troll?" asked Caroline.

I grunted. "I'll hook up with D.T. when I arrive. I'll want you and Bill to meet D.T. at the boulder. Fill him in on what I intend to do, and when you see a transport truck driving up to the parking lot on the east side of the park, it will be me, Dave and a trailer full of pissed-off statues."

"Sounds like a plan... sort of. What do we do in the meantime?"

I grabbed the staff and slung my satchel over my back. "You still have that old Volkswagen Beetle, don't you, Caroline?" I asked.

"Yeah, it's in the garage out back," she said. "I haven't driven in over two years, but I start it up once a month, so the engine won't seize up."

"Perfect," I said as I glanced at my watch. "It's 7:30 now, so head over to Nose Hill Park at around 9:00 o'clock."

Caroline waved her hand. "What if there are people in the parking lot? I can't just jump out of the beetle with a rifle slung over my shoulder. And of course, there's the other issue of my appearance. I kind of look like a zombie."

I threw on my leather jacket and walked to the door. Caroline shuffled behind me, her fuzzy slippers scraping against the hardwood floors.

"Strip down your rifle and carry it in a backpack," I said, putting my hand on her shoulder and smiling. "As for your appearance, well, you *are* the hottest family lawyer in Calgary. I've been in your bathroom, and I know for a fact that you've got enough lipstick and foundation underneath the sink to do a makeover that Oprah would be proud of."

Caroline snorted. "So?"

"So, don't you think it's time you changed your look?" I said as I opened the door. "Get dolled up… or as close as you can to getting dolled up, and look for the semi-trailer coming up the east hill."

Caroline shrugged her shoulders and grunted. "Fair enough… see you then."

CHAPTER 37

It was past 8:30 P.M. when I pulled my Maxima onto Bow Trail. I'd had just enough time for me to collect the remaining spell ingredients from my condo and head downtown. The sun would be setting shortly after 9:00 P.M., and I hoped like hell that Dave would get to the Board of Education on time.

It had been a whirlwind thirty-six hours since I'd first learned of the missing grain bin, and now I was facing a pseudo-biblical apocalypse with the goal of wiping out everyone in Calgary and summoning Satan. Yeah, I was way out of my element, but it didn't matter. I'd throw the best of my limited knowledge of spellcraft and alchemy at Mago and hope that between Fifty-Dollar Bill, the statues, a dwarf troll mage, and a zombie, I'd have an edge.

And I needed an edge — there was too much at stake.

What if we were unsuccessful? Was there a way to stop Mago, outside of divine intervention? I chewed my lip furiously as I passed Mewata Armory and headed down 9th Avenue East.

"How the hell does North Korea come into all this?" I asked myself. "The guy uses gold to pay an ogre, and it's traced back to North Korea's central bank. What the hell does a secretive dictatorship want to attack Calgary for, and why is this guy going to attempt to summon Satan?"

I was still having problems getting my head around magic becoming a weapon of choice among terrorists and enemy nations, because there was just as much risk for those who employed dark magic to achieve a political aim. Mago, for example, could easily be double-crossed by a minor demon — forget about Satan. While the dark mage possessed arcane talents that made my abilities seem like a fart in the breeze, a demon lord, for example, could mop the floor with pretty much anyone, sorcerer or not.

Evil beings are called evil for a reason: you can't negotiate with them in good faith, they always have an ulterior motive, and perhaps most importantly, they're generally working for someone else — someone more powerful and far more sinister. Vishesh had provided me with scant information about Mago, so I couldn't examine what his motives were. This couldn't be more than an insane mage with delusions of hell on earth: there *had* to be someone in the background pulling the strings, and no matter how I sliced it, I just couldn't see the head of any state or terrorist organization wanting to make a deal with the Prince of Darkness.

I turned on the radio, hoping to hear the weather forecast, because electrical storms provide a constant source of ammunition in the hands of a skilled mage. All I heard was the faint hiss of dead air. I pressed the seek button, and my little stereo cycled through the entire FM band, but it was all the same: dead air.

"This is just like when the airwaves went dead last night," I said to myself. "Only this time it's happening before dusk."

As I passed the Calgary Tower and pulled into the left turning lane to head down 2nd Street, the radio made a loud crackling sound as the hissing subsided, and I heard a voice.

"You carry my staff," whispered a disembodied female voice, in a heavy east-European accent.

A jolt of panic shot through my chest as I spun the steering wheel hard to the left and jammed my foot on the brake. The car screeched to a stop after nearly sideswiping a minivan full of nuns.

"C-Come again?" I asked, staring at the radio.

The radio hissed and popped loudly as the sound of static filled the interior of the Maxima.

"You carry my staff... *mage*," said the voice, with emphasis on the word 'mage'.

It was the shade.

I gulped and turned on my hazard lights, then slunk down in my seat. "I-Is this Elena Orlowski?" I asked, nervously.

"I am who I was," the voice said. "The night will bring about death to all who dwell in the shadow of the great hill. It pleases me that you have found my staff; through it you will wield a power that can destroy the one called Mago."

"B-But I don't even know who Mago is."

"He knows *you*, mage — and make no mistake, though you call yourself an alchemist, clarity tells a different story. It is clear as a fencepost on the horizon. It burns with intensity that is rare among those in the mortal realm. You are most surely a mage."

I glanced at Elena Orlowski's staff on the passenger seat. The entire shaft glowed in waves of shimmering emerald light that pulsed through the engravings at the sound of her voice.

"Take my staff into your hands. I will reveal knowledge of Mago and how you might destroy his dark plan."

"But how are you contacting me?" I said, nervously. "I thought you were under Mago's control."

"He controls my will as it relates to what he has stolen from the earth and to the purpose of his spell," said the shade, angrily. "He does not control that part of my will that dwells inside my staff. Take it into your hands, mage. Time is short, and there is much to be revealed."

I didn't need to be asked again.

I gently grasped the staff in my right hand and closed my eyes. Instantly, the feeling of being seated in my car gave way to a floating sensation, as if gravity itself had disappeared. A sense of contentment washed over me like a steaming hot shower on a cold day, and I could swear I caught a whiff of freshly baked bread.

I opened my eyes and suddenly I was in a field of waist-high wheat that bobbed and weaved to a gentle breeze. Ahead I saw a familiar looking house with a small door framed by a window on either side. The tiny farmhouse had a fresh coat a white paint, trimmed in emerald green, and there was a small poplar fence with a white gate that clattered noisily with each gust of wind. Beside the house was a large vegetable garden with corn growing in neat, weed free rows. Tomato plants grew to more than three feet in height with fruit as red as a freshly boiled lobster, along with cabbages as big as basketballs.

"This is Elena Orlowski's home, only it's new, and I'm not really here." I whispered as I walked through the gate.

I could hear a woman's voice coming from behind the house. It sang a mournful song in Ukrainian, and though I don't know a word of Ukrainian, I somehow understood what she was singing.

Tam v haiu, pry dunaiu, solovi shchebeche
Vin svoiu ptashynochku do hnizdechka klyche.
Tam v haiu, pry dunaiu, tam muzyka hraie
Bas hude, skrypka plache, molodets' huliaie.
Tam v haiu, pry dunaiu, khodzhu samotoiu
I plachu, I rydaiu myla/mylyi za toboiu.

In the forest near the Danube river,
There is a nightingale singing,
He sings to gather everyone from his family
In the forest near the Danube river,
There is a bass vibrating and a fiddle crying,
I think of a place where my lovely one is strolling now
In the forest near the Danube river,
I am sick with my loneliness,
Crying, I want to fly like a bird,
To where my lovely one is now.

I followed the voice, and as I walked around to the back of the house, I saw the soddy, only this time it stood more than eight feet high, and it was adjacent to large clay oven that billowed white smoke into a cloudless sky. A door attached to the front of the sod house opened, and out walked a thin woman with penetrating, dark eyes, carrying a large ceramic bowl filled with dough. She wore a scarf tied in neatly around her chin, similar to Hutterite women. She was dressed in a wide skirt that dropped to her knees, a thin black coat with armhole slits, and embroidered sleeves that she'd rolled up to her elbows.

"Hello, mage," she said, placing the ceramic bowl onto a makeshift table that stood next to the clay oven. "Welcome to my home."

She motioned for me to sit on a handmade bench that rested neatly against the front of the small sod house. I nodded politely, then sat down and watched as the young woman began shaping the dough on an enormous wooden paddle. She flipped it a few times and then slid the paddle into the clay oven and pulled out a fresh loaf of rich, golden bread.

She wiped her hands on her apron and sat down next to me.

"E-Elena Orlowski?" I asked, astonished.

She nodded once, and I couldn't help but be drawn to her intense, brown eyes.

"I am who I was," she said again. "This was my home when my husband and I began to raise our family. We cleared this land with our bare hands until we were able to afford a team of horses. I baked bread every day for my family... you should bake bread, young mage; it will help your focus. A good mage must know their focus, for it will save them during dark times."

I laughed a hearty, self-deprecating laugh. "Oh, Mrs. Orlowski," I chuckled. "I can't bake to save my life. I have been known to burn water when it's cold... that's how bad I cook."

She smiled warmly and took my hand in hers. I was struck by how rough and calloused her skin was, given that her visage appeared younger than I am now.

"Time is short, mage," she said in a somber voice. "The one called Mago gathers his power into a spell that will open a door for the Prince of Lies to come into your world."

"But why?" I asked, trying not to sound frustrated. "The bible foretells the end of the world… this can't be it, can it?"

She shook her head. "Mago seeks the end to all things. Whether he can undo prophecy with this spell remains to be seen, but know this: he seeks counsel with Lucifer and is an emissary for a union of those who wish to tip the balance of power to their favor."

"A federation?" I gasped. "Who?"

She squeezed my hand. "Those who care to challenge Kings and nations. Some are zealots, and many represent those whose interests contrast that of the west. As a group, they are known as the *Conclave* and they have members that number in the thousands. Some are practiced in the darkest of arts, while others possess no magical pedigree."

I blinked a few times and said nothing.

"They come from both the mortal and non-mortal world — Conclave's leaders. They have formed numerous associations with like-minded beings from both worlds, and make no mistake, the Conclave is comprised of smaller factions. These factions include New Covent Witches, whose craft rivals that of the most powerful wizards. There are Upper and Lower House Vampires who wish to farm humans. Their human minions, promised immortality in exchange for carrying out Vampire affairs during the daylight hours, live to serve their undead masters. Indeed, there are some who have infiltrated governments in the mortal realm — those are the ones who will smile politely as they lead you to their masters and ultimately, your doom."

"But why Satan?" I asked.

Her face became a mask of stone. "Mago, as emissary, must offer tribute to Lucifer," she said. "If he is successful, those who dwell in the shadow of the great hill will be condemned to the dark place, and the Conclave will have strengthened their hold on a world that is already rotting from the inside."

I stared at Elena Orlowski for a long moment and tried to process what she'd just revealed.

There existed a shadowy world of beings who sought to upset the balance of power to their favor, and the Conclave was the final piece of the puzzle. Now I understood why Mago had paid the ogre with North Korean gold and why he intended to summon Satan: he was an emissary acting on behalf of the Conclave. They were seeking to increase their influence with the most powerful force of darkness the world has ever known, and the price of Satan's counsel was a million human souls.

"Who besides me knows about this?" I asked.

Elena gave me a hard shrug. "The Conclave used to be common knowledge," she said. "That which you now called folklore was once a way of life. For centuries, wizards and those trained in magic were an integral part of the human world. Kings and nations sought their counsel — indeed, most sovereigns kept their own practitioner to defeat those who would threaten their reign."

"So this is just the twenty-first-century version of something that's been going on throughout history?" I asked.

She nodded. "Yes, but now the stakes are much higher for the mortal realm. Shadowy figures can instantly communicate with the click of an electronic device. International commerce generates far more wealth now than at any time in human history, and developing nations in the throes of civil strife are an easy target for corruption from the Conclave. Given time, they will control entire nations, with drastic consequences for the mortal world."

I doubted that Vishesh knew about the Conclave; in fact, I doubted whether anyone in Government Services and Infrastructure Canada had ever heard of it. It was too fantastic sounding to be real, yet there it was, laid out in a tight little package. My instincts told me to run as fast as I possibly could, to hide out at the cottage with my parents and pretend none of this was real. But if Elena Orlowski's spirit could find me, so could this Conclave.

Elena stood up and walked into the soddy. She came out moments later holding what looked like her staff, but without as many carvings on the surface.

"This is my staff as it was at the time I lived in this house," she said, proudly. "The carvings represent the key to my entire life's work. All books in my sanctuary are guarded using the set of spells I've spoken into the carvings."

I nodded silently.

"Through my staff, you can channel magical energies that can free that part of my spirit that is bound to his will."

"And then what happens?" I asked. "Won't it be too late?"

She shook her head. "I am but the catalyst for the spell that will transform those magical energies into the fog of death that he will turn on the innocent. My staff can break the spell that binds me to his dark purpose. When I am freed, I will set upon him, and he will die," she said, bluntly.

I let out a weary sigh and pursed my lips. "Before you

show me how to do this," I said. "I'd like to know why you're a shade. Why didn't you cross over?"

Her shoulders slumped, and suddenly her face took on a look of despair.

"Because there were none to carry on my life's work," she said. "After my mortal life ended, I transformed into a shade and have held vigil over the lands of my children and my children's children — to protect them, yes… but also to protect this sanctuary. I needed someone to pass on my life's work. You, mage, are the one I have chosen."

Me?

I felt honored that she'd selected me to be the recipient of her sanctuary, but I didn't feel worthy. Maybe it was because I'd never encountered wholesale evil on this kind of scale before, and maybe because I'd always valued a way to find a peaceful solution to a conflict. Her revelations about the Conclave only added to my already heightened sense that I was in way over my head. Yet somehow, she saw something in me that I couldn't. I don't know what it was, and I didn't ask — I didn't think it would be right to ask. Elena Orlowski was a powerful sorceress, and she had spent her life protecting those she loved. Now she was asking me to take her knowledge and protect a city's worth of innocent people.

I gave her a helpless look, and she smiled at me. I took a deep breath, focused my mind, and stood up.

"Alright," I said, in a voice filled with determination. "Tell me what to do."

CHAPTER 38

I became transformed.

There is no other word I can use to describe the surge of renewal that flowed through my body and mind. My thoughts were clear of any lingering self-doubt about stopping Mago, despite a constant wariness that I might wind up dead, along with everyone in Calgary. I felt strengthened somehow, as if my encounter with Elena Orlowski's spirit had provided me with a better understanding of my abilities.

Yes, Mago was a powerful mage. Yes, he was likely a master of dark magic. Yes, I might die, but it didn't matter. I felt completely focused on what must be done, and for the first time since I'd learned of his plan, I had a sense that he *could* be defeated.

I came to behind the wheel of the Maxima. I ran my hands over my face and chest, just to make sure I wasn't in another dreamscape, that I was in the here and now. I glanced at the staff and then at the clock on my stereo. It was flashing 10:02 P.M., and I realized with a shot of panic that I'd been out for more than an hour. I spotted something fluttering underneath my windshield wiper, so I stepped out of the car and snatched it.

It was a parking ticket that was issued at 9:18 P.M.

"But I was inside my car," I said, quietly. "If the cop had seen me there, he would have told me to move, unless… "

I stuck my nose into my sleeve and inhaled deeply. I could smell wood smoke and a faint hint of bread and spices.

"Unless I wasn't in my car!" I gasped.

Out of body experience? Time travel? I gave my head a shake and hopped behind the steering wheel, then turned the key. As the Maxima roared to life, I turned on the radio again, wondering if I'd hear Elena Orlowski's voice. The hissing of dead air filled the interior of my car, confirming that all the radio stations were still out of commission, and I didn't hear the shade either.

"So much for the weather forecast," I muttered as I slipped my car in gear and headed down 2nd Street.

I rounded onto 5th Avenue and then turned left onto McLeod Trail. I could see the statues in front of the Calgary Board of Education ahead, so I parked the Maxima in front of a warehouse and grabbed my satchel and Elena Orlowski's staff. It was shortly past dusk, and the moonlight threw distorted shadows along the grass beneath the twenty-one foot tall behemoths. Dave hadn't yet arrived with the semi-trailer, and that gave me time to prepare the impartation spell.

The sidewalks were empty, which made sense. This wasn't the part of downtown Calgary where barflies and the nightclub crowd liked to hang out. I was a stone's throw from two of the seediest drinking establishments in the city, and anyone wandering around would either be three sheets to the wind or a homeless person. Still, I made sure the park was empty and looked for a spot to begin the spell.

"Crap," I whispered as I realized that a semi-trailer pulling up onto the grass at the Calgary Board of Education would attract the attention of anyone driving south on McLeod Trail. "What I need is a blackout."

Suddenly Elena Orlowski's staff began to glow, and I could hear her resolute voice in my head.

"Draw that which surrounds you through my staff," the voice whispered.

I didn't even have to think about it.

Instinctively, I raised the staff over my head and drove the tip into the grass. I visualized the staff drawing all the electrical current from the buried cables and overhead wires into a compressed ball of energy, then releasing itself into the atmosphere. My grip tightened along the shaft as the hair on my forearms stood up. I could feel a pressure building from directly beneath the staff as I gritted my teeth and whipped my head up to let loose.

"In Divum!" I bellowed, my voice echoing like Charleton Heston's in *The Ten Commandments*.

A ball of electrical force shot through the base of the staff and flew out of its highly polished crown. I closed my eyes tightly as a blinding flash of white light turned everything photonegative. The air crackled loudly, giving way to a blast of thunder that shook the ground and nearly knocked me flat on my back.

Then it was over.

The air smelled of ozone as I slowly opened my eyes and looked onto McLeod Trail. My car wasn't bathed in the yellow glow of streetlights. Every light in every office building surrounding me was out, and the air was filled with the sound of car alarms and honking horns.

"That should keep away unwanted attention," I said, feeling immensely satisfied. I glanced at my watch. It was 10:15 P.M., and Dave would be arriving within minutes. It was time to try the impartation spell on the statues, and if everything worked out, they'd be hitching a ride in the back of a semi-trailer for a short trip to Nose Hill Park – and whatever Mago was planning.

I took a deep breath and drove the tip of the staff into the grass, then dug a circle about eight feet in diameter. I cleared my mind and stepped inside the circle, immediately feeling the magical barrier snap to a close. I carefully pulled Elena Orlowski's book on impartation out of my satchel and flipped to page twenty-three.

The book said that I was to radiate living energy through my staff and that I could channel the life force of any living thing into an object. It also said that in order to work, I'd have to surround the object in a circle that would magnify those energies until the object took on human characteristics, and then the spell would only last for three hours.

"This is going to be one big frigging circle," I muttered as I closed the book and stuffed it back into my satchel.

I knew I could channel the energies in the grass and trees surrounding the statues; that part would be easy. The challenge was to ensure that the statues were in a cooperative mood and would assist in taking down Mago. I'd also have to make a circle big enough to surround the statues in order for the spell to work, and I only had one small stick of chalk in my satchel.

I chewed my lip and considered digging a circle with my staff, but the area surrounding the statues was more than fifty yards in diameter and the circle needed to be constant: it would have to be a uniform depth. I glanced at the Maxima.

Paint.

I had one gallon of 'Flamingo Dream' Easy Latex' that I'd intended to use in my bedroom (yeah, it's pink and girly, so what?) after a moment of divine inspiration while watching Home and Garden Television. I scanned the area surrounding the statues and decided there might be enough to complete a circle, so I raced across McLeod Trail, grabbed the four cans and a brush, and then raced back to the statues.

I popped open the lid with my buck knife and grabbed the can and a paintbrush. I hustled over to the statue closest to me, being careful not to spill any paint, started on the circle. In the distance, I could hear the unmistakable sound of a semi-trailer, which I assumed was Dave. I continued the circle until the two inch wide pink lines met. I exhaled hard and walked the entire perimeter of the circle to make sure it was uniform and complete, then tossed the paint brush in the empty can and raced back to my car.

A black semi-trailer pulled up on the left side of McLeod trail, and I could see Dave smiling at me from inside the cab. I ran around to the driver's side, and Dave rolled down the window.

"You've got pink on you," he said, grinning.

I looked down and saw that paint had splashed onto my jeans and covered my Danner boots. "Dammit," I winced. "These boots cost me two hundred dollars."

Dave pointed to the statues. "If the plan was to paint gang tags all over town, you could have at least picked a better color."

I rolled my eyes and stepped up onto the fuel tank. "Dave, I need you to open the trailer and don't ask questions," I said, trying to sound authoritative. "You're going to see something happen in a few minutes that will probably freak you out, and if you plan on ending our relationship because of it, I'll put a curse on your gonads and shrink your pecker... *got that*?"

Dave's smile disappeared, and he stared down at his crotch. "You know, I think that might hurt," he said. "Listen, Val. I don't exactly know how you can do what you do, and God knows I've seen some pretty weird stuff since we've been together. But I stole a truck for you, and I'm here, and I l – "

I put my hand on his lips. "Don't say it yet, okay?" I interrupted.

"Lesbian," he huffed. "I was *going* to say lesbian!"

I climbed off the truck and gave him a hopeful smile. "I lesbian you too, Dave. Now open up the back, and for crying out loud, don't have a stroke when you see what we'll be hauling."

Dave nodded and opened the door. I ran back to the statues and stepped inside the circle. Instead of it snapping shut, this time it felt like someone slamming a door in a fit of anger. I grunted agreeably, relieved the circle was complete. So long as nobody disturbed the integrity of the circle, I'd be able to complete the spell.

I opened Elena Orlowski's book and flipped to page twenty three. I drove the staff into the earth and grasped the shaft with my right hand. I dug my left hand into the earth and built an image in my mind of my body acting like a giant sponge, absorbing all the surrounding living energy. I shut my eyes tight and spread my fingers wide, feeling for pockets of living energy. My mind collected them, molding the energies into a tight package that vibrated with growing intensity as more and more power fused together, ready to burst.

I made a mental image of each statue freed from more than forty years of being frozen in place, taking their first tentative steps. The head of the staff glowed white as jolt of energy surged up from the earth, ready to be released.

The spell was ready.

"EXISTO ET LIBERUM!" I shrieked,

What happened next can only be described as a miracle.

The staff shook violently, and I threw my other hand onto the shaft and pushed down hard into the earth. The shaft, which had been glowing bright red until now, immediately transformed into a brilliant, white bar of pure energy, which shot out in ten different directions, eventually hitting each statue square in the chest. I ground my teeth together, bearing the weight of my entire body down onto the staff. A wave of intense heat, like a hot wind at the height of summer, kicked up dust devils that swirled around the base of each statue. My head pounded like a jackhammer on steroids as I fought to control the living energy until it had run its course; the problem was, I had no idea how long it would take.

Suddenly, the air filled with the sound of creaking metal. I turned and looked hard at the left hand of the statue closest to me and saw the long bony fingers begin moving, as if the statue were awakening from a long sleep. The earth shook some more, and the statue slowly straightened its back, then the left arm rose up in a grinding sound that split the air. The statue raised its hand to its face, and that's when I finally understood the true scope of Elena Orlowski's power.

The statue's face, which up until moments ago was devoid of human features, began a metamorphosis. A pair of human-like, grey eyes pushed out of the cold hard aluminum. I saw a thin horizontal line form about two thirds down the face, and a mouth formed itself into an O-shape. A nose pushed out with a tinny sound and the statue began to examine its hand.

It reared back its chest, pulled its elbows in tight and screamed into the night sky.

"FREE!"

It stepped outward with its right foot, testing the ground. Then slowly, it lumbered forward and began to walk in careful, deliberate steps. I looked around; each of the nine other statues was engaged in a similar process as the blinding light from the staff dissolved into the darkness.

I scrambled to my feet and raced to the middle of the circle.

"Family!" I bellowed. "Allies… hear me!"

The statues ceased their movements and arched their long thin necks over their narrow shoulders.

"Sorceress," the one closest to me said, in a deep, bass voice that I felt in my bones. "What have you done?"

"All the birds have left us," said a female statue, as it knelt down and examined me as if I were a toy. "The sky has been silent for one day… where have the birds gone?"

"A mage!" I shouted. "He practiced a dark spell on the very creatures that allow you to see and hear the city. He has killed all the birds, and tonight he plans to kill all the mortals. Please… I need your help to defeat him."

Another statue took a long, clumsy step, nearly tripping over its feet before steadying itself. "Then we seek the right of vengeance," it said in a voice that sent a jolt of fear down to the pit of my stomach.

I pointed my staff northward and motioned for the statues to draw close to me.

"The highest point in the city is where he will unleash death itself upon the mortal realm," I said. "I don't know who his allies are, but we're not alone in this. Friends wait for us, but we cannot defeat the mage without your help. I have imparted life onto you, as I consider you to be my friends, and you have always come to my assistance in the past. I know this fight is not yours, but should the mage succeed, a terrible evil will fall onto this place, and all who dwell in the shadow of the great hill will die."

The statues looked at each other, and their expressions ranged from mild curiosity to anger. They began talking amongst themselves, and I had no idea if my appeal would fall on deaf ears. I looked over at McLeod Trail to see the trailer doors wide open and Dave, standing there with a look of either horror or wide-eyed shock on his face — I couldn't tell which. He gave me a tiny wave of his hand and grimaced, giving me a sinking feeling that I'd be onto another boyfriend by the time the night was through.

You know, assuming we survived.

The statues stopped talking, and the one carrying the baby took a cautious step forward.

"We have known about a great evil that would befall this city," it said, in a somber voice. "But we are not immune to magic — the spell that freed us from our place in this park has proven that."

"I understand," I nodded.

"You must also understand that we could be turned by a dark spell. This mage might set his will upon us, and while we cannot be killed, we could be forced into acting against you if his power is strong enough."

The statue was right, of course.

Mago might possess enough skill to turn the statues into twenty-one-foot-tall killing machines, but he'd have to use the right kind of spell. Moreover, I'd imparted life on them for only a few hours; after that, the statues would again be immobilized. There were other factors to consider, like what if we hadn't defeated him before the spell ended? They'd be stuck on Nose Hill Park until someone with a flatbed and a crane moved them back downtown.

"Oh, the hell with it," I said, flatly. "The risks are there, allies. But the danger outweighs the risk. Will you join me in this fight?"

The statues looked at each other again, and slowly, they nodded in agreement.

"It is done," the first statue said. "We too have a stake in this fight and many of us seek vengeance on he who killed the birds. What would you have us do this night, sorceress? Where is this mage?

I let out a huge sigh of relief and pointed to trailer. Dave was still standing there with a stunned look on his face.

"Climb into that trailer," I said, as my lips curled up into a confident smile. "We have a date with a mage."

CHAPTER 39

Dave was silent as we headed up Edmonton trail.

Actually, scratch that, he'd been struck dumb.

He'd literally *fled* across McLeod trail and ducked behind my car while the statues climbed into the trailer — a reasonable action, all things considered. He was frightened, and though fear isn't exactly a quality I find myself attracted to in a man, he had every reason to be afraid: this simply wasn't his forte. (Bear in mind, he didn't race across the road screaming like a little girl; *that* would have been a huge turn off.)

"Are you going to be alright?" I asked, quietly.

He glanced at me through the corner of his eye and shifted down as we crossed Memorial Drive. "About as alright as I'm going to get, I guess," he said, in a near whisper.

I reached over and placed a reassuring hand on his cheek. His skin felt cold, and I realized he was really shaken by what he'd seen.

"I'm scared too," I said. "We're going up against a dark mage named Mago, and he's going to try and kill everyone in the city."

He glanced at me again and let out a nervous sigh. "If you're worried that I'm going to break up with you, you're wrong," he said. "Like I told you earlier, I don't understand what it is that you do, and sometimes I think life would be a hell of a lot easier if I'd never met you — but then I wouldn't get to see your bright, brown eyes every day, and I just couldn't live with that."

I beamed at him, no... actually, I glowed.

"Dave Webber," I gushed, as my eyes welled up with tears. "That is the most wonderful thing any man has ever said to me. I just want you to know that now is the time."

"Huh?"

"Now," I said again.

"I l-love you?" he asked, in a hesitant voice.

Okay, it wasn't a Hallmark moment, but it was close enough for me.

"And I am *in* love with you," I said with a pathetic sounding sniffle. "I've been in love with you since that first beer and pizza outside the Jack Singer. I just want you to know that..."

He rolled his eyes, and his lips curled up into something resembling a forced smile.

"Listen, don't say something sappy, like 'you complete me', okay?" he said, half-sarcastically. "Now that we love each other, would you care to tell me what just happened back there? Better yet, would you tell me what the hell is happening tonight? I don't steal semi-trailers for every girl, you know."

I nodded and wiped my tears on my sleeve. "I used a spell from an old gypsy sorceress, and this is her staff. There's a dark mage at Nose Hill Park who is going to channel the energy of a shade, which is really the gypsy sorceress' corporeal visage, and he's going to wipe out Calgary and summon Satan. I don't think they plan on going for a beer after they're done, either."

Dave was silent for a moment and clenched his jaw tightly. "Well, that sounds about right,. Is there anything else I should know?"

"Yes," I exhaled.

"Want to let me in on it?"

"We'll be meeting with a two-thousand-year-old troll, and I'm his apprentice. We're also going to meet up with a zombie named Caroline, who has a sniper rifle and a sickle." I blurted out.

He nodded a few times and arched his eyebrows. "Well, of course there's a zombie; there *has* to be a zombie."

"And Fifty-Dollar Bill," I said, blowing my nose. "Don't be mad, okay?"

"I'm not mad," he said, quietly. "Overwhelmed a bit, sure — but definitely not mad. What are the statues for?"

"It's complicated," I said. "Remember those birds that died? That was the mage. He's using the shade to create a wall of energy that kills organic matter. The statues aren't organic and can't be killed, so the plan is to have them go in there and kick his ass."

Dave looked over his shoulder at the trailer through the rear window. "And the statues are cool with that?"

"They wouldn't be here if they weren't."

We drove in silence for another few minutes, and Dave turned right left onto McKnight Boulevard. I could see the east slope of Nose Hill Park ahead, silhouetted by a haunting, grey glow that blurred the horizon line.

"Looks like this mage guy is hard at work," said Dave.

"He's likely preparing the spell. It's just after 11:00

o'clock, and he can't release the spell until midnight. That gives us enough time to unload the statues and get ourselves ready."

"What do you want me to do?" Dave asked.

Without hesitating, I stuck my thumb out the window and pointed in the opposite direction. "Get the hell out of town until I call you." I said.

Dave shook his head. "That's not going to work for me, Val," he said. "Listen, I don't know any of this magical, freaky-deaky stuff that you do, but I'm not leaving you… got that?"

I couldn't force him to leave, and I understood why he wanted to stay, but I couldn't ask him to put himself in any more danger. If there were an opportunity to survive the night, I wanted him to take it.

"Okay," I said. "You'll stay in D.T.'s sanctuary. It's protected by some pretty hard-ass magic, and you need to know that if things go badly for us, everyone except for the statues will be high-tailing it in there."

"Will it protect us from this mage dude?"

"Probably not," I said. "But at least we'll be together when the end comes."

Dave nodded again and turned onto 14th Street. He signaled left, then geared down and pulled into the left turning lane.

"Just pull into the parking lot and kill the lights," I said. "When we stop, I want you to wait here until I come for you."

"Don't send that ghost guy, okay?" Dave asked. "You come and get me."

"Alright," I said, as we pulled into the parking lot and came to a hissing stop.

I hopped out of the cab and slipped my satchel over my shoulders. Aside from Caroline's Beetle, the parking lot was surprisingly empty. I looked out onto the city to see the entire downtown core was black, and smiled. Apparently, my spell had been a little more powerful than I'd bargained for.

"Stay here, Dave," I said, pointing at the ground. "I'll be back soon."

Dave nodded, and I clutched the staff tightly as I headed up the path leading to D.T.'s boulder. The higher up the hill I climbed, the more I felt the terrific slurry of magical energies in the air. I'd been in Nose Hill Park at night many times before, but the energy this night was different — almost deliberately tinged with a whiff of panic and a smattering of malice. It was also cold, but not the dry cold that prairie dwellers like me are used to. There was a dampness that clung to my skin like a wet towel, and I could feel the malice in my bones.

When I got about fifteen yards away from the boulder, I felt a tingle of electricity in front of me. I stopped in my tracks and held my hand out as a hum of magical energies vibrated against my fingertips.

"I can feel your shroud, D.T." I said. "Is everyone here?"

I heard a muffled *pop,* and the magical barrier disappeared. D.T. stepped out of the circle, limping more heavily than usual.

"Greetings, ally," he grumbled. "Thy staff is not the one I gave thee."

I gave him a pensive shrug. "It's a long story… where's Caroline and Fifty Dollar Bill?"

The little troll pointed to his cavern. "The ghost is circling the hill, and the creature is inside my dwelling."

"Why?"

"It is feeding," said D.T.. "Thine ally felled a deer."

My stomach pitched to the left at the thought of Caroline sucking the marrow out of deer bones. "Fair enough," I said. "Hopefully she will find Mago and take him out with one clear shot."

"Mago?" asked D.T., his voice laced with surprise. "What of the shade?"

I recounted the entire story of learning the name of the mage from Vishesh, the attack by the ogre, the fact that the shade was the spirit of Elena Orlowski and finally, Mago's plan to summon Satan.

"Elena Orlowski," said D.T., as he scratched his scraggly white beard. "Aye, she was a powerful mage."

"You knew her?"

"Aye," he nodded. "We fought together and defeated certain agents of darkness. She is bound by the will of this Mago, is that correct?"

"That's right," I said. "I've got a nasty surprise for Mago inside that trailer at the bottom of the hill."

D.T. frowned and looked down at the trailer. "That is very powerful magic, apprentice. What is thy plan?"

I craned my neck and searched the sky for a sign of Fifty-Dollar Bill, but he was nowhere in sight. "Assuming Bill locates the mage, we'll unleash the statues and destroy Mago before his spell envelopes the park and everything in it."

"Thou must surely know this mage has enough power to remain hidden, should he choose," said D.T. "But he must reveal himself to cast the…"

Suddenly, we heard an explosion that sliced through the air like an artillery shell. Instinctively, I dove onto D.T., and we hit the ground hard. I looked up to the direction the sound had come from and noticed a haunting, orange glow that silhouetted a stand of poplars more than five hundred yards ahead.

"I think the battle is about to begin, D.T.," I whispered, "Not sure what that explosion was about."

D.T. crawled out from under me and got back to his feet. "The enemy draws near," he said, pointing toward the million-dollar view of Calgary. "He senses thy presence."

I grunted as I stood up and saw huge blocks of lights all over the city extinguished, until the entire city was shrouded in darkness. The sound of screeching tires filled the air, followed by emergency vehicle sirens of every description. "Blackout," I said, gripping the staff. "Would you say that sound came from just north of us?"

"Aye," said D.T. "Not far."

I heard a familiar grinding sound as the boulder behind us rolled to the side. The ambient glow from inside D.T.'s sanctuary shot out of the tunnel in a beam of orange light, and out hustled Caroline, dressed in combat fatigues and a ball cap, sniper rifle at the ready. An olive drab, cotton duck backpack bulged heavily atop her shoulders, and the sickle dangled against her right thigh from inside a tight leather sheath attached to a web belt.

"What the hell was that noise?" Caroline growled. "I was just finishing up a meal, and there was an explosion that knocked me flat on my ass!"

"Mago knows we're here," I said, pointing the staff in the direction of the explosion. "I hadn't counted on that."

"Does this change the game plan?"

I chewed my lip. "Probably — though I don't want to get those statues out of the trailer until we're absolutely ready."

A gust of wind blew through the waist-high grass, and D.T. knelt down, motioning for us to do the same.

"Listen," he whispered.

A high-pitched warbling sound started pulsing through the air, as if being projected through stereo speakers. I looked at Caroline as she took pulled a pair of what looked like binoculars out of a canvas bag. She flipped a small, silver switch, and a little red light came on.

"What are those?" I asked, thinking that Caroline had a secret life as a high-tech mercenary.

"Infrared binoculars," she said, peering through the eyepieces. "They're not as good as thermal imagery goggles, but they'll do in a pinch."

"See anything?"

"Not yet," she said. "But I have a pretty good idea where this Mago is — have a look."

She handed me the binoculars, and I held them up to my eyes. The scenery was bathed in a mint green color, and as I looked up over the horizon line, the green tinge gave way to a bright white glow that took up most of my field of vision.

"Everything looks green except for the big white spot," I said, handing the binoculars back to Caroline. "What is it?"

"Night vision collects light particles and processes them; that's why everything is green," she said. "The white light is what happens when there's too much light to process, and I'd bet dollars to doughnuts that's where Mago is located."

Just then, I felt a jolt of cold surge through my body and I shuddered. I spun around and spotted Fifty-Dollar Bill sitting on the ground against the boulder.

"Sorry about that." he said, his face knotted with worry. "I came in low because the explosion very nearly sucked me in."

I crawled over to the boulder and crouched down beside Bill. "I take it you found Mago," I said. "Where is he?"

Bill bugged out his nearly transparent eyes and appeared to let out a heavy sigh, no mean feat, since he is a ghost, and the last time I checked, ghosts can't breathe.

"It isn't so much where Mago is located that matters," he said, in a somber tone. "It's far more a case of *why.*"

I gave Bill a helpless look. "What are you talking about, Bill?"

The old ghost pointed to the highest point of the park, and a defeated look washed over his face.

"Beyond the apex of this hill, young lady, there is a fissure in the earth. It bears a distinctive yellow hue, I might add."

"Yellow hue?" Caroline groaned. "What the hell is he going on about?"

I motioned for her to settle down and sniffed the air.

"Sulphur?" I mused.

D.T.'s features darkened as he gripped his staff and knelt down.

"Nay, apprentice," he sighed. "'Tis brimstone."

Caroline cocked her rifle and squared her ball cap over her waxen brow. "That fissure must be a gate for you-know-who," she said grimly. "Looks like this Mago guy has opened a doorway that leads into hell, and you know what that means Val…"

A stab of panic shot into my chest as the first of what was probably going to be a number of nasty surprises dawned on me: Demons.

Perfect.

"How soon?" I asked, turning to Bill.

"I'd say you have five minutes," he said in a matter-of-fact voice.

D.T. flew into action. He raced to the crest of the hill and whipped his staff around his head like a propeller. I could feel an intense magical energy drawing out of the overcast sky as he bellowed an evocation.

"GLACIALIS!" He roared.

It was at this point that I was introduced to difference between an apprentice and a true sorcerer.

Instantly, the temperature began to drop. Actually, that's the wrong word: It *plummeted.* All the moisture in the night air transformed into ice crystals that drifted down from the sky like powdery flecks of snow. D.T. spun his staff in one hand like a baton twirler at a football game as he closed his eyes and reached out with his left hand. With his tiny, green right hand, he made a slow, almost elegant waving motion across the front of his body, and a bone-chilling breeze came out of nowhere, collecting the ice crystals, blowing them up to the crest of the hill.

And D.T. wasn't done yet.

He spread open the fingers of his right hand and pushed outward, as if he were pushing against an invisible wall. The swirling cloud of ice crystals began crackling loudly as they fused together into a barrier of pure, glacier-colored ice that shot up from the ground and stretched across the highest point of Nose Hill Park for five hundred yards in both directions.

"Release thine allies, apprentice!" he barked. "Time is short, and the enemy draws close!"

I didn't need to be asked twice, because the look on D.T.'s face told me that all hell was about to break loose. I spun around and started racing down the hill, frantically waving the staff and calling out to Dave.

"Open the trailer, Dave!" I screamed at the top of my lungs, until I almost started coughing.

Dave's head was sticking out the passenger-side window with his patented dumb-struck look on his face. I sent a jolt of energy out the tip of the staff, which landed with a flash next to the right front tire, and that shook Dave out of his stupor.

"Open the trailer *now!*" I shrieked.

He scrambled out of the cab, very nearly landing face first in the dirt as I stopped running and drove Elena Orlowski's staff into the ground. I focused my thoughts for a brief second, and the knotted wooden head lit up like a beacon, illuminating the entire east-slope of the hill. Dave gave me a panicked look as he slid the latch on the back of the trailer and swung it wide open.

"Get up here, Dave!" I snarled. "I want you inside D.T.'s sanctuary."

"Gotcha!" he shouted back, as he started scrambling up the hill.

The trailer started rocking back and forth as the air filled with the sound of creaking metal, then I saw a long, cold, metallic pair of legs emerge through the rear doors. The statue took a few steps and turned around clumsily, then reached its long, branch-like arm inside the trailer and started helping the other statues out.

One by one, each of the Family of Man emerged from the trailer and started up the path, drawn by the light from my staff. I spread out my arms and almost instinctively, the

265

statues formed an extended line. Together, we marched up the hill, ready for whatever was going to burst through the ice barrier D.T. had made.

Yeah, right.

CHAPTER 40

Gunshots.

I don't know where Caroline had disappeared to, but something was getting its head blown off, because a percussive series of loud cracks rang out and echoed across the hilltop.

I pointed to the hole leading into D.T.'s sanctuary and gave Dave a wary glance. "Get inside that tunnel and wait for me," I ordered.

He stood beside the boulder, staring at the wall of ice, his jaw wide open, and wouldn't move.

"Dave, let's go *now!*" I growled, and still no movement.

D.T. ran down from the crest of the hill and whacked him in the shin with his staff. Dave yelped, then doubled over, rubbing his shin and met D.T.'s determined eyes.

"Mortal," he snarled. "In what manner of magic art thou practiced?"

Dave looked D.T. up and down for a second, seemingly recognizing the little troll.

"Y-Yoda?" Dave gulped, in astonishment.

I rolled my eyes. "He's not a mage, D.T.," I groaned. "He's my boyfriend."

D.T. gave me an impatient sneer and fixed his eyes again on Dave. "Then what use is he? Flee this place, unless thou art willing to die in battle with the darkness."

The statues stood a few feet back from the wall of ice, ready for whatever Mago was sending. I nudged Dave with the heel of my hand and pointed to the tunnel.

"We're about two minutes from a company's worth of demonic foot soldiers, Dave," I grumbled, impatiently. "I love you dearly, but we don't have the luxury of time here. Get in that hole!"

A soul-destroying, unified roar suddenly sliced through the night from behind the wall of ice. I gave Dave another hard shove. He shook his head a few times and looked up to the crest of the hill.

"W-What was that?" he whispered.

"A demonic war cry… honey, *get in that hole!*"

D.T. let out a frustrated breath of air, the vapor forming a miniature fog that floated above his head. He dug a small circle around Dave's feet with the tip of his staff, and then tugged at Dave's jacket. When Dave glanced down, he made a small waving motion with his right hand and said, "Sleep, you fool."

Dave dropped to his knees and then did a face plant in the cold grass. He was out like a baby. D.T. gave him a disgusted look, shook his head, and then whispered a few magical words and Dave vanished behind a shroud. He would be safe, for now.

"Apprentice," D.T. said as he reached into the deep pocket of his tunic and pulled out a long silver chain. "Where is thine armor?"

I swung my satchel around off my back and poured the contents on the grass. I looked up, saw dozens of shadows nearing the ice wall, and frantically searched through the pile of the supplies for an amulet.

"I-I don't have one," I growled. "Dammit!"

D.T. again shook his head and readied his staff. He tossed the silver chain at me and I caught it with one hand. "Gather thy focus into yon chain," he ordered. "The magic I do now may catch the enemy off guard. Protect the sanctuary."

I was about to protest, because I was never one to back down from a fight, but D.T. didn't give me time. A loud cracking sound began to spread across the hilltop as the demons threw their bodies against the ice barrier in an attempt to smash through. D.T. stood atop his boulder and spread his arms wide. He shut his inky black eyes tightly, and the head of his staff immediately glowed white. I glanced up at the barrier and saw the wall was about to shatter like an enormous windshield, and that's when D.T. declared war on the netherworld.

"Incendia ex abyssus!" the little troll roared.

A pillar of blue flame burst form the head of D.T.'s staff, roaring like a squadron of F-16's, and into the center of the wall of ice. I felt a wave of intense heat flash over my body, and I ground my teeth as I pushed my magic into the silver chain, forming a protective bubble around Dave and me. Grass instantly burst into flame beneath the column of spectral fire, and D.T. was just getting warmed up.

The wall of ice immediately melted into a boiling stew of scalding water two feet thick, stretching across the hilltop. D.T. reached up to the sky and literally *pulled* a gale force wind out from the clouds. He arched his arm back and launched his body in a throwing motion, sending the gale screaming up the hill and into the bubbling wall of water. As soon as it hit, he released his grip on the wall, and a torrent of water and muck poured across the hilltop, capturing the twisted bodies of dozens of demons and sending them down the hill in a flood.

He dropped to his knees, exhausted. I lowered the shield, and that's when the statues went to work.

They moved forward, keeping even distance from each other, stomping the demon bodies into brownish pulp and grinding them into the ground. I stuffed everything back into my satchel and raced up the hill. I could still hear a steady series of loud cracks every few seconds, and I knew Caroline was busily making quick work of anything that had red skin and a tail. When I got to the top of the hill, I dove into a defensive position, so that I wouldn't silhouette myself along the hill's crest. The statues threw themselves on clusters of four or five demons at a time, stepping on them and tearing them apart with cold metal hands. Ahead I saw the fissure in the ground, bubbling and belching jets of yellow-orange sulphur high into the air.

I let out a hopeless gasp.

It was as wide as a bungalow and glowed a deep crimson, and every few seconds, one or two demons clawed their way into the mortal realm in a hideous parody of birth.

D.T. crawled up beside me to take a look.

"Mago opened a rift to the dark place," I said, sounding deflated. "Those demons will keep spawning unless we can close it somehow."

D.T. let out a weary sigh. "Yon chasm will not be closed without the black arts. Thou surely must know that even with our combined power, we carry no malice with which to destroy it."

My heart sank.

Neither D.T. nor I possessed a malicious bone in our body, and since Mago was a demonomancer, we'd have to resort to black magic if we were to seal the rift.

"So that's it?" I huffed. "Mago wins, and we're just supposed to roll over and die?"

The little troll shook his head. "I know not, apprentice. The hour grows late, and the black mage is nowhere to be seen."

I scanned the battle zone; it was carnage on a staggering scale.

The statues were laying waste to everything in their patch. The demons, each the faceless embodiment of pure evil, poured out of the hole. Their bodies, bloated and distorted into grotesque effigies of former human beings, clawed and gored the twenty-one-foot-tall behemoths, but to no avail. The statues were relentless, snapping the demon's backs in their hands like they were twigs, then casting them aside as they lumbered forward.

A large group of demons, each carrying a double-edged axe, swarmed one statue, toppling it onto its back. They swung their axes down hard on the statue's torso as it kicked and swatted other demons as if they were mere insects. With each blow from a battle-axe, a loud clang rang out amid a shower of sparks, and it only seemed to make the statue angrier.

It rolled over onto its side, squashing a group of four demons into a bloody, spectral goop, and then pushed itself back onto its knees. It reached over its back, grabbing a handful of the creatures, and hurled them at another group that was bearing down, their axes reflecting the crimson glow from the rift.

I glanced at my watch; it was 11:40 P.M.

In twenty minutes, Mago would cast the dark spell that would descend on Calgary in a fog of death. I chewed my lip and wondered how we were supposed to fight through wave after wave of demons and somehow locate Mago. I didn't even know what the guy looked like, and here we were, twenty minutes from oblivion, with no game plan.

Game plan?

"Football!" I nearly cheered. This is freaking football!"

D.T. threw me a confused look. "What is this foot *ball*," he said, enunciating the word 'ball'.

"It's a sport that humans play," I said, with a tinge of optimism in my voice. "This is just like a blitz in the fourth quarter."

"I know not of quarters and blitzes, apprentice. What is thy plan?"

I gave D.T. a friendly nudge on the shoulder and beamed. "The blitz is a team defensive maneuver, in which one or more linebackers or defensive backs, who normally remain on the defensive team's side of the line of scrimmage during a play, are instead sent across the line to the offensive side to try to tackle the quarterback or disrupt his pass attempt."

D.T.'s confused look became one of pure befuddlement. "I know not of what thou speak," he said.

I drew a rectangle in the mud and explained.

"The line of scrimmage is that pit," I said, drawing a small circle. "The demons are the linebackers and defensive backs that are crossing the scrimmage line onto the offensive side. We're the quarterback, and we have the ball. In football, our job would be to get the pass to one of our receivers, but the demons are trying to disrupt our pass."

"Aye," D.T. said. "It is a feint."

I nodded. "That's precisely what this is. Mago is in front of us somewhere, probably behind a shroud. He's sent his blitz out to distract us long enough for him to get the spell ready. Those demons are just a ruse."

"Then we must set upon his magic and detect his shroud before it's too late," D.T. said, with a look of determination in his shining black eyes. "But surely we cannot go through the field of battle."

I clasped my hand on his shoulder and gave him a reassuring squeeze. "We won't," I said in an optimistic voice. "We'll do a flanking."

CHAPTER 41

We doubled down into the low ground and headed north. Around us, the sound of crashing metal and crunching bones filled the air, but we hadn't been detected by the demons that were busy getting their collective ass handed to them by the statues. I gripped the silver chain in my fist, if something attacked us, the power of D.T.'s amulet combined with the chain would be more than enough to block a Howitzer shell, forget about magic.

We rounded a small copse of trees and crawled onto our bellies through a maze of broken undergrowth and shrubs until we spotted a small coulee that veered sharply to the left. It was far enough away from the belching chasm that we wouldn't be seen by the demons, and it offered excellent cover should anything attack us from the rear.

"This is where I'd be," I whispered, scanning the ground below us for any signs of movement.

"Aye," D.T. nodded. "I feel the enemy's presence — his shroud renders him invisible, but his magic flows through yon valley like a river."

I reached out my hand and concentrated. Jolts of spectral energy crackled against my skin in a steady, rhythmic pulse, a sure sign that somewhere nearby, Mago was hiding.

"What does a dark mage need to project a spell of this magnitude, D.T.?" I asked. "Shouldn't we be looking for a circle or a pentagram carved into the earth?"

D.T. shook his head. "Nay, apprentice. He uses elemental magic and bends the forces of nature to his dark will. That with which he killed the fair birds must descend from on high like an invisible fog of death. It creeps toward thy unknowing body and seizes thee before thou hath time to render fear."

I chewed my lip. Somewhere in this coulee, Mago was putting the finishing touch on his spell. We had only minutes to find him and disrupt the spell, but I couldn't pinpoint his precise location.

"How can we find Mago?" I said, my voice growing desperate. "I can feel his magic, but it's so uniform. There's barely a ripple."

D.T. said nothing and instead frittered with the leather wrapping on his tiny staff with his thumb. I held out my hand and intensified my concentration, hoping to feel something, anything that would offer a clue about where Mago might be shrouded, and still nothing. I exhaled heavily and dug my hand in the ground, hoping that if I could draw some of the earth's natural energies, it might lead us to the dark mage. I spread out my fingers and closed my eyes, intensifying my thoughts and feelings on Mago. I whispered a word of magic and instantly, I felt a tiny, rhythmic pulsing of the earth's elemental energy, like a faint heart beat.

"That's not right," I whispered, glancing at D.T. through the corner of my eye. "This is Nose Hill Park — the magical energies should be off the scale, and all I'm getting from the ground is a weak pulse."

D.T. gave me a surprised look and dug his fingers into the ground. "Aye, the enemy draws from the earth to help fuel his dark plan."

I nodded. "If he's drawing power from the earth, there might be a way to disrupt it. Any ideas?"

D.T. frowned and glanced at Elena Orlowski's staff and then at my satchel. He scratched away at the ground with a tiny finger and shrugged. "'Tis possible thy satchel is the key," he said, grimly. "Where art thine ally in spirit?"

"You mean Fifty-Dollar Bill?" I asked, giving D.T. an impatient look. "Why?"

"The spirit will be needed by and by," he said, pointing to my satchel. "Thy purse carries earth from whence the mortal remains of yon shade is buried?"

"I've got a Tupperware container filled with soil from where the grain bin disappeared at Orlowski's farm," I said. "It's not from the actual burial site of either Elena Orlowski or her husband."

D.T. grunted as he started to dig a small hole in the ground. He whispered an incantation I'd never heard before, and suddenly the small hole gave off a twinge of spectral energy.

"Earth is never the same," he whispered, as he began adding small broken twigs and grass to the hole. "That which thou parcel in thy purse is not of this place or time."

I pulled the drawstring on my satchel and reached inside for the Tupperware container. I tightened my grip on Elena Orlowski's staff and handed the Tupperware container to D.T.

"Are you suggesting that because the soil in that container is not from Nose Hill Park, it would somehow cause a short circuit to Mago's spell?"

D.T. nodded, but his face took on a cautious look. He pulled the lid off the container and poked a finger inside. "This earth is not of this place," he said, concentrating. "Soon the very life of this place will yield unto death as is the dark mage's wont. Yon shade is the spark through which thine enemy will bring forth the end of all things that dwell in the shadow of the great hill. Know this: the enemy cannot render magical energies of a foreign source. We cast lots with chance, so pray the earth from whence the shade once lived and worked her magic during life yields a confrontation. We know not if this will bring about victory, but draw the enemy from his shroud my magic surely will."

I let out a nervous, long breath. D.T. knew everything about Nose Hill Park, because he'd lived there all his two-thousand years. He also knew something about the source of magical energies, and if he said the soil from Orlowski's farm would short circuit Mago's spell, then this was our best shot. What would happen once the spell was disrupted would boil down to a good old-fashioned knuckle-duster between a dark mage, a three-foot tall dwarf troll, and an outclassed novice.

Yeah, our chances sucked, but we didn't have a choice. I watched as D.T. took a small handful of earth from the Tupperware container and dropped it in the hole. I held out my hand to feel if there were any disruption in the magical energies surrounding us, but still the uniform hum of Mago's magical signature continued unabated.

"It's not working yet," I said, my voice dripping with desperation. "What's Fifty-Dollar Bill got to do with this?"

D.T. ran a cautious hand through his white beard and started kneading the soil from Orlowski's farm into the hole with his fist. "Thine ghostly ally will act as a sentinel for the spirit in bondage," he grunted.

"You mean the shade?" I asked.

"Nay, apprentice," he said, his voice sounding more determined than ever. "Thy spiritual ally must bring forth the soul held as ransom — summon him."

I nodded silently and shut my eyes tight. I focused carefully on Fifty-Dollar Bill's residual presence and gritted my teeth.

"William Lyon Mackenzie King, I summon you," I said, in a quiet commanding voice.

A jolt of cold passed through my body, and a faint spectral glow appeared beside me. It slowly took shape, and within seconds, Bill's visage materialized.

His pudgy, translucent face had a look of genuine fear, and I knew instinctively that Bill didn't want to be here. Hell, I didn't want to be here, but it didn't matter. I knew he'd protested doing anything in the past that might put him in peril, but I had to believe there was some measure of courage in the old spirit's soul.

"I'm not supposed to be here, young lady," he said, curtly. "This is your battle, not mine. Good heaven's, haven't I helped you enough by now?"

I gave him a resolute glare and clenched my jaw. "I know, Bill," I said, the panic in my voice ready to boil over. "I need your help… everyone in Calgary needs your help."

"Again, not my battle," he said, digging in his heels. "I'm a sentient spirit of a wily old politician — *not* a sorcerer."

I held up my hand in protest. "Bill, I don't give a rat's ass if you're not a sorcerer," I snapped. "Once upon a time, you led a nation; all I'm asking you to do now is lead a fellow spirit in bondage to freedom."

"Absolutely not," he snapped back. "If this Mago can pull spirits through the other side and into the mortal realm, only to imprison them, he'll make fast work of me."

D.T. flashed with anger. "Spirit, thou art compelled to carry out this task for the sake of all that's good. My apprentice and I will keep the dark mage at bay long enough for thou to lead that which is in bondage to freedom."

"Bill," I pleaded. "D.T.'s right. The shade is bound to his will so long as he keeps her husband's spirit hostage. You can be the hero, here… tonight. You can save more than a million innocent souls from falling victim to the Conclave. Think about it, Bill — your entire life was one of dabbling with the occult and leading a secretive life. I can't change that you're dead, I can't change that a whack of political scholars think you were a nut job, but one thing I know about Mackenzie King is that he led Canada through the darkest period in its history. Mackenzie King led a nation through a world war with an enemy as vile and malicious as they come. Please, Bill, for the love of everything that is good, help us save lives. Help *me*, Bill… I need you."

He stared at me hard for a moment and opened his translucent mouth to say something. Then, as if he'd just seen a ghost himself, his eyes bugged out.

"I-I can feel him," he said, in an astonished voice. "I can feel the presence of Bogdan Orlowski… he's nearby."

"Then go to him, Bill," I said, trying to sound patient. "Go find that ghost, and when we disrupt Mago's spell, you'll know what to do."

Bill stood up and straightened his tunic. He narrowed his eyes and, for half a second, looked fearless. "You, young lady," he said, fixedly, "Had better make certain this works. Goodbye and good luck."

He disappeared in an instant, and I turned my head to D.T. He'd finished kneading the soil into the small hole and stared out into the coulee with a look of hard determination. "Take thy staff, apprentice," he said. "Fix all thy will upon yon tiny hole, and drive thy stake into the heart of the dark one's plot against all who dwell in the shadow of the great hill."

I blinked at him. It took me a few seconds to register what D.T. wanted me to do, and I flushed with embarrassment at not acting instinctively. "All right, D.T.," I said in a quiet but purposeful voice. "It's time."

I got to my feet and stood before the tiny hole. The air hummed with the constant vibration of magical energy being sucked into Mago's spell, and behind me, I could hear the occasional gunshot as well as the blood-curdling screeching of demons.

I fixed my gaze on the head of Elena Orlowski's staff and raised it high over my head. I stared down at the hole and gathered my thoughts into a tempest of energy, and then I drove the stake into the hole.

There was a blinding, white flash for half a second and then an enormous tremor that rumbled out from the tiny hole, straight into the heart of the coulee.

I felt my body surge with power, and a curious sense of peace wash over me simultaneously. Then, another blinding, white flash arced high into the air, followed by a storm of electricity that seemed to rise in a wave from a fixed point about two-hundred yards in front of me.

A hunched figure dressed in a black cloak with a hood cocked its head over its shoulder and glared at the source of the tremor. The figure raised a hand and then pushed outward, as if it were shoving someone at the start of a fistfight. A wave of compressed force sailed up the hill and hit me square in the chest, sending me sailing through the air and into the trunk of a very large and immovable poplar tree.

I slid to the ground and dropped to my knees.

Then, blackness.

CHAPTER 42

I don't know how long I was out.

I opened my eyes and blinked a few times. A warm trickle of blood slowly dripped from both my nostrils, and my brain felt like it was victim to a hundred hangovers. I shook my head and wiped my nose with my sleeve as I tried to stand up.

"Mago," I whispered, as the nausea in my stomach splashed about. "I-It worked."

I felt disoriented and slightly dizzy, but otherwise I was fine. I spotted my staff lying on the ground about a hundred feet in front of me, so I dashed up the small incline and then dove onto the ground. A bubble of emerald light blazed in the center of the coulee, giving everything a haunting green glow. I saw a lash of fire shoot straight across the coulee, and I spotted D.T. in the throes of a furious battle with a cloaked figure, which was easily two and a half times his size.

The figure threw out an arm, and the fire splashed in every direction, deflected by some kind of shield. He spun around as if he were throwing a discus, and an arc of emerald energy twisted itself into a column of force and then blasted across the coulee like a rocket. D.T. held out his amulet, and the energy beam bounced off like a ricocheting bullet into the night sky.

"Be thou at thy most vile," D.T. shrieked, his voice bouncing off the coulee walls. *"Thou shalt take no innocent souls this night!"*

He swung his staff like a baseball bat, and a ribbon of blue flame spun itself into a compressed ball, then jettisoned at Mago with blinding speed.

The dark mage held up a hand and shouted, *"INERMIS,"* dissolving the ball of force as easily as sugar dissolves in water. D.T. gave him a surprised look and made a lifting motion. The ground shook violently, and a mound of dirt formed at Mago's feet. Less than a second later, a geyser of soil erupted, sending the mage hurtling high into the air, landing hard on a bramble of twisted undergrowth.

"Fiero!" shouted D.T. as he shot a jet of fire into the bramble, which burst into flame. I raced down the hill as the fire spread across the bottom of the coulee, nearly tripping over my feet and almost landing face first in patch of Russian thistle.

"I-Is that it?" I panted, getting back to my feet. "You destroyed him?"

D.T. kept his shining black eyes fixed on the blaze as it grew in intensity, and exhaled slowly.

"Nay, apprentice," he said, his voice sounding strangely weak. "Behold."

A column of acrid white smoke floated into the sky, and suddenly, the edges of the fire that had spread across the coulee floor began to fade. Orange flames that just seconds ago burned as high as ten feet receded into the now blackened grass, as if someone with a giant candlesnuffer had smothered it out. Dried blood clogged my nostrils, and I began coughing as the smoke suddenly descended on D.T. and me, blinding us from Mago.

I gripped the sliver chain tightly in my right fist, expecting the mage to lash out with another blast of emerald force, while D.T. leaned against my right leg.

"W-Where is he?" I coughed.

"I know not, apprentice," the little troll hacked. "Be thou on thy guard!"

I readied myself in a defensive posture and grasped the staff with both hands. Stinging tears ran down my cheeks, and my eyes felt like someone had poured vinegar in them.

"On your guard *indeed,*" a voice chuckled. "Your worst nightmares are but the tiniest glimpse of the horrors that await you both."

Instantly, there was a gash of searing pain deep inside my head, and I screamed as I doubled over onto my knees. Razor sharp fingers clawed into my brain as I ground my teeth together, trying desperately to focus.

"Your minds are all I need," the voice continued. "Why should we battle in such an uncivilized way when there is so much to do in such a short span of time?"

I felt myself spinning. Myriad images flashed through my brain in what seemed like an eternity, yet my instincts told me it was instantaneous. I saw a wispy, billowing mist begin to roll from the highest point in Nose Hill Park, out over John Laurie Boulevard. It crept forward, deliberately enveloping homes and buildings, and I felt the presence of a vile, malevolent pleasure. It was almost as if the mist itself was somehow alive, aware that its presence brought instant death to everything in its wake. I felt the life energy of organic matter sucked dry, as all around, grass and leaves turned black as the fog lumbered forward.

I watched in horror as it wafted through the ductwork inside a sleeping child's room. It rolled slowly across the carpet, crawling up the footboard and across the bedspread until it met with the sleeping child's face. It was a young girl, no older than a toddler. She took a deep breath, and the mist flowed in through her nostrils. *"No... you son of a bitch, no!"* I screamed.

The little girl exhaled slowly, almost contentedly, and her head canted slightly to the right. Her blonde bangs hung limply over her left eye, and her hand fell out, onto the side of the bed.

"Breathe, damn it... breathe!" I shrieked.

I reached out to the child, my hands gripped her shoulders hard, and I shook her. I shook her and kept screaming,

"Breathe! For the love of God, please... breathe!"

The dark mage cackled like a hag at a homeless shelter.

"The mind is always the weak link of the chain," it said, in a strangely sensual voice. "I very nearly destroyed you while you slept, but this time you won't be so lucky."

Darkness surrounded me; I felt like I'd been pushed into a room with no light and narrow walls. I held my hand in front of my face and saw nothing but an inky, impenetrable blackness that threatened to swallow me whole. I ground my eyes shut and tried desperately to clear my thoughts. I tightened my abdominal muscles and coiled myself down like a spring, then I lunged outward into the void, but the darkness only seized me tighter.

"D.T.," I shrieked, as I felt the air being squeezed from my lungs. "Help me, p-please."

"The troll is in his own little world," Mago, hissed. "Surely a cagey young woman like you knows there is nothing that can stand in the way of my work this night."

I opened my eyes, and tiny electrical synapses burst in flecks of blue and white. I couldn't tell if what I was seeing was real or just more of Mago's dark magic, so I pulled my buck knife out from its sheath and held it over my palm. I grated my teeth and then sliced into the center of my hand, waiting for the sharp, stinging pain of the cut. One, two seconds... no pain. I looked at my palm and realized there was no blood; he was still in my head.

"None of this is real!" I snarled. "You're trying to control my thoughts, but your magic is weak, Mago... if you were half the dark mage you've been made out to be, you'd have killed me by now."

"Perhaps," the voice said. "Or perhaps I am like a cat that enjoys toying with its prey."

"Why toy with me when you have an emissary's work to do?" I shot back. "Here's little old me thinking you wanted to summon the Prince of Darkness."

I had to buy time. Fifty-Dollar Bill was out there somewhere, and I knew that if he could bring the spirit of Bogdan Orlowski into the mortal real, Mago's hold on the shade would be ended.

I thought up a lie.

"I know who you are, Mago," I shouted. "I know about the Conclave."

The darkness surrounding me seem to thin somehow at the mention of the Conclave. I decided to press on.

"I know that I've been drafted into some bullshit peacekeeping force of the hell-knows-what, and that the people who pay me have been lying to me for a long time."

There was a moment of silence, and I imagined that Mago was contemplating a response.

"And I am to now believe that you're interested in learning about the true nature of magic," he sneered. "You'd have me believe that your powers could be a benefit to the Conclave."

"Who knows?" I shouted. "You wouldn't have attacked me on two separate occasions if you hadn't felt my magical signature."

The darkness separated like a curtain opening at the movie theatre. I saw a cloaked figure approach, his hands hidden beneath his long sleeves. I felt him release his grip on my thoughts, and the darkness peeled away to the acrid smell of burned grass and smoldering wood. I glanced to my left. D.T. hunched over into a squatting position, his face a mask of intense pain.

"The troll is still a prisoner," said Mago, as he stopped a healthy distance from me. He reached up to his hood and pulled it back, revealing a pasty, white face with a shaved head and a series of intricate tattoos that covered his entire scalp. His thin lips curled up into a confident smile that pushed the skin on his face back over a set of sharp, almost pointy cheekbones. His eyes were milky blue and gave him an almost predatory look.

"What about your summoning spell?" I asked, trying to cloak the panic that stabbed at my chest. "I believed you to be an emissary for the Conclave. It's past midnight; aren't you supposed to be summoning the Devil or something?"

He folded his arms and frittered with a pentagram amulet that hung loosely from a gold chain.

"You have much to learn, novice," he said, in a belittling voice. "I can summon the full extent of the netherworld any time I please."

"Then why haven't you killed me yet?" I asked, trying to match his tone. "I am, after all, a novice."

He nodded slowly, and his creepy smile didn't falter. "Call it my own curiosity," he said. "Or perhaps I care to indulge my ego enough to learn if you are indeed what they claim you to be."

I stared at him hard, my face a mask of determination.

"Who are *they*?" I said, in a voice that came within a whisker of sneering.

"Why my contemporaries," he said. "Surely you don't believe for a second the Conclave doesn't keep track of those with certain gifts."

"The gift of what?" I huffed.

He started to circle me, like a cat that is considering the best way to pounce. "The gift of clarity," he continued. "Your magical signature is much like gold that has been refined to absolute purity. Do you think a dwarf troll mage can teach you the true extent of your abilities? Look upon the pitiable creature! He's lived for over two millennia, and a mere mortal has subdued him."

Clarity.

The first time I'd heard it was in the presence of Elena Orlowski, but whatever the hell this gift was, it hadn't registered. Now Mago has used the word, and things became abundantly clear. Now I understood why all my life, I'd seen the undead and those who dwelled in the preternatural world were attracted to me. Now I understood why D.T. had wanted me as an apprentice and why the government had an interest in my activities.

I should have felt angry, but I didn't, because in the grand scheme of things, whatever gifts I possessed would change nothing. If I survived the night, the Conclave would continue to target me and those I loved. I decided in an instant that when all this was over, I would resolve to explore this so-called 'clarity' under the watchful eye of a two-thousand year-old troll. I'd hone my skills to near surgical precision, and I'd lay waste to anyone or anything with a dark purpose.

I clenched my jaw tightly and stared through Mago. I had played to his ego and won. Now all I had to do was keep him talking long enough for Fifty-Dollar Bill to find Bogdan Orlwoski.

"I've never heard of this *clarity,* but I'm sure you're going to tell me about it," I said. "God knows those I work for have been keeping me in the dark on all this hocus-pocus crap."

He gave a hearty chuckle and continued circling me. "Oh, clarity is so much more than magic words and phrases, novice. Clarity exists in only two people in the spectrum of mortal practitioners. The Conclave is host to one of them, and I believe she'd be pleased to take a true apprentice under her wing."

I blinked a few times and chose my words carefully. "If I had this clarity you're speaking of, why did you try to kill me in my home and at that farm?"

He drew closer now and took a couple of cautious steps toward me. "The ogre was a spy," said Mago. "He wasn't supposed to attack, but you know how utterly stupid ogres can be. I would have destroyed him for his incompetence, but you apparently beat me to it. As for what happened in your home, that was my attempt at measuring the level of clarity you possess. For example, had you been a normal mortal, you would have never survived my initial incursion into your subconscious. That you met my will and prepared to engage in psychic combat speaks well of your resilience and is a true sign that you are indeed gifted."

I grunted. "And who is this person in the Conclave that would act as a mentor?"

"Nice try," he chuckled. "She keeps her name secret for reasons that you know full well. Nobody knows her real name, but what I can tell you is that only she has the ability to help you reveal the true nature of your power."

I slowly ran my right hand along my belt until I could feel the hilt of my buck knife. Mago took another step closer, his eyes never veering from mine.

"You know," I said, sounding impatient. "I never asked for any of this, and I'm tired of people trying to control my life. Who's to say this unnamed clarity chick won't use me as this troll has used me. Hell, everyone has been using me for something or another. I work for a government that thinks it can do whatever the hell it wants with me; I've been told that I have to be an apprentice to the troll, and you know, I'm just wondering if maybe someone, anyone, can deal me straight in life."

"She can guide you toward your *own* choices, novice," he said, taking another step. He stretched out his claw-like hand and reached for my shoulder. "She can help you find the meaning of your magic, and you'd be exalted within the Conclave."

He rested his hand on my bicep, and I cringed at his touch. I wrapped my hand around the handle of my buck knife and took a step toward Mago.

"It's pretty clear I can't defeat you," I said, trying as hard as I could to sound deflated. "Perhaps we can broker a deal with respect to the Conclave and your work as an emissary this night"

He gave me a confused look.

"What's the bigger prize to the Conclave," I continued. "A meeting with Mephistopheles or recruiting someone who would strengthen your ranks. Perhaps a bargain can be struck."

He exhaled slowly and nodded. "I believe my work as an emissary can wait until another night... what is your proposal, novice?"

I pulled the buck knife out of its sheath and drew so close to Mago that I could smell his foul breath.

"My proposal is... *THIS!*"

I swung the buck knife around my waist and drove it hard into Mago's stomach, and then I grabbed a handful of his cloak and pulled him down on the blade with all my strength.

He gushed out a mouthful of stale air and clutched his stomach with both hands. I glanced back at D.T. and saw that he'd come out of his stupor, but he was severely weakened.

"You fucking bitch!" Mago screamed as he staggered forward. *"You'll fucking burn for this."*

I gave him a disgusted look and shouted. "Not tonight, asshole... *Bill, if you can hear me, this would be the right time!*"

The familiar cold rushed through me, and I heard Bill's voice.

"I thought you'd *never* ask," he said flatly, materializing before me. "Valerie Stevens, I give you... *Bogdan Orlowski!*"

Elena Orlowski's staff started vibrating in my left hand. Suddenly, her engravings glittered with every color in the spectrum as the visage of a young man clad in traditional Ukrainian peasant garb appeared at Bill's side. His penetrating dark eyes, the same eyes I'd seen in the old wedding photograph at Orlowski's farm, materialized out of the darkness, staring at the crumpled form of Mago with a look of pure, unbridled hatred.

"Elena! Ya hocu pobacytysya z toboyu!" he cried out into the darkness.

The staff flew out of my hands and landed at Bogdan Orlowski's feet. He reached down to pick it up, and his hands passed through it.

"Elena!" he cried again. *"My pobachymos'a znovu?"*

The rainbow of colors shot out in a single pillar of concentrated spectral energy that formed a fissure in the darkness. Brilliant, white light spilled through the crack, and a pair of delicate looking, female hands pulled the fissure wide enough for the spirit of Elena Orlowski to emerge into the mortal realm.

"Bogdan!" she cried, racing to him, her arms outstretched. *"Tse najkrash'ij den' u mojemu zhytti!"*

The two spirits embraced in a blaze of sparkling colors, their energies entwining together, reunited, even after death.

Mago lay in a pool of inky black ichor as he stared at the bittersweet moment. His milky blue eyes blinked flatly, as his breathing became more and more faint. His hands still clutched the handle of my buck knife and I knew it was a matter of minutes until he died. The spectral pair separated for a moment, and Elena Orlowski, the shade, the Roma *chovihanis*, smiled and floated to the dying body of the dark mage.

She reached a translucent hand out and stroked Mago's face, then, with a smile she whispered, "The dark place calls you home, vile mage… go now and be with souls of the damned."

Mago's eyes rolled into the back of his head and suddenly, his entire body became engulfed in a spectral torrent of fire and ash. He screamed in a voice that could have shriveled God's testicles as the blaze consumed him, until his body was nothing more than a small pile of smoldering, gray ash.

She returned to her husband, and together they beamed at me. "Young apprentice," Elena said, her voice gushed. "I told you that you'd know what to do when the time came. Care for my sanctuary and master that which I used to protect this realm from those who would threaten the innocent. I thank you; *we* thank you for reuniting us."

D.T. took my hand in his as tears welled up in my eyes. I nodded in deference to the spirit of the Roma sorceress, and I smiled softly. "Cross over, Elena and Bogdan Orlowski. Cross over, and may you never again be parted."

Together they bowed and then floated into the fissure as Fifty-Dollar Bill dabbed at his eyes with a ghostly handkerchief.

It was over.

CHAPTER 43

We climbed to the top of the coulee in silence. D.T. hobbled more slowly than usual, so I cut my pace and held out my hand.

"Want a ride?" I asked, concerned by how weary he looked.

"Nay, apprentice," the little troll said quietly. "Thine enemy's attack on my spirit weakened these old bones."

I grunted and dug my staff into the ground as we traversed a small copse of trees and headed into the low ground, to the spot where the statues had laid waste to countless demons Mago had summoned. I'd expected to see hundreds of demon carcasses, but all around us were small pools of ectoplasm that reflected the moonlight, giving the battlefield a ghostly, frozen appearance. Ahead was the ridge where D.T. had created a barrier of solid ice, and I spotted the statues on the crest of the hill, but they weren't moving. I glanced at my watch; it was only 12:30 A.M., and my impartation spell should have been strong enough for another two hours.

"The statues aren't moving," I said, pointing my staff to the crest of the hill. "I must have done something wrong when I brought them to life."

D.T. shook his head. "Nay apprentice," he said, his voice almost distant. "Thine allies drained thy spell's energy in their battle with the darkness. In time, thy power will mature and strengthen thy spellcraft."

I grunted. At least the statues appeared to have returned to their original sculpted positions.

We climbed the steep slope to the crest of the hill, and I spotted Caroline sitting on top of D.T.'s boulder, cleaning her sniper rifle. She had a look of smug self-satisfaction on her face and whistled an old *Huey Lewis and the News* tune as she ran a long rod through the rifle's barrel.

"Hell of a night, Val," she chuckled, her eyes fixed on her rifle. "You two are still alive, so I'll assume Mago is dead."

I forced a smile and walked up to the boulder. "He's dead," I said.

Caroline pointed her thumb over her shoulder and motioned that I should look down the east slope of the park. "Your boyfriend is wandering around like a lost puppy," she sneered, her voice laced with sarcasm. "Apparently he's scared of zombies."

"I see him," I huffed and then started to jog down the hill.

When I got to him, he had a dazed look in his eyes and was chattering on about finding a girlfriend who didn't hang out with dead people. I threw my arms around him and gave him a hard, loving squeeze.

"Dave… sweetheart, it's me — it's Valerie."

He cocked an eyebrow and gave me a confused look for half a second.

"You put me to sleep!" he growled. *"You and your Jedi Master put some kind of spell on me."*

I got up on my tippy-toes and kissed his nose. "We had to, Dave," I apologized. "We didn't have a choice."

"Uh-huh — is it over?"

"Yeah," I said, beaming at him. "It's over."

"I'm going to need therapy, you know," he grumbled. "I'm just a frigging dump truck driver, for shit sake, I'm not used to giant statues that come to life and people trying to kill the woman I love."

I pursed my lips and nodded again as he put his arms around my waist and pulled me close. He leaned in to give me a kiss but stopped an inch from my lips.

"You smell like crap, Valerie," said Dave as his mustache curled up into a smile. "This is *not* making me horny."

I grinned and kissed him good and hard. Then I punched him in the shoulder.

"I just helped save a city while stopping Satan from entering the mortal realm, and you're worried about getting laid?" I asked, in a voice dripping with mock sarcasm.

Dave's face flushed red, and he gave me a sheepish look. "I don't know, Val," he said with a grin. "A girlfriend like you tends to make a man feel like a… "

"Shut up, you moron," I groaned, rolling my eyes. "Listen, do you have anything in that trailer we can use to get those statues back to the Board of Education?"

Dave stared at me blankly. "You're kidding, right?"

The look on my face told him I wasn't kidding. If I couldn't get the statues back to their original location, Vishesh would tear a strip off me that would probably leave a permanent mark.

"I'm serious, Dave," I huffed. "Got anything?"

He looked up the hill to the statues and shook his head. "Val, if you can't use your magic and bring those statues to life again, the only way they're getting back downtown is with the crane and a flatbed."

I let out a defeated sounding groan and kicked at the dirt. I was too physically and spiritually exhausted to take on the impartation spell again, and I knew there was no way D.T. could do it in his weakened state. It looked like the statues were going to have to stay, and Vishesh would once again have to work an administrative miracle.

I reached into my Mickey pocket and grabbed my handheld. I pressed the power button, and the blue screen blinked a few times before it died.

"Crap," I grunted. "Damned thing is fried... got your cell?"

Dave grabbed his phone from his belt and handed it to me. I punched in a classified number so Vishesh would know it was me, and texted him the following:

Crisis averted. Clean up crew requested at Nose Hill Park. Bring flatbed and crane. You'll be pissed with me... deal with it.

Valerie.

I snapped the cover shut and handed the phone back to Dave. I gave him a serious smooch and told him to get the truck back to Demarco's. I'd hitch a ride with Caroline and meet him back at my condo in a few hours.

In the days following the clash with Mago, the local news media was out in full force, combing over the two or three blackened hectares of Nose Hill Park, trying to find the source of the mysterious blaze that could easily have grown into an inferno, which would have threatened the million-dollar homes bordering the great hill. It didn't help that Calgary's mayor lived in one of those miniature mansions, and he'd taken to the airwaves promising swift action against, you guessed it, *shiftless teenagers*. If only he knew the truth.

The statues were returned to their original spots in front of the Calgary Board of Education. I visited them about a week later and thanked each one for their help. Surprisingly, they felt indebted to me for freeing them to walk in the world of the living, even though they'd spent the bulk of their time kicking serious demon ass.

Caroline asked me about my promise to reanimate her body and was mad as hell that I couldn't deliver. She left me an angry voice mail and accused me of reneging on our arrangement, so I paid her a visit to try to smooth things over. She let me into her flat only after I promised to bring her some live chickens, and soon I found myself sitting on her sofa explaining myself.

"You promised to help me, Val," she grumbled. "I put my neck on the line for you!"

I motioned for her to calm down. "I can't do it yet, Caroline," I said, my voice filled with genuine disappointment. "I'm not saying I will never be able to do it, but I need to focus on developing my skills. I'm not a necromancer — you know this."

She stomped a slipper clad foot into her Berber carpet. "I do *not* want to live like this!" she snapped. "I've always been there for you in the past, Valerie. I've lost my family, my friends, and half the time you look at me with fear and distrust. The least you can do is try something... *anything* to get me better."

There was no escaping the fact that I'd been dishonest with Caroline, and I felt like a Class-A heel. I had needed her to back me up against a force that could have wiped out a city, and I'd dangled the prospect of a normal life like a fishing lure to a trout. She'd believed in me, and I'd let her down.

"Caroline," I sighed heavily. "You have no reason to trust me, because I used you, but I'm asking you to believe in me now. I promise you with all my heart; I will put every effort into finding a cure for your condition."

She folded her bony arms across her chest, and her dead eyes bore straight through me. "You *will* find a cure for this, Valerie," she snipped. "I've seen a whack of crazy stuff since I was turned, and the answer is out there somewhere."

I nodded and tried to give her an optimistic smile. "I'll need your help," I said. "I'll bring you books from Elena Orlowski's sanctuary, and we can start our search there. Somehow, we'll get you back to the way you used to be."

She sniffed and wiped her eyes with the back of a chalk white hand. "I don't have any friends, Val. I've lost everything, and I've even thought about putting a bullet in my head, but I can't do it. I'm terrified of going back to the dark place."

I put my hand on her shoulder and squeezed. "You're making amends for whatever it is in life that sent you there, Caroline. I have to believe there is a supreme being who knows that you're solidly on the side of good. There's a hell of a lot of evil in this world, and you are a big part of what keeps it at bay. Never forget that."

She sniffed again as I reached into my Mickey pocket and pulled out a beige envelope.

"What's that?" Caroline asked.

"Open it," I grinned.

She ran a long, sharp fingernail through the side of the envelope and tore off the end, and then she reached in and pulled out a gift certificate.

"A five-hundred-dollar voucher for live chickens from Quarrydown Farms," she read aloud. "Gee, Valerie — are you trying to butter me up here?"

I gently grabbed her cold, dead hands and gave another squeeze. "I couldn't get a coupon for poodles, so this will have to do," I said, quietly. "Caroline, don't ever once think that you're alone in this. I am and will always be your friend, even if I blew it this time."

She sniffed again and nodded. "You're not forgiven, Valerie… five-hundred dollars' worth of live chickens isn't going to cut it."

"I know."

"Just fix things, okay?"

I nodded and smiled warmly. "I will, Caroline. Somehow I will."

D.T. decided it was time for a change.

With the permission of Peter and Bernadette Orlowski, the little troll took up residence in the old soddy at the Orlowski farm. I didn't even try to protest, because apprentices aren't supposed to question the wisdom of their mentors. I wouldn't have protested either way: Elena Orlowski's sanctuary was now Valerie Steven's sanctuary, and there was a lifetime of spellcraft on those old, wooden shelves. Who better to help me master my skills than a cranky old troll with a penchant for Player's unfiltered cigarettes? I'd seen the true nature of D.T.'s power during our battle with Mago, and with the revelations regarding the Conclave and this dark sorceress who shared something called clarity with little old me, I was going to need all the help I could get.

As we entered the sanctuary for the first time, D.T. whispered a word of magic, and the candles on the old table lit up, giving the old soddy a haunting, orange glow. He carefully hobbled down the steps and hopped up on the bench seat of the table.

"Thy sanctuary is a wealth of treasure," he said as he stroked his white beard and looked around the place. "Be it known to thee, no apprentice until this moment owned a dwelling such as this."

I sat down opposite the little troll and smiled warmly. "Try to think of it as *our* sanctuary, D.T." I said. "Mr. Orlowski is going to add another chamber, so we can move all your stuff from Nose Hill Park."

He nodded his head and gave me a cautious look. "Then thou surely must know the path of an apprentice is fraught with peril," he said, grimly. "This old mage grows weary with every passing day ,and thine enemies grow in number."

"I know," I said, matching his somber tone. "The Conclave is a threat that not even my employer truly understands."

"Then it is upon thy powers to persuade those in the mortal realm of the dangers that lie ahead."

I hesitated about asking D.T. if the clarity Mago detected in me would put those closest to me in danger, but I kind of knew the answer to that. In the weeks following the battle with Mago, D.T. had slowly revealed that clarity offers a pure magical signature unlike anything in the preternatural world. It was because of my clarity that the shade had been able to locate me, not to mention Mago himself. I shuddered as I remembered how quickly Mago managed to break into my mind and play with my thoughts with surgical precision. It was only my ability to tempt the tempter that had saved me — and ultimately, the entire city of Calgary.

Well, that and an eight inch Buck Knife.

I hadn't asked for the gift of clarity, and after a few weeks of soul searching, a large part of me wanted to resign from Government Services and Infrastructure Canada, disavow magic, and live an anonymous life, listening to Mozart with the man I loved. Unfortunately, there was no hiding from my gift. My magical signature would always place me and those I love in mortal danger, so if this were to be my lot in life, I had to master every aspect of elemental magic to survive and protect others.

I decided that since my options were limited, it might be a reasonable expectation to renegotiate my contract with my employer. I sat at my computer and put the finishing touch on a letter that I'd send to Vishesh via e-mail. It was a Sunday afternoon, and my entire condo was filled with the sounds of *Don Giovanni*. I smiled warmly as Dave tried to sing along — off key, of course. I could smell the rich aroma of steaming hot spinach and tangy feta cheese baked in phyllo, and my stomach rumbled agreeably. The letter read as follows:

Dear Vishesh:

Please find the attached contract for your consideration. I'm sure you'll find it fair and reasonable.

In the past few weeks, I've contemplated the numerous revelations regarding an organization known as the Conclave, the nature of my relationship with my employer, and information that has been deliberately kept from me due to security concerns. During my investigation into Peter Orlowski's missing grain bin, it became very clear to me that I must be fully briefed as to the extent of Canada's involvement in arcane matters if I am to continue as an employee of the Federal Government. There are forces at work in this world that I'm not yet convinced either you or the Prime Minister's Office truly understand, and the threat is very real. That said, if you have deliberately kept me out of the loop, be advised that you can consider this letter to be my formal resignation.

In the meantime, I am willing to meet with you to discuss my further involvement, and I would be grateful for a briefing on our so-called "peacekeeping" activities. I'm still in the dark about that.

> *Regards,*
> *Valerie Stevens*

I clicked "send" and let out a relaxed sigh as I spun around in my chair. Imagine my surprise at seeing Fifty-Dollar Bill seated on my bookcase, with a look of self-importance on his face.

"That was an exceptional letter, young lady," he said. "My staffers couldn't have written it better."

"Thanks, Bill," I said, cocking an eyebrow. "You do realize that I have a date, right?"

He nodded politely and frittered with his tunic. "I do indeed," he huffed. "I've come to tell you that I found our little adventure in the park to be among the most thrilling challenges I've experienced."

"And?"

"And that I've decided a young lady like yourself needs a heroic figure in her life," he said proudly. "That, and I've grown quite fond of you."

I rolled my eyes and walked over to the bookcase. I gave Bill a very stern look and was about to tear a strip off him, but I thought better of it.

He *had* been helpful, actually.

Fifty-Dollar Bill was the one who had found the names of the four spirits I'd originally thought the shade dragged into the mortal realm. He provided valuable intelligence on the afterlife, and he'd freed the spirit of Bogan Orlowski. I chewed my lip as my stern features dissolved into something resembling mild affection, and I gave him a polite smile.

"Fair enough," I said. "If you intend to hang around, there's going to be some new rules for you to follow. And you *will* follow them, you old ghost."

"Go ahead, Valerie," he grunted agreeably. "I am at your service."

I cleared my throat to emphasize my points. "You will *not* come into my home without announcing your arrival or advanced warning. You will *not* watch me shower. You will *not* hover above the bed while I am being intimate with my boyfriend, and you *absolutely will stop* being such a colossal pain in the ass."

Bill bristled at my tone and gave me an indignant glare. He was about to say something smart but caught himself and gave me a reluctant look.

"Very well," he huffed. "I agree to your terms."

"Good," I grunted again. "Now, would you get lost? I want some quality time with Dave, okay?"

Bill nodded and began to fade away.

"Oh and... Bill?" I called out. His head materialized through the ceiling.

"What is it *now*," he sighed, sounding impatient.

I threw him a sharp frown, and then my lips curled into a grateful smile.

I grinned at him. "I couldn't have done it without you."

The old ghost's pudgy face had a look of genuine amusement, and I thought he might chuckle, assuming he had a sense of humor.

"I... *agree*," he said with an aristocratic sniff, and then he was gone.

I rolled my eyes so hard I thought they'd get stuck in the reverse position and turned on my heels to head into the kitchen. Dave stood at the doorway to my office wearing a lime green t-shirt that said *"Mozart Metal Fest '07"* and my pink oven mitts.

"Dinner is served, madam," he announced in a snooty voice. My stomach let out a loud gurgle, and I flushed with embarrassment as I hustled across the floor and threw my arms around Dave.

"The lady wishes to dine in front of the TV," I gushed; the warmth of Dave's chest felt like heaven against my cheek.

"Then dine you will," he said, doing his best Errol Flynn. He swept me up off the carpet and carried me into the living room, and then said, "Oh, and that stomach gurgling thing? *So hot.*"

I plopped out of his arms and yanked him down to eye level by the collar. I gently placed my hands on his cheeks and pulled his lips against mine. Then I softly kissed him for what seemed like an eternity as Dave rested his pink oven mitts on my waist and pulled me close in a deep, soul-enriching embrace.

My name is Valerie Stevens, and I'm love with a dump truck driver.

How cool is that?

THE END

TURN THE PAGE FOR
A SNEAK PEAK AT

FUNERAL PALLOR

THE NEXT IN THE
VALERIE STEVENS SERIES

AVAILABLE JULY 2010, FROM

SNOWBOOKS

CHAPTER 1

"There it is again," I whispered, as I crouched behind the garbage bin. I was knee-deep in torn-open trash bags, and I could have sworn I felt a something scurry across the back of my legs.

Rat-free Alberta, my ass.

The evening started out alright. I'd been downtown watching a new cellist's debut at the Jack Singer Concert Hall, alone I might add, because my ever-lovin' boyfriend Dave was up in Fort McMurray working on a new oil sands development. (Yeah, the evil global-warming oil sands that environmental groups and half the staff of the CBC complain are the greatest threats to human life as we know it. I deal in more immediate human destroying threats like demons, dark magic and plain old bad juju.) We'd been arguing for two weeks since he announced he was going, and though I'm not the kind of person to tell someone how to run his life, Dave's reasons for working up in the back forty for six weeks simply didn't make sense. There was plenty of work at the Demarco construction company, and, sure, I know there's a quick buck to be made up in Fort Mac, but Dave doesn't need the money. He owns his house free and clear; his only debt in the world is for a home renovation loan for about $30 thousand dollars, and even that was about eighty percent paid off. Still, he was insistent about it to the point of walking out on an argument and not calling me for a day and a half.

Was I mad at him for going? Well, yeah – but what really bugged me was that he just arbitrarily laid down the law, and that was a side of him I'd never seen before. It was a side to a lot of men I'd dated in the past, and that's one of the reasons I'd dumped them. But Dave is supposed different. He's the only guy I've ever been with who isn't afraid of me, and that jettisons him to the top of the list in the quality male department, because there's a lot about my life to be afraid of.

I'm Valerie Stevens, and I'm an alchemist, or apprentice mage, or something in between the two – I'm still trying to figure out which one it is. I work for the federal government in a benign-sounding ministry called Government Services and Infrastructure Canada, and I deal with the things that go bump in the night and eat your face.

I'd just hopped in my car in a parking garage about a block and a half away from the abandoned warehouse when my ghostly accomplice informed me about the creature, so I grabbed my staff and the rifle bag from the trunk and shrouded myself behind a magical veil, since I was pretty sure the Calgary City Police might take issue with someone creeping around the crummy section of town with a loaded weapon.

Fifty-Dollar Bill's spectral eyes squinted behind a pair of vaporous, wire-rimmed glasses. "Are you quite certain, Valerie? It could well be a homeless person, you know. There have always been homeless people in Victoria Park, even back in my day."

I gripped my staff tightly in my right hand and adjusted the shoulder strap of my rifle. I'm not big on guns, but it was a gift from the past President of the Bow Valley Sharp Shooter's Association, and she'd been giving me lessons near my sanctuary at the Orlowski farm. Her name is Caroline, by the way, and not only can she can fire a bullet into the neck of a beer bottle from five hundred meters away, she also packs her own ammunition.

Oh, and she's a zombie — sort of like the guy Fifty-Dollar Bill and I were watching as the pile of trash I was standing in seemed to come alive with rodents scurrying across the toes of my Danner boots.

"You're a ghost, Bill," I grunted. "And frankly, I think your homeless person is as dead as you are."

"Because he's staggering around like a drunkard?"

I pointed with my staff. "No... because there's a dismembered human leg on the ground beside him, and from the look of it, I'd say that about sixty percent of the flesh has been chewed off."

Bill squinted again and nodded agreeably. "Good show, young lady. I didn't quite catch that at first glance. What do you propose we do if he is one of the undead?"

"He's a zombie... vampires are undead," I said sourly, as I swung the 7.62 MM FN FAL rifle around and screwed a silencer on the end of the flash suppressor. "The last time I looked, the best way to deal with a zombie is to shoot it in the head."

"Right, then," said Bill, as his corporeal visage floated back a few feet. "Do try to actually hit it, won't you?"

I ignored my accomplice's snide comment as I lifted the butt of the rifle against my right cheek and peered through the rear aperture. I checked my breathing and flipped the safety off with my right thumb and took aim. I was just about to squeeze the trigger when a primal-sounding groan cut through the silence of the alleyway like a chainsaw, and something gripped my calf and pulled me back with near superhuman strength. A loud crack rang out as the barrel of my rifle bucked skyward and the silencer flew twenty feet in the air. I felt myself lose my footing as I stumbled over a rusted oil drum, landing on stack of empty boxes. Not the smartest move with a loaded rifle in your hands, but then whoever said I was smart? I'm just a lowly civil servant, and the only difference between the thousands of other federal government employees and me is that I'm the only one who's calling card has a pentagram next to the government of Canada logo, and I can see dead people, as the nature of my relationship with the ghost of Canada's tenth Prime Minister will attest.

Of course, William Lyon Mackenzie King's spirit wasn't intent on eating me, whereas the recently embalmed corpse I'd been planning on shooting was. I fired a glance to my original target and saw that it was shuffling forward in my direction; the sound of a rifle going off generally attracts the unwanted attention of zombies. But that was the least of my problems. The rat that I'd felt scurrying around my legs wasn't a rat at all. No, it was a zombie in a Commissionaire's uniform, who, during the last few moments of his life, probably came out to do a security check – the poor bastard. I clenched my jaw and hoped like hell I remembered the snap shooting lessons that Caroline gave me because if I couldn't nail both creatures between the lookers, then I'd have to resort to magic. You know, really ugly, fast and wildly inaccurate magic that could wind up torching the adjacent warehouse.

I dropped to one knee and brought the rifle to my shoulder. I'd just stared down the iron sights when I noticed the end of the barrel had been flayed open like a fish. The bullet obviously destroyed it when it blew off the silencer so the only thing my rifle was good for was as a makeshift club. Zombie number two, the one that had tripped me up, hopped forward on one leg. A bloody, pulpy stump with about four inches of femur and dangling tendons dripped gore onto the cold wet pavement of the alleyway. At least now I knew whose calf I'd seen only moments earlier. He was a fresh kill, no more than perhaps thirty minutes past death, and I shuddered as I realized how quickly he'd transformed from innocent victim of the living dead to a one-legged killer who'd rip me to pieces if given the chance.

Of course, where there are one or two zombies, there's bound to be more, because that's just how things work in my happy little life. I spun around as four more rotting husks lumbered forward through the loading bay doors of the old warehouse. The sound of shattering glass followed by a chorus of throaty, unearthly groans filled my ears as three more zombies literally forced their way through a plate glass window like a trio of Boxing Day shoppers pushing through a crowd at Best Buy. It was clear I'd walked into a nest of zombies who'd claimed the warehouse, and even if my rifle had been undamaged, they'd be on me before I'd have a chance to attach another twenty round magazine.

I slung the rifle over my shoulder and scurried across the alleyway, staff in hand, through an opening in the chain link fence that formed a perimeter around the warehouse parking lot. I was planning on the zombies following me and filtering one by one through the hole in the fence, which would give me enough time to nail each of them with a blast of magic. Of course, Fifty-Dollar Bill just had to pipe up and scuttle my plan.

The jerk.

"You've got about twenty of them meandering across the parking long, Valerie. It might seem more practical to perhaps consider a hasty retreat."

I glanced over my shoulder as a platoon of the walking dead fixed their inhuman gazes at me and, as if on cue, let out a chorus of blood curdling groans that told me two things: they were hungry, and I was in big freaking trouble.

"That's... what, like thirty zombies?" I squeaked, as I tore across the parking lot.

"Twenty-nine, actually," Bill piped up. "You know, when I was Prime Minister, we made sure the education system across Canada taught basic math skills, young lady."

"Stow it, Bill!" I snarled, as I leaped over a cement barricade and headed for what used to be a boarded up doorway.

The old ghost followed the contours of the exterior walls on the dilapidated warehouse and I ran like hell up an old loading ramp, feverishly scanning my surroundings for a place where I could have something resembling a tactical advantage. If I had a hope in hell of surviving what was fast becoming an incident that could easily spread beyond the warehouse's corroded chain link fence, I needed to funnel the creatures inside the building and go for a far less surgical zombie removal remedy than shooting.

You know, like bringing the building down on top of their decaying heads.

The downside, of course, was that once I was inside the building, my chances of finding a zombie-free escape route were significantly reduced. I glanced over my shoulder and saw the creatures had wandered into a large gaggle and were menacingly shuffling across the parking lot. Their throaty, lifeless groans filled the air in a refrain of primal hunger as a wave of nausea and panic twisted itself in knots deep in my bowels. They were about a hundred meters back when I kicked in a plywood-covered doorframe and ran into the old warehouse. The only light inside the building came from two hanging light pots that cast an eerie glow across the floor, so I did a quick scan of my surroundings and spotted a wrought iron gondola about thirty feet above a trio of doors. There was a rickety-looking wooden ladder attached at the north end of the gondola, and I noticed a pair of boarded up windows on the east side of the building. I decided I'd have a better chance of destroying the creatures from up high, since zombies can't exactly fly, and they're notoriously bad at climbing. I'd kick out the rungs on the ladder so they wouldn't be able to make it up to the gondola, and when I'd destroyed them, I'd just make a hasty escape through the boarded up windows.

It sounded easy in principle, or so I thought...

ACKNOWLEDGMENTS

A huge thank you goes out to Anna Torborg for her fantastic cover art. I told her it would be cool to have a book cover that is completely different than other urban fantasies with a strong female protagonist, and Anna delivered big time. Thanks to Emma Barnes and everyone at Snowbooks for all their support and encouragement.

My great thanks to the 3 Day Novel Contest, as Shade Fright's first draft was written during a coffee-fueled and sleep-deprived Labour Day weekend in 2007.

A big hello goes out to my biggest fan, Jodi Hughes, who loves everything I write. Special thanks to Nancy Holzner and Doug Knipe for their kind words about my book.

Finally, I am so very grateful to Cheryl, who is the ultimate sounding board for my crazy story ideas. She's a bigger geek than I am (if that's possible) and believed in this book from the very beginning.

ABOUT THE AUTHOR

Sean Cummings is a comic book geek of the highest order and self-described nerd. His interests include urban fantasy, science fiction, the Borg, cats with extra toes, east Indian cuisine and quality sci-fi movies/television. He lives in Saskatoon, Canada.